SCENT OF MURDER

SCENT
OF
MURDER

AN ISSY CASTILLO MYSTERY

CAROLINA DOW

LEVEL
BEST BOOKS

In memory of Barbara Steiner, the best writing teacher ever, whose perspicacious comments and unflagging encouragement and support have made me a better writer. Your influence shines on.

Praise for Scent of Murder

"Carolina Dow's *Scent of Murder* is a carefully crafted puzzle, rich with witty dialogue and colorful characters…including Issy's six-times-great-grandmother, who periodically makes an appearance from the spirit world to offer sage advice and clever clues…This engaging…debut murder mystery kept me turning the pages and guessing whodunnit right to the end."—Skye Alexander, author of the Lizzie Crane mystery series

Chapter One

"Hay un remedio para todo menos la muerte."
"There's a remedy for everything except death." — *Miguel de Cervantes*
(1547-1616), Spanish Author

I am Issy Castillo, a first-time Spanish professor at Gold Mountain University in Boulder, Colorado. On this lovely full moon evening in May, I have become a suspect in the murder of a colleague. A colleague with whom I was hoping to begin a romantic relationship tonight.

Instead, I found myself kneeling over Eddy Calderon's body, clutching my own scarf with which the drama professor had been strangled. Forget my aspiration to return to my hometown to teach after earning my doctorate back East, reconnect with family and friends, and explore my Hispanic roots. Put aside my desire to build a career as a respected Latina academic. No! First and foremost on my agenda is finding the killer and clearing my name before the police arrest and charge me, and bring shame upon me, my school, and my entire family. *Ay, Qué lío!* What a mess!

I was in my campus office Saturday night, the picture of innocence. Which I was! I was writing a letter of recommendation for a student. But the words didn't flow. Little noises—creaks, rustlings, clanking pipes, imagined or real footsteps above my head—disturbed my concentration.

When the phone rang, I almost jumped out of my skin.

"I'm back in my office finishing up some business," said Eddy. "Come up soon, and we'll go for that pizza. Eddy Calderón, Spanish theater professor and new friend, had invited me to go with him for a late snack after rehearsal for a medieval morality play he was putting on for a department fundraiser. I knew Eddy was interested in me personally. We'd even kissed once. But I'm getting ahead of myself.

"I'll be there in a few minutes," I said. "I want to finish writing this letter."

"Listen. Suzanne, Dolores, Javier, and maybe Miguel want to join us." He sounded apologetic about inviting the head of the teaching assistants, the Portuguese lecturer, and two graduate students, all of whom were involved in the play. "Suzanne's been itching for us all to get together. And social interaction does help build cast solidarity. We won't stay long with them, I promise."

"No problem," I said, but my heart sank.

"Also, I keep forgetting to mention that your scarf has been hanging on the back of my door since Baldo's party."

Baldo, or Baldomero Vigil, was department chairman. He'd held a kickoff summer barbecue last Sunday at his home to foster faculty solidarity. Which it didn't.

"*Gracias.* I forgot I left it in your office after the party. I'll get it when I come up."

"*Cruz!*" I exclaimed aloud while attempting to tame my wild hair and apply fresh lip gloss in the bathroom. Somehow, I'd managed to let twenty minutes slip by writing that letter.

I sped through the basement, up the two flights of stairs, and down the corridor to Eddy's office as fast as my sandal heels could take me. Not wanting to appear too eager, I slowed my pace as I got closer. His door was ajar, and the light was on.

"Sorry I'm late." I announced, "but it took forever to finish that…" I stopped short as I collided with something solid. Eddy was stretched face-up on top of his Indian rug with my scarf wound tight around his neck. His red-rimmed eyes stared sightlessly at the ceiling, and his face and neck had turned dark red.

"Eddy!" I cried.

I knelt by him and, with one hand, ripped away the scarf that had left a deep horizontal contusion around his neck. I bent close to his face and registered a cloying, sweet scent. Putting my shaking hand to his nose and mouth, I checked for breathing, then felt for a pulse. Lifeless!

Shivering almost uncontrollably and blinking back tears, I scrambled in my purse for my cellphone. At the same instant I heard the voice at 911 come on the line, Suzanne, Dolores, and Javier appeared at the doorway. On seeing Eddy's body and me, crouched over it with my scarf in one hand and phone in the other, their faces blanched.

"What have you done?" shrieked Suzanne.

"You've killed him!" shouted Javier.

Dolores screamed, "Murderer! Murderer! Murderer!"

* * *

In fewer than five minutes after I dialed 911, both campus and city police, sirens blaring, rushed to the scene of the crime. I must have been numb from shock because an officer had to pry the scarf from my hand and heave me to my feet from my kneeling position. With Dolores', Suzanne's, and Javier's accusations keening in the background like a Greek chorus performing at an Irish wake, the police hauled me to the station. The other witnesses rode in a separate car to give their statements.

The not particularly cordial officers deigned to let me call Papi, my father, before tossing me into a windowless room with a mirror covering one wall. The furniture consisted of a metal table and four uncomfortable-looking plastic chairs. And a reeking ashtray full of stubbed-out cigarettes. Inconsequentially, I puzzled over the ashtray because smoking is prohibited in most of eco-friendly Boulder's institutional spaces. But this was not the moment to voice an objection, even if I'd had the heart to complain.

I paced the small space and waited together with my dark thoughts. Like a film noir DVD stuck on replay, the nightmarish scene repeated in my mind: Eddy, lifeless, his dusky face turned cherry-red, stretched belly-up on his exquisite Indian rug like a piece of rejected cat kill. The same rug with the animal figures I'd seen in one of my intuitive dreams I sometimes have. Why hadn't I intuited something like this would happen and put a stop to it?

Too late, I understood the significance of the blood-red background color. The many murder mysteries I've devoured over the years didn't prepare me for the horror and helplessness of seeing, feeling, and touching the still-warm dead body of a friend in real life. I shivered so hard my teeth chattered.

Get a grip, girl, I admonished myself. *Blot out that horrible vision and focus on something else. Like asking questions.*

Who would want to kill Eddy? As far as I knew, he was everybody's friend, kind and thoughtful, always helping people with advice about their lives and careers. At least, that had been my experience in the short couple of weeks I'd been at my job. And what was the motive?

The question thing wasn't working. Somehow, I couldn't shake the memory of the scent that surrounded the body when I leaned over to check for a pulse. Even in my distraught state, I remembered something my other new friend and aromatherapy instructor, Elsbeth MacLeod, said in class about how saints' bodies in medieval times and even the corpse of the Mexican Colonial literary genius Sor Juana de la Cruz were said to exude such a fragrance. Back then, people called it the "odor of sanctity." Poor Eddy! Such a good person.

Exhausted, I slumped onto one of the chairs, still shaking, and awaited my fate. All my years of study and hard work flushed down the tube in an instant because I stumbled on the corpse of a friend. One who might have become more than that and now never would. I kept asking myself, how did I get into this colossal *lío*—a pickle of all pickles? I had only myself to blame.

I started thinking back to how it all began and if I could have done something to prevent this disaster. Then, sitting under the bright LED ceiling light, I lay my head on the table, and things got a little hazy.

Chapter Two

"Nadie es adivino del mal que está vecino."
"Nobody can know what evil lurks around the corner." —*Spanish Proverb*

It began with me not paying attention to my intuition or my spirit ancestor Doña Isabella's warnings. For now, though, I'll put aside the topic of my ancestor and concentrate on the intuition angle.

On a clear, high altitude early May morning, I was about to step across the stone footbridge to my first job as a college Spanish professor, when I paused. I'll never know whether I did it to admire the view of Colorado's Front Range of the Rockies or if I had a premonition of the horror to come. But at that moment, I experienced a kind of flash that off-balanced me.

I've always wanted to possess a psychic's gift. Even as a kid I dressed up like a fortuneteller every Halloween, much to Mami's and Papi's chagrin, who preferred I costume myself as a princess. Over time, my yen to peer into the future buried itself under a clay *olla* as I went about my business growing up and getting an education. Until recently, when I started getting plagued by these sudden flashes of things to come, along with a vision of an ancient Indian woman.

Anyway, a minute before, the sun shone bright in a cerulean sky with a transparency that only occurs in medieval paintings or in Colorado on sunny mornings. While pausing, I admired a dozen hummingbirds, their wings flashing silver in the sunlight, buzzing the richly fragranced lilacs overhanging College Pond. Then a small but vicious-looking black cloud materialized like an evil genie from a bottle and blotted out the golden sunshine. And I got the flash again. Annoyed, I squinted up at the cloud and stumbled. The two-inch heel of one of my dress sandals buried itself between two wooden planks on the bridge and snapped off.

"Demonios!" I cursed softly and bent to pull the broken heel loose. I ended up limping my way across the bridge. Just when I wanted to put my best foot forward, I was going to have to clump around all day like Quasimodo.

Preoccupied with grumbling, I didn't notice the scene unfolding outside the main entrance to the Spanish and Portuguese Department until I was almost on top of it. Under the red-tiled roof of the two-story sandstone building, two guys, who, from their youthful appearances, I took to be students, were arguing. I hobbled over to join the gaggle of onlookers who, undoubtedly glad for any diversion from their studies, had gathered at a safe distance to view the entertainment.

"You have no right to say such cruel things," one adversary, a fireplug of a youth with a muddy red face, snarled through full, thick lips.

"You pay too much attention to gossip." His opponent, a smooth-looking guy with large, dreamy green eyes, gave a scornful sniff with his patrician nose.

The first student backed against the heavy oak door flared the nostrils of his flat nose like a cornered bull and flexed his muscles so they rippled beneath his blood-red top. "You are the one who spreads the *chismes*! I demand you take back every word." He took two steps forward and pawed the ground with his Asics running shoe.

The other student, who in the insouciant manner of a toreador sizing up his quarry, had what looked like a red J Crew windbreaker slung carelessly over his shoulder. He said nothing but transferred the outer garment to lay over his arm. An amused smile spread across his male model-handsome face. I negotiated my short frame between the backpacks of two spectators to better watch the show.

Latinos tend to create nicknames for everybody, and I'm no exception. Not sure why we do it—there's no malice intended. Maybe it's simply to distinguish one person from another. And if truth be told, we enjoy interjecting a bit of humor into situations, especially trying ones. So, the guy with the windbreaker became "Toreador" in my mind. He tossed his jacket on a nearby juniper bush and shifted to face his accuser head-on. *"De veras, Javier?* Make me!"

Though I stood sheltered behind the crowd, I moved my shoulder purse across my chest for protection. Onlookers held their collective breath. Somewhere, a cellphone tinkled the Lone Ranger theme song, but nobody answered it.

The door to the Spanish Department swung open, and a man with his hair drawn back in a ponytail strode out. Before the door shut, I glimpsed a reedy woman with stringy black hair and a pale, pinched face lurking in the shadowy hallway.

Toreador shifted his attention to the older man, but Bull didn't realize anybody was behind him. In an instant, Bull saw his advantage. He charged his opponent, smacking him on the nose with a neatly executed right jab.

Toreador leaned forward and cupped a hand to his face. Blood oozed between his fingers and ran down his crisp blue Oxford cloth shirt, dripping at his feet on the sidewalk. A gasp rose from the crowd, and I covered my open mouth with my hand.

Ponytail stepped between the opponents with an agile movement. He held back Bull, gripping his shoulder.

"Guys, enough!" Although he hadn't raised his voice, it vibrated through my body like a tuning fork, and I'm embarrassed to admit I tingled as if I were the one being reprimanded. "If you two have a grievance, take it off campus. Michael," he addressed Toreador, "you'd better have a doctor at the clinic take a look at that nose."

The professor released his grip on Javier the Bull's shoulder. Now, I recognized the teacher as one of my interviewers at the Modern Language Association job fest. He took a tissue from his pocket and gave it to Michael to help staunch the bleeding. "Want me to report this to university police?"

Michael spoke through cupped hands as if into a muffled bullhorn. "It's not worth reporting." He clicked his tongue in disgust at Javier, whose coal-black eyes sparked danger from under shaggy eyebrows. Then he took off across campus.

With the histrionics over, bystanders lost interest, turned, and shuffled away.

The professor focused on Javier. "I would have expected better behavior from you."

"But *Profesor Calderón*, it is a matter of *pundonor*. Honor and integrity. Miguel was besmirching the reputation of—"

Have I wandered into an eighteenth-century play of manners? Nobody uses the term "besmirch" anymore. There's something weird about this guy.

"I don't care whose reputation is at stake," the teacher broke in with a curt wave of his hand. "There are better ways to settle differences than resorting to violence."

Then he noticed me for the first time, listing to one side on my good shoe like a sapling bending in the wind. "Ah, Professor Isabel Castillo," he said. "Our new medievalist has arrived." He dismissed the student with, "If you want, we can discuss this later in my office."

Javier glanced at me, gave the teacher a nod, and rumbled off.

The professor stepped over the blood and flashed a dimpled smile at me, which did nothing to assuage the butterflies that were competing with the breakfast huevos rancheros Mami had brought me because "you must fortify yourself for your first day at work." Those eggs were now threatening mutiny in my stomach. "Welcome to Boulder and Gold Mountain U." He extended a well-padded hand. "I assure you things aren't always so exciting around here."

The handshake, though warm, felt overpowering. A subtle scent of musky aftershave clung to my fingers after he released his grip.

"I imagine you prefer to keep the drama in your classroom," I joked to cover up the unsettling feeling the incident had produced.

Eduardo Calderón, Assistant Professor of Spanish and Latin American Theater, eyed the once again cloudless sky that framed the landscape in robin's egg blue. He shook his head. "Springtime in the Rockies is unpredictable in so many ways." The rich olive color of his smooth skin deepened but lightened again as he looked back at me. "If only my students were as passionate about the plays of Lope de Vega, we might get some lively discussions going." Then he focused on my foot. "*Dios mío*, what happened to your shoe?"

I felt my cheeks turn pink. I shrugged. "It's nothing. I broke a heel."

The dimples widened, and Calderón looked ready to break into a belly laugh. "Why, that won't do at all, Professor Castillo. Not on your first day." He offered me his arm in a grand gesture. "Fair lady, allow me to escort you into the ivory tower to my official abode, where a lowly, but useful bottle of epoxy awaits your command."

I took in his deep-set mocha eyes that twinkled as if he'd told a joke to which only he and I were privy and was disarmed. "I look forward to making said bottle's acquaintance, Professor Calderón," I replied in kind as I took his supportive arm.

"Please call me Eddy."

* * *

So, what was my famous intuition doing at that moment? To be fair, it wasn't totally lolling in a river of forgetfulness. I had an inkling that something was up. After all, two students coming to blows over the concept of honor and integrity wasn't what most people of that age would consider actionable. And the drama prof? Let's say I wasn't used to such open-hearted friendliness on first meetings with the opposite sex. But my orderly, logical left brain hushed me into believing I was overreacting.

* * *

A familiar voice was calling my name. I felt my shoulders being rocked—no—shaken.

"Isabel. Wake up!" Boulder Police Chief Lucio Mondragón had entered the room. The frequent restaurant patron, Papi's good friend and my *padrino*, was a rangy man with a long nose and even longer mustache perpetually turned down at the corners. His drooping shoulders looked burdened with the weight of the world. A female detective had also slipped in without my noticing to videotape the interview. I rubbed the sleep from my eyes and straightened my cramped body in the chair.

The Chief was courteous, but his manner was cold and distant like he was making sure he was doing everything by the book. At that instant, it was as if he'd never sat me on his knee when I was a toddler and showed me how he could make a quarter disappear from his fingers and reappear behind my ear.

This new Chief Mondragón, from whom I now had mentally distanced myself by calling him by his title, grilled me about my relationship with the deceased. How had I found the body? What was my scarf doing in Professor Calderón's office? What was my purpose for going there so late in the evening? Had Calderón and I quarreled? Were we lovers? *How could he even think of asking me something like that?* He made me seem like a courtesan out of the medieval Spanish *La Celestina* comedy. Only this was no comedy.

Over and over, I insisted I didn't know Eddy well and, therefore, had no reason to kill him. Why wouldn't Tío Lucio take me at my word?

Because, according to the other three witnesses, I was once seen driving off with Eddy after play rehearsal to lunch in another town. And I was spotted another time in a restaurant with him near campus, where he was seen massaging my neck and shoulders. And he'd taken me on a date to a department party, all within the space of a couple of weeks. This was true as far as it went. But just because we went to a party together didn't mean we were lovers. Absolutely not. I needed to wait for my head to clear before I could revisit those episodes.

For now, I was not to be deterred. I went on repeating my story for probably the fourteenth time, when another officer stepped in, and the Chief left the room with him and the female cop. After a few minutes, the officer came back and told me my father was waiting outside. I was to be released to his care with the strong suggestion not to leave town in case they had more questions.

Papi, unshaven, his complexion the color of a young eggplant turning purple around the edges, met me with eyes that pierced me through like two jagged pieces of onyx. Grim-faced, he drove me to my condo to pick up a few overnight things, then brought me to their home. The only time he spoke during the trip was to tell me that because I'd already dialed emergency before the other witnesses appeared, the Chief chose not to charge me and lock me up.

Chose not to charge me? Really? How about the fact that I was innocent, and Mondragón knew me well enough to understand that I wouldn't hurt a fly? *Por el amor de Dios,* in high school I used to solicit donations from the Chief for PETA. Besides, I'd only been teaching here for a couple of weeks. How would I have the time to develop an ongoing relationship with a colleague, then get furious enough with him to kill him?

I was too drained to protest about being driven to my parents' little blond brick Fifties ranch house. If truth be told, I wanted to hide away in my closet and never come out again.

Feeling numb, I let Mami fuss over me. After downing the hot chocolate she insisted on making, I revived enough to call Olivia, my new university friend, and nineteenth-century Spanish Lit professor. Better she hears it from me than on the News or the Internet. Or worse, from Suzanne or Dolores. After Olivia absorbed the shock, she offered to cover my classes for a couple of days and not talk about the incident to anybody, although we knew it would be all over campus in a few hours. I thanked her, rang off, and went straight to bed in my old room without bothering to remove what makeup was left on my face. I slept for ten hours straight.

Chapter Three

"Ten en cuenta que el gran amor y los grandes logros involucran grandes riesgos."
"Remember that both great love and great achievements involve great risks."
— *Spanish Proverb*

When I awoke, and over the next couple of days, when I was too exhausted to think, I spent my time mulling over how the events had unfolded and what I could have done to prevent them from happening. In my mind's eye, I once again traveled back to my first day on campus, entering the department with Eddy.

* * *

As Eddy opened the door for me, a hulk of a young woman in a black muumuu with frizzy hair gone prematurely white, squeezed past us. She shot a look at our entwined arms that Mami would call "giving us the fisheye."

"Hey, handsome!" the woman honked to Eddy and batted eyes with lids and lashes heavy with purple eye shadow and mascara.

"Hey, Suzanne!" He called to her retreating backside as she lumbered down a staircase, the flip-flopping of her rubber sandals echoing behind her.

Guiding me along the hall, Eddy explained. "Suzanne is in charge of the TAs, our underpaid and overworked Teaching Assistants."

"Are the guys who had the argument TAs, too?"

"No. We turn here." He ushered me around the corner. "Can you manage a staircase?"

I disengaged my arm, brushed away a black lock that had fallen across my eye, and drew my frame up to its full five-foot-two-inch height. "I am not injured. It's only a mishap." Trying to look as unconcerned as possible, I clasped the banister for support and limped up the stairs. "And the guys?"

He looked blank. "The guys?"

"The punch-out."

"Oh, them. They're grad students. Javier Malecón was once a Golden Gloves boxer, as you may have gathered from his lightning-quick moves. He grew up in Boston."

"And the neo-preppy?"

Eddy raised one eyebrow, then burst out laughing. "As good a way as any to describe him. Michael Kent or Miguel de la Madrid. He prefers to use his Spanish name to let everybody know that his ancestors were among the first families to settle in Colorado, although he spent his own childhood back East."

We were traversing one of the most elegant academic corridors I'd ever seen. I sniffed appreciatively at the intermingled scents of fresh paint, varnish, and books, taking in the low, timbered ceilings that reminded me more of a stately home than an institutional building.

Eddy stopped at one of the solid wood doors built with square panels that flanked the hallway every twenty feet or so and inserted a key in the lock.

"Welcome to my humble home away from home." He doffed an imaginary hat and stepped aside to let me enter first.

If I hadn't been treading carefully because of my broken heel, I might have reeled in wonder. This place took my breath away. Light cascaded in from two south-facing windows that, when the summer heat struck, could be shaded by the rich burgundy velvet drapes. In a corner sat not one, but two state-of-the-art computers.

Squinting with my slightly myopic eyes, I strained to read some book titles in the cases that lined one wall. They were filed according to category and internally alphabetized. Covering the floor was an exquisite wool rug with images of *alebrijes*, those fantastic creatures of Native American and

Mexican myth, which must have set the prof back a few thousand. The office of a careful and precise man. I could hardly wait to see mine.

"Sit, sit." Eddy waved me over to a plush loveseat, probably an antique, and went behind his big mahogany desk to rummage through drawers.

Not wanting to take the loveseat, but not seeing chairs other than the one behind the desk, I glanced at the door. At least he'd left it ajar. In grad school, I'd given a wide berth to those occasional notorious elderly profs, known among us Latinas as *viejos verdes,* dirty old men, who put the moves on students and young female faculty. Not that Eddy Calderón was old. He probably wasn't more than six or seven years my senior, and I'm twenty-eight. Perching on the edge of the loveseat, I eased out of my broken shoe.

"What an elegant office," I said to the top of Eddy's head because he was bending over a low drawer.

A muffled reply came from the region of the floor as he slid drawers open and closed. "Keeping a decent-looking office is one of my few indulgences. It helps me forget some of the rough treatment we poor profs sometimes put up with around here." He raised his head enough to cock one nut-brown eyebrow in my direction.

Hmm.

I got distracted by a movement outside the door and thought I saw Javier milling around in the hall.

"I think someone is waiting to talk to you," I said.

"Huh?"

"The student called Javier."

I saw Eddy's shoulders shrug from the back. "It's not office hours now. He can wait." He went back to searching through a drawer.

Okay, then. Evidently, this guy's concern for his students only extends so far.

Eddy sprang from the floor, waving a small bottle high in the air. "*Epa!* This stuff claims to bond anything instantly. Shall we test it?"

While Eddy busied himself, gluing the heel to the shoe, I studied him. In his guayabera shirt, khaki pants, Doc Martens, and single earring, Eduardo Calderón gave the impression of an easygoing guy. Perhaps too easygoing for a professional, in my candid opinion. Yet the meticulous attention paid to detail in his office pointed to someone who liked being in absolute control of his environment. Someone like a theater director.

To push my mind off that track, I said, "I'm originally from Boulder and looking forward to teaching here."

Eddy looked up from his repair. "You're a rare bird. We don't see many natives around here. Our transient academic population makes it easy for those of us with shady backgrounds to keep our true identities secret. It's one of this town's more attractive features." He wiggled one eyebrow in mock conspiracy. It made him look like Stephen Colbert.

I shifted my uncomfortable position, scrambled to think of something to say, and failed.

Preoccupied with his task, Eddy pressed the glued heel to the shoe in silence, then took up the previous conversation. "Javier and Michael are rare birds, too, in different ways. You'll see them in your literature class this summer since they need it to graduate."

I rolled my eyes. "I hope they don't try jousting in my classroom."

He smiled, and little crinkles appeared around his eyes, indicating that he smiled a lot. "The only jousting they're likely to do is in the medieval Spanish morality play I'm putting on as part of the department fundraiser. Both are taking principal roles as knights. Michael's parents are flying in from the East Coast for the event."

I gasped in delight. "A medieval morality play! That's right up my alley since I'm teaching medieval poetry during both Maymester and the two summer terms."

"The play's coming along rather well if I do say so. I'm hoping for a successful debut so we can take the show on the road as the first production of the Gold Mountain University Ambulatory Hispanic Theater. Hey, maybe you'd like to stop by rehearsal sometime and see our students do something other than take jabs at each other."

"I'd love to."

He left the desk and knelt before me to replace my shoe, his fingers lingering a fraction too long on my ankle. "Perfect! Now try walking on it."

We were still in that position when the door opened wide to reveal Uma Thurman poised on the threshold.

16

Chapter Four

"Ya que estamos en el baile, bailemos"
"In for a penny, in for a pound." — Spanish Proverb

"Sorry. Didn't know anyone else was here." The svelte blond wasn't Uma Thurman but could have passed for her movie double. Except, I considered, maybe for the hardness around the mouth. And the eyes with their large black irises. Raven's eyes, sharp and predatory.

Uma Clone, as I decided to call her, fixed a bead on Eddy and me. We stood quickly as if we'd been caught out in something. Eddy's olive skin darkened a shade, then lightened again.

He cleared his throat and said, "Barbara Pomodoro is a senior majoring in Spanish. Barbara, this is the new medieval Spanish literature professor, Isabel Castillo."

The supple Amazon advanced on me. She extended an octopus-length arm tanned to golden perfection that made my own look like a bowling pin. I'm used to Angla six-footers in the university environment, so I wasn't intimidated by the girl towering over me. I just wish these students wouldn't grow so tall so I wouldn't have to practically throw my neck out of joint to look up at them. I put it down to too many growth hormones in their genetically modified cornflakes. They should nosh on organic breakfast burritos instead. Much healthier.

"Everyone calls me Bibi," she said. "I've been dying to meet you, Isabel," she gushed in honeyed tones, further irritating me by using my first name.

Wondering why Bibi Pomodoro thought she would expire if she didn't meet me, I put on my most brittle professorial smile. "As soon as I get an office," I said, "you're welcome to visit."

Bibi's irises expanded as if they were taking digital photos of the room and its occupants for a divorce lawyer. "Awesome! I'll come back when you're not so busy, Eddy." She turned, and I watched the back of her size 2 Boyfriend jeans and clinging tank top disappear out the door.

After a beat, Eddy said, "Bibi is one of our more precocious students."

Time to escape. "Must be running along, too," I said. "Thanks so much for fixing my shoe. If you could point me toward the main office, I'd like to get a key so I can settle into my new digs."

After showing me the way, he said, "If you can spare the time, come to Saturday's rehearsal at the Charles B. Kent Theater. Yes, that Kent. Don't look so surprised. Michael's parents are major donors. Our troupe cranks up around 10 AM. We'll do lunch afterwards."

"I'll try to make it. And please call me Issy."

As my sandal heels clicked over the polished hardwood floor, I considered my new colleague. Good-looking and personable, but a tad overbearing like many Latino guys. Yet there was something indefinable, almost mysterious about him. If he were a woman in fashion or show business, people would say Eddy had "it." I decided to call him "Enigma Eddy." And the student would be "Uma Clone." What was up with those students anyway? I shrugged and turned into the doorway marked Main Office. With any luck, if the ones I'd met took my class, they'd graduate at the end of the summer, and I'd be rid of them for good. Little did I know how prophetic that desire would be.

* * *

I was leaving the main office with the key to my office when I collided with someone entering.

"Halloo!" a beanpole of a man who looked to be in his early forties blurted without apologizing for running into me. "You must be our new Erato come to dole out pearls of poetic wisdom to the ardent Lotharios."

He grabbed my hand and pumped it as if it might produce oil. "I'm Clive

Strange. I teach literature of the Southern Cone." He accentuated the roundness of the vowels. "But my passion is clocks."

"Isabel Castillo," I managed over the pumping. "Most people call me Issy."

He let go of my hand and combed long-nailed fingers through his flaming red hair, moussed into fingerling carrots. From behind the thick lenses of black-framed glasses, he stared at me in open curiosity with eyes that looked like blue-colored ping-pong balls. A mass of freckles on his malleable face danced a polka in the light from the overhead chandelier.

He leaned forward, and when he grabbed my arm, I caught a whiff of bay-scented hair gel. "Dear lady, let's steal a look at the timepiece on your wrist. Ooh!" he squealed in delight. "It shows two time zones. Clever!" He made the last word sound like two. "But it's running two minutes slow. This will never do." He shook his head in chagrin. "How will you ever get to your classes on time? What's your sign?"

I'd been following this barrage wide-eyed. "Ah…I'm a Scorpio."

He drew back. "Beware the venomous scorpion. It rustles through the woodwork and strikes when one is least aware."

As Clive was making that pronouncement, I thought I heard rustling in the corridor behind me. "Hmm, I'll bear that in mind. Right now, I want to get to my office," I said as if putting off a student who had asked for the tenth time when I would get those grades posted. I stepped around Clive.

"Toreadors, bulls, women in muumuus, enigmas, Uma Thurman clones, and now Mr. Carrot Top," I muttered, moving along the hall. What was up with these people? Instead of following up on my apprehensions, I concentrated on the tranquil palm frond-green walls that looked like they belonged to an upscale restaurant rather than a school. The softly gleaming lights from the Craftsman-style chandeliers overhead lulled me back to my normal good humor.

* * *

I should have guessed it wouldn't be all dark chocolates and red roses for me. My nascent intuition had been making irritating little "yips" like an insistent kitten all morning, but I chose to ignore the warning. Even when my heel broke off my shoe, I failed to pay attention.

My office wasn't located within the lofty emerald and golden precincts, but on a lower level. Okay, the basement. On my way downstairs, I met two women coming up. One was the waif with the phantom-white face and stringy black hair, who I glimpsed lurking in the doorway during the student altercation. As she flitted by, she glowered at me like a seething ghost jealous of one who had poached on its private haunt. I'd been on campus for a mere hour and already managed to get up somebody's nose and had no idea why.

Her companion was the woman in the muumuu who had greeted Eddy in the doorway. "Hey," she acknowledged me with less enthusiasm than she'd shown the drama professor and introduced herself as Suzanne Selos. In her jet-black tent dress and fly-away white hair, she reminded me of Hecate after a rough night at the Oracle.

"We're practically roommates," she said with a wink. "Your office is next to mine." Behind pointed frame glasses, her gaze darted around me like a ferret sizing up its next meal.

"*Maravilloso,*" I said, trying to sound enthusiastic, but fearing it came out as sarcastic.

"Gotta catch Dol." Suzanne shambled up the stairs. From the landing, she belted out a cheery, "Have fun with all the living things down there!"

I shrugged and continued my descent.

The basement was a step below the polished hardwood and spiffily painted upstairs. The once whitewashed walls had turned gray with dust and mold, and the tired, leathery brown linoleum flooring buckled at the edges. I sniffed the cold, clammy atmosphere that smelled vaguely of mouse and sneezed. Here was the TA bullpen crammed with desks, bulletin boards, and one jangling landline that nobody bothered to answer. Beyond the communal quarters, like last season's clothes pushed to the back of the closet, four office doors crouched along a narrow, ill-lit hall.

I unlocked and opened my door to a puff of stale, dusty air and an ominous scrambling in a corner. Maybe this was what Suzanne meant by "living things." Or perhaps it was Clive's reference to scorpions. I shuddered and turned on the light, which—*gracias a Dios*—functioned.

The space was slightly bigger than my condo's walk-in closet. At least a modicum of natural light struggled in through the north-facing, barred basement window well. A big old blond wood desk with a matching swivel chair dominated the center of the cramped quarters. In one corner were crammed a gunmetal-gray filing cabinet and scuffed bookcase, and in the other, an ancient typing table. A blast from the past straight out of the TV series *Mad Men*.

I dusted the office chair that squeaked when I sat at the desk and opened my briefcase. I extracted my framed doctoral graduation photo and placed it left center of the desk. Gazing at it brought back sweet memories. First in my family to earn an advanced degree, my graduation was an occasion for family pride. Everyone attended, even my soldier brother Tony and his family, who lived in another state. The Castillo clan had gathered for the photo, blinking at the watery East Coast sunshine. And there was I in the middle, trying to look dignified in my cap and gown. What a glorious day! I sighed. And so, from triumph to ignominy, and in such a short interval. The hope for success of the eldest daughter and so-called role model for her teenage sister was in danger of crashing and burning up on takeoff. A sob escaped my lips, and a tear trickled down my cheek, plopping like a raindrop on the dust-covered desk. I buried my head in my hands.

The standard issue black and white wall clock made a loud single tick as the hour changed. I glanced up and noticed that it was running thirty-four—no—thirty-six minutes slow, according to my watch. Wouldn't Carrot Top Clive have a fit? His ping-pong ball eyes might pop right out of their sockets at this sacrilege. The image was so ridiculous that I began to laugh. Once I started, I couldn't stop until tears of belly-wrenching laughter made little rivulets run like brooks over the dusty desert of the desk.

I fished a tissue from my purse, wiped my eyes, and blew my nose hard. Then I squared my shoulders. As a Latina striving to be respected in Academia, I'd surmounted such challenges before. Like I had to endure the sideways glances, whisperings, and even a few pointed insults from those who judged that the only reason I'd earned a full fellowship to a prestigious Ivy League school was because the university needed to fill its quota of minorities. This criticism didn't just emanate from Anglos; some Latinos were equally vicious in their condemnation.

And nobody, not even my parents, ever learned how despite the fellowship, I worked while in Graduate School as a part-time translator and tutor. I did this so I would have enough to get started on proving my worthiness by living independently.

From my briefcase I took a pen emblazoned with the Ivy League university name where I earned my doctorate. I rolled it between my fingers, remembering a couple of incidents when people said unkind things about me. Determined to overcome the stereotype, I buckled down to work, intent on becoming a stellar success.

On practically day one, I was lucky to meet smart and sassy fellow grad student Ana Torres, who was a couple of years ahead of me. This funny, sometimes outrageous, worldly Jersey girl of Cuban descent became both a friend and something of a mentor. She wised me up to the fact that for my preliminary oral examination, the committee would ask me all sorts of questions about Aristotle, Plato, and other philosophers and scientists of antiquity. Having graduated from a good but small Western regional school, I'd never been required to read about those intellectual giants. So, I studied, studied, studied, read, and absorbed a book a day in both my field and about the Classics until the words on the pages swam before my eyes. I was *not* going to embarrass myself in front of the committee.

Now, here I was once again, facing up to prejudices, petty jealousies, and ignorance. Well, I was accustomed to fighting adversity on all fronts in the past and would do so again. This morning's episode did not represent the entire film of my career. I hadn't even made it through the first act. I refused to close the book on it because of a few badly edited initial scenes. My whole life lay before me, and I would enjoy it to the fullest, come what may.

Thus ended the first day of my first teaching position. Little did I know that worse would follow. Much worse!

Chapter Five

"Estas son las mañanitas/ Que cantaba el rey David..."
"These are the early mornings/ That King David sang of..." — Latino Birthday Song

My cellphone crooning the strains of the perennial Latino birthday party song roused me from my Saturday morning reverie in my condo. I'd slept poorly all week, plagued by dreams that featured an ancient Indian woman with a raspy voice spouting indecipherable Spanish proverbs. I put this down to not being used to living alone without roommates or family.

Edgy and sleep-deprived, I struggled to unlock my legs from their pretzel-like position on my living room floor and staggered to my feet. Grabbing my half-drunk espresso from the floor, I stumbled around the boxes I hadn't yet unpacked and reached for the phone charging on a side table.

Mami's voice rang out loud and clear. "We missed you at dinner last night, *mi amor.*"

"I ate with you on Sunday," I reminded her. "I got too busy this week."

"Too busy to call your mother? *Bah!* I set a place for you, and everyone was anxious to hear how your first days went."

By everyone, she meant she and Papi. I was certain my fourteen-year-old sister Angela couldn't have cared less. I tried to keep my voice even. "Mami, I can't stop by every day now that I'm working. There's been a lot to do this first week of school."

If an electric current could have been coaxed to crackle out of the receiver at Mami's behest, it would have. "I do not understand why a *hija* of mine living in the same town will not spend time with her family. This is a bad habit you picked up from your Anglo college friends."

I drained my now cold cup of espresso, covered the phone's mouthpiece, sighed, uncovered it, and said, "I do want to spend time with you all, but we've already decided I'll come over on Wednesdays and Sundays."

"You missed this Wednesday."

"I know, but this first week has been insane. I'll settle into a routine now."

"And call me every day."

"As often as I can," I promised as I paced the minute area cleared of boxes. I felt my mother shrug her plump shoulders at the phone.

With a quick intake of breath, she was off on her next agenda item. "I wish you would stick around home more for Angela's sake. With those skimpy tops she wears, not to mention the tattoos, even though they are only henna ones, I know. I do not like the image she is presenting. Mark my words! She will fall in with bad company one day."

My activist sister probably already had fallen in with bad company, but I wasn't about to point that out.

"She does not pay attention to a word we say. *Ni una palabra!*" Mami lamented as if such behavior were unheard of in a teenager. "She is probably gone deaf from the loud music on that iPod she is pasted to." With her Spanish accent, she pronounced it as "ee-pohd." Plus, Angela was generations ahead of I-pods, but I wasn't about to enlighten my mother about the latest technology either.

"There's nothing wrong with Angela's hearing," I said. "I know she's been acting flaky, but what can I do about it?" It was my turn to shrug.

"Come around more; provide a role model for her, *hija*. She respects you and your achievements so much."

Right. But I said, "I'll be over tomorrow for Sunday dinner. Gotta go now. Lots of unpacking to do this weekend. Love to Papi and Angelita."

Barefoot and still in my nightgown—after all, it was only eight o'clock—I padded into the kitchen. I prepared a second cup of espresso from the deluxe machine I'd bought to celebrate landing my first teaching job. Taking my coffee to the living room and brushing aside a pile of books on the sofa, I plopped down, out of steam.

My thoughts strayed to last Sunday's disastrous homecoming dinner. Papi had glared at me from across the dining room table, a forkful of chalupa gripped in his fist.

"*Demonios*, Issy," he swore. "You're not the daughter who left Boulder four years ago to get her doctorate. You've even let your appearance go with that New York frizzy hairdo you've got sticking up all over your head."

The comment about my fashionable hairstyle was a low blow, but I knew it masked his real criticism that I'd taken advantage of the fact I had no college debt because I'd been awarded a full fellowship. And so, I'd chosen to buy a two-bedroom condominium near the university with a picture-postcard view of the Flatirons, the mountains that tower over the city, instead of moving in with them. This, despite now being saddled with a mortgage the size of the State of Colorado. Not to mention the fact that I could already tell how lonely and isolated I might feel here without family and friends surrounding me. Sure, I worried about the mortgage and could foresee the time I'd be obliged to take in a roommate so I could make payments. But right now, it felt so good to be free and independent.

Sipping the chocolaty brew and rubbing the tension knot that had developed at the back of my neck, I looked around my silent living room that seemed to be waiting for me to make my impression on it with my life story.

I understand my parents' problem with me. As a traditional Latina, I'm a failure. I burn the tortillas, haven't been to confession in *Dios sabe cuánto*, donkey's years, and refuse to let macho men boss me around. People know better than to ask me to sew on a button, let alone create a precious little outfit for a saint. That comment about my East Coast Anglo friends means my parents probably think I'm jumping the bones of anything on campus with a heartbeat. *Vaya!*

At that thought, a vision of the slim but well-muscled Eddy Calderón, dimples and all, rose before my eyes like a playful devil. How many times had I heard Papi, the restauranteur, warn his employees at The Hot Tamal,

"You don't get your meat where you get your bread!" I shivered despite the balmy day. Sunlight streaming in through the picture window warmed everything it touched but me.

For a few minutes, I stared at the jumble around me. Then something strange happened. A ray of sunlight found its way to one of the few pictures I'd managed to hang and made the landscape sparkle and dance around. It was a well-executed painting of an Indian pueblo that caught my eye at a flea market because it looked so serene yet also intriguing. The pastel colors ranged from the mud brown and tan of the adobe dwellings to the celestial turquoise, pink, and lavender of a morning or evening sky. The rutted road full of texture complemented the pastels and divided the two sides of the pueblo. Somehow, that road looked familiar as it meandered mysteriously into the distance. Almost as if I'd been there before. And I swore the painting buzzed in my hand when I touched it but had no idea why. Anyway, the picture attracted me and was dirt cheap, so I bought it.

Then, as suddenly as the sunray was there, it was gone. I shook my head to clear away the mental cobwebs and stood. If I was to get any unpacking done before my quasi-date with Eddy took place, I'd better quit daydreaming and get a move on.

* * *

The Chamber of Commerce claims that Boulder has 350 sunny days; it's one reason people want to move here. In reality, the weather is volatile. On some of those days, the sun only peaks out for a few minutes. At other times, it beats down mercilessly. Today was one of those days that had turned hot and dry, at least for May, our allegedly rainiest month. So, when I stepped inside the Charles B. Kent Theater, the cool air swirling around my shoulders felt as refreshing as the breeze from an orange grove.

Theater aromas assailed my nostrils. Greasepaint and old costumes mixed with sweat and tempura drying on scenery combined with dust rising from the velvet proscenium curtain that sparkled under the hot lights. I inhaled deeply. Maybe I should have gone into acting. Not! Teaching had its elements of theater, too, and it paid, if not necessarily better, more consistently. And I'm sure teaching is a much more acceptable career to my parents. Underneath, I know they prefer I marry and teach elementary school for a while until "the baby" comes along.

Two of my high school girlfriends did that. They both married after graduation, one to the star quarterback and the other to a champion boxer. Neither went to college and one is now saddled with an alcoholic husband and three kids. Haven't heard what's happened to Marirosa, the second one, but rumor has it he's become a heavy for The Low Riders, our local mob. I shivered for the second time that morning.

The blazing footlights and spots blackened the auditorium, so I felt my way into a seat to let my eyes adjust. Onstage, Suzanne and Javier lounged on two platforms suspended by support ropes approximately three feet from the floor. They leaned against the ropes, and their feet dangled off the sides, making them look like two aging children on swings.

In the second row, Bibi Pomodoro's blond curtain of hair swished over an open playbook. A woman named Olivia Oakes, who had introduced herself earlier in the week as the nineteenth-century Spanish literature professor and assistant play director, stood onstage between the platforms. With her back to the audience and arms akimbo, she stared up at the ceiling. In blue chinos, a big white shirt, Saucony running shoes, and hair the color of washed brown suede swept into a neat knot on top of her head, she looked ready to tackle any challenge.

Olivia called into the vast upper reaches of the stage. "I think we've got the actors positioned okay. Now it's up to you to raise them slowly and smoothly."

A stagehand yelled something indistinguishable from a catwalk, and the platforms began to move upward in short, jerky motions. Suzanne and Javier clutched the ropes to keep from falling off.

"Watch it, moron!" Suzanne yelled. "This isn't a bucking bronco." She huffed and rearranged her gypsy skirt, a riot of color and pattern that made her look like a Ukrainian Easter egg Humpy Dumpty perched on a wall.

"They are supposed to be fluffy clouds transporting us to Heaven," Javier put in with an expressive wave of a hand.

With that, the platforms ground to a halt, suspending the actors ten feet in the air.

The specter-like woman who had grimaced at me on the staircase and who Suzanne had called Dolores materialized from somewhere in the wings. In one hand, she held a piece of shimmering cloth, probably a costume, and in the other, a needle and thread. In a quavering voice that sounded more like a question than a statement, she called to the technician, "The platforms can't make such jerky movements. At the finale, they rise up as if the White Knight and Fair Lady Inés are being pulled in one deft motion by the hand of God."

My eyes had adjusted to the dimness of the auditorium. As I left my seat and made my way up the steps to the stage, I heard a technician mutter, "God, schmod!"

The platforms lowered, and Suzanne and Javier jumped off.

"What's all this about raising the actors to Heaven?" I smiled a greeting to the cast gathered on center stage.

Olivia got distracted by the technician on the catwalk, who called down to her about how he thought he'd better increase the ballast on Javier's side to compensate for Suzanne's weight, so Dolores answered me.

"In this scene," she said, "Dona Inés is married to the White Knight." She pointed to Suzanne, who curtseyed. In so doing, the young woman's bright yellow peasant blouse dipped to reveal enough ample bosom to put the ladies at Hooters to shame.

"The White Knight is played by yours truly." Javier made a Beau Brummell-style bow. Today his cleanly pressed, Cherokee-red cotton shirt worn over black tights and his relaxed expression made him look, if not handsome, pleasantly presentable. Not the raging bull I'd encountered on my first day at work. I also noticed that when he wasn't arguing with Michael or sulking in the back of my classroom like he had all week, he had a soft voice. Apparently, he felt at home in the theater.

"When The White Knight trots off to the Crusades," Bibi directed her comment to me as if explaining the concept of laughter to an autistic child, "the Black Knight, Miguel, tempts Inés to commit adultery."

"Being a faithful little homemaker," Suzanne put in, batting her eyelashes at Javier, "I resist the evil one's advances."

"The Black Knight is *furioso*," said Dolores, "and so, he resolves to abduct the object of his desire."

"But I return in the nick of time and slay the Devil incarnate!" Javier raised his arm with a flourish and grinned at Dolores. She giggled, and her face transformed from dour spinster teacher to enchanted maiden.

"Because Javier kills 'the Devil incarnate,'" said Olivia, who had finished talking to the technician and returned to the group, "and because Dona Inés remains faithful to her husband, the Archangel Gabriel elevates them both to Heaven. Hence, the platforms. We use them throughout the play to highlight scenes taking place in Hell, on Earth, or in Heaven, thereby taking advantage of all zones of the stage."

"Explaining it sounds more complex than it is," said Bibi in a tone that could be taken as either disparaging or informative.

"I understand," I said. "You're being true to the spirit of medieval symbolism."

"Have you met everybody?" Olivia asked.

"I think I know everyone except for you." I indicated Dolores.

"Dolores Lopes," she said, sounding as tired as if she'd just taught six first-semester Spanish classes back-to-back. "I'm sewing the costumes."

"You also translated this play," Javier reminded her, his eyes gleaming with pride.

I extended my hand, but Dolores, her eyes cast downward, didn't take it. "Don't you also teach Portuguese?"

"More or less." Dolores pressed the costume to her thin chest like a shield.

"What are you doing here?" the forthright Bibi asked me.

"Eddy invited me to the rehearsal."

Suzanne and Dolores exchanged narrow-eyed glances, and Dolores moved downstage.

"How nice to have a medievalist here," said Olivia. "Eddy's going over musical scores with Georgina." She gestured upstage left. "Go through that gap in the curtains, and you'll find him."

As I passed between two heavy black drapes, I saw Javier catch Dolores from behind and pull her hair. Then I heard Olivia say, "Let's take it from where Javier kills Miguel. Since we need Bibi as prompter and Miguel's not here yet, Dolores, can you play the dead body?"

I was about to give up on finding Eddy in the clutter of props and scenery when he appeared out of nowhere like a *deus ex machina*, decked out from head to toe in black leather.

"*Válgame Dios!*" I almost backed against a chair. "Where did you come from?"

He chuckled. "Didn't I mention I grew up in a haunted house in Santa Fe?" he said. "I learned a trick or two about invisibility from the ghosts."

"*No lo creo!* You're pulling my leg."

"Would I do something like that to such a gorgeous lady?" He laughed. "Of course, I would. Truth is this theater is riddled with hidden passageways and compartments."

Placing a proprietary hand lightly on my shoulder, he guided me toward the back of the theater. As he talked, he gave the impression that we were the only two people in the building, perhaps in this entire make-believe world.

"Theater folk by nature possess a flair for the dramatic," he said. "They've been known to build such devices into the walls. They're useful for storing props and getting a person from one side of the stage to the other during a performance. The privileged few know which button on a decorative molding to press or what book to remove from a shelf to have a secret compartment or even a crate swing open."

I smiled. "Very Charlie Chan. Or maybe Nancy Drew."

Nearby, Clive Strange was painting wide swaths of scenery with a big brush. At the sound of our voices, he swiveled around. "Hail and well met again, dear lady!" He bobbed his carrot top and waved his brush at me.

We arrived at a table near the stage door where a woman in a gray pantsuit stood, leafing through a pile of musical scores. She wore sturdy brogues and had steel-gray hair chopped short as if to brook no nonsense from wayward curls.

"Georgina Rampage" (he emphasized the last syllable of her surname, pronouncing it as "ahj") "is our twentieth-century Spanish and feminist literature specialist," said Eddy, picking up a sheet.

Georgina looked up from the music. Without removing the pen from her mouth she'd been sucking, she extended an icy, skeletal hand ending in crimson-painted fingernails that matched her lipstick. "Ahem. Yes," she mouthed. Her gray eyes swept over me, then glanced away as if she had evaluated me and seen enough not to be bothered.

At that moment, a brawny man with a cordwood brown beret pulled halfway over his face burst through the stage door.

"*Qué demonios es eso?* I heard about you meddling in my affairs," the intruder thundered at Eddy. "You have no right!"

Clive dropped his paintbrush. He, Georgina, and I stood transfixed like a tableau in a murder mystery after the detective declares, "Someone in this room committed the fateful deed." Slowly, Eddy placed the sheet music he was holding on the table and turned to confront his accuser. As he had done when he broke up the student row, he kept his voice low and even, but authoritative. "I have every right under the law, Juventino, and you know it."

Juventino, his eyes bulging like a demented toad, reared up. For a moment, I feared he was going to pummel Eddy with his powerful fists. In a voice thick with contempt, he uttered, "You have no respect for the downtrodden." He whirled around and stalked out the door.

Eddy's olive complexion had turned gray; I couldn't tell whether out of fear, consternation, or anger. Then he fixed on me, and the color flowed back.

He said, "Well, Issy, you've gotten a taste of how some of our faculty behave when they are crossed. That was Juventino Guerrero, professor of Mexican, Chicano, and Caribbean literature and resident department rebel. I would have introduced you, but he seemed in a hurry."

Clive picked up his brush and started painting again, whistling a tune that could have been a dirge.

With trembling fingers, Georgina took her pen from her mouth and placed it on the table. "It's not your fault, Eddy," she clucked, transforming from cold cod to mother hen. "He's the one causing trouble."

"He thinks I have no sympathy for his cause," said Eddy. "At least I'm from a working-class family. Not some rich Mexican trying to atone for his sins. What he's doing will hurt us all."

The others appeared from the stage. Javier and Dolores were linking arms. Bibi's eyes, as quick as a velociraptor's, scanned the room.

"We thought we heard a commotion," said Olivia. "Is everything alright?"

By now, Eddy had regained his composure. "It depends on your point of view," he replied with a short laugh. "As the Spanish saying goes, 'What can't be cured in a year can't be cured in an instant.' Listen, gang, I'm taking the afternoon off."

"But I thought we were all going for lunch at that new Italian place," Suzanne whined.

"And what are we going to do about rehearsing lines with Michael not here?" Bibi reminded him.

Eddy thought for a minute, then came to a decision. "Here's the plan. Georgina, I think we'll use the score from *El Concierto de Aranjuez*. Even though it wasn't composed during the Middle Ages, it's powerful. Please get copies to the conductor and the musicians. Suzanne, you need to stay with Dolores for a fitting, then go back to rehearsal.

"Bibi, you can take the role of Dona Inés for now. And please call that undergrad friend of yours with the good Spanish accent, Joe Binks. You know, the kid from the crowd scene. Ask him if he'd like to understudy Michael's role so Javier can practice his lines, and Olivia can figure out the blocking. Javier, be mindful of your tendency to upstage."

Javier's face turned a muddy color. "*Lo siento*, I am sorry to make mistakes, but I am new at acting."

"You're doing fine," Eddy, all smiles again, said and patted Javier on the shoulder. "Is everyone clear?"

They nodded like military recruits.

"Okay. We're out of here. Let's go, Issy."

Over his shoulder, he called, "And Clive, don't think I didn't see that

Daliesque clock face you've painted into the forest. You're going to have to rub it out."

Chapter Six

*"El amor es invisible y entra y sale por donde quiere, sin que nadie le pida cuenta
del hecho."*
*"Love is invisible and comes and goes wherever it wants without anyone held
accountable for its action." — Miguel de Cervantes*

Outside, Eddy had parked a big old Harley like the one my soldier
brother Tony rode before he deployed.

"Where are we going?" I asked.

Eddy's dimples dissipated the remnants of cloud that still lingered from
his encounter with the Mexican literature professor. "Seeing you're from
around here, I thought you'd like to take a trip down Memory Lane and up
Boulder Canyon to Nederland. Hope you don't mind taking my motorcycle."

"I love Harleys!"

I was glad I'd opted for a casual look with jeans, tank top, and moccasins
instead of my usual sundress with bolero jacket and sandal heels. And
gladder still, that Eddy presented me with a safety helmet to keep my
rebellious mop under control. I hopped on, wrapped my arms around
his trim waist, and we were off into the Front Range of the Rockies.

Zipping up the canyon, I nuzzled against Eddy's ponytail that extended
below his helmet, inhaling the clean fragrance of his herbal shampoo. Spring
green grasses and meadow flowers cascaded by in a profusion of color
reminiscent of an Impressionist painting. Masses of yellow, pink, and white
blooms sent brilliant splashes of paint against the amethyst-gray canyon
walls. They wrapped around me like a womb, welcoming me home. Without

a car's body to impede it, the wind blew around us and bore on its wings the clean scents of conifers intermingled with flowering plum, apple, lilac, and iris, an ardent blend of freshness, sweetness, and spice. Soon, we crested the canyon at Barker Dam, the reservoir that holds Boulder's water, and eased past the speed trap into Nederland.

Once a high-altitude mining camp at 8,300 feet above sea level and later, a sleepy tourist town, Nederland used to nod off in the summer heat and tuck in during winter blizzards. I'd been away for a while and, to my chagrin, realized the place had been "discovered." As we rode into town, I stared in disbelief at the surrounding hills. Well-heeled, out-of-state city folk who relished the spectacular views and pristine air had been snatching up high-altitude lots at an alarming rate. Mini-McMansions sprouted like wood and stucco mushrooms over the pine-covered, drought-vulnerable hillsides.

I shook my head. Those houses provided a whole new category of fodder for the forest fire that would engulf them one day. Still, I admitted, the town itself retained much of its Colorado rustic charm.

We parked on a dirt street lined with clapboard businesses fronted by a rickety boardwalk and hitching posts. Strolling along the walk, we window-shopped at a rock and fossil store, organic grocery with a live Tabby snoozing in the window, and a Western antiques emporium. I was admiring a sweet-faced porcelain doll posed in a child's rocking chair in a display window when Eddy said, "I just glimpsed a colleague in the window's reflection. Mind if I go after him?"

"If it's someone from the department, can I come with?"

"Uh…you stay here and browse. I'll be back in a jiff."

I shrugged but smiled in assent. After all, it was Eddy's business who he felt comfortable introducing me to. In the window, I watched his reflection shimmer through a gap between two buildings and down a lane empty of pedestrians. The alley appeared to house a collection of repair places, including an ironmonger, clockmaker, shoe and leather repair, and incongruously, a modern copy shop, among other establishments.

I'd immersed myself in an old book of English mumming plays plucked from a rack outside the antiques store when Eddy returned, out of breath from the altitude.

"No luck," he said, avoiding eye contact again. "My friend must've slipped away." He took a bandana from his pocket and wiped his brow. Then he turned his full, brown-eyed attention to me. "Anyway, I'm starving. How 'bout lunch?"

"I can always eat." I scanned the street for a restaurant and saw the landmark Pioneer Inn across the way. From the mass of shining chrome parked outside, I assumed a bunch of born-to-be-wild bikers had made the venerable eatery their destination for the day.

"As I recall, that place does good Mexican food," I said, "but it looks busy."

Eddy followed my gaze. "I know a cozy café along the Peak-to-Peak Highway that rustles up to-die-for paninis."

"What are we waiting for?"

A short ride brought us to a log cabin restaurant on the roadside nestled among stands of fir. Soon, we were seated on a sunny wooden deck at a small round table covered with a blue-and-white checkered cloth. A little fired clay vase of columbines graced the table's center.

A teenaged server in cutoff jeans, halter top, and full metal smile for which she was probably paying by waitressing, bounded over to take our order. After she'd gone, Eddy clasped his hands behind his head, leaned back in his chair, and took in the view of the mountains carpeted with lush, mossy-colored growth. With his face and body language free from stress, he looked ten years younger.

"I hope you don't mind me bringing you up here," he said. "I needed to get away from the university and the Boulder scene."

"I'm happy you did," I said, breathing in the scrubbed smell of freshly washed plant growth. "The drive reminded me of how much I've missed the mountains." I sipped my mineral water and looked out at the tourist traffic snaking along the road. "I hope that Professor…Juventino's?…outburst doesn't have anything to do with the play."

"Nothing like that." His eyes wandered again. "Ah, here's our food already."

The waitress arrived with our orders in record time. Ah, to be sixteen again with all that energy! On the other hand, I'd be engulfed in an ocean of pubescent crises. Realizing that the high-altitude air had made me ravenous, I bit into my warm ham-and-cheese panini and savored its fragrant gooeyness.

Eddy tucked into his hickory burger and focused on me with eyes that reminded me of warm, spiced cognac. "So, how are you settling in?"

"Okay, I guess. I haven't had a chance yet to look up old friends from high school who may still be around. But I've met a few nice people, including our Head Administrative Assistant, Mrs. Webber, and Olivia Oakes, who seems like she could be a lot of fun."

"They're two of my favorites," he spoke through a mouthful of food. "Olivia is her own person; she doesn't toady up to The Powers That Be. She's half-Hispanic, by the way. Oakes is a married name, although she's a widow now. And don't let Mrs. Webber's old-school look fool you. True to her name, she's a genius at managing our office's communications spider web. And she's taken on the role of spiritual advisor to us all. I suspect she's the reincarnation of Della Street of *Perry Mason* fame, that is, if a fictional character can reincarnate."

"Now you mention it, she does remind me of Della with her Eighties pantsuits and tight permed curls."

"She's as smart as Della, observant, and very savvy. And she's earned her place in Heaven for putting up with Baldo."

I felt my mouth go dry from the sandwich and took a sip of water before speaking. "I take it you're referring to our chairman, Baldomero Vigil. It's strange, but I haven't been able to wrangle an appointment to meet him yet."

Eddy laughed so abruptly, he almost choked on his burger. "Believe me, you're not missing much."

I felt a tinge of pink in my cheeks and straightened in my chair. "I don't understand. I'd expect the department chair to show at least some interest in a new faculty member." Having gobbled my sandwich like a famished construction worker, I now tried to redeem my femininity by delicately dabbing the corners of my mouth with my napkin.

Eddy leaned across the table and shook his head in mock dismay. *"Ay, Issy!"* You have a lot to learn about Academia. Consider yourself lucky Baldo *doesn't* pay you any attention. Unless you have a trust fund to donate or are bosom buddies with the president of an Ivy League university, I'm afraid our esteemed Chair won't concern himself much with you."

"Oh." I dropped back against my chair and went silent for a long moment.

The ever-ready server skipped over to take our coffee orders, whisked away our plates, and bubbled off.

Maybe I, too, needed to get away from town and the dream job that was fast becoming something which, if not quite a nightmare, had developed decidedly hinky overtones. Or perhaps it was because I happened to be sitting across from a sympathetic, handsome face in the rarefied, pine-scented air. Whatever the reason, I made up my mind to air some concerns.

"Another person I don't understand," I said, "is Dolores Lopes. Even before we met officially, it seems I ticked her off."

Eddy shook his head again, only this time, he looked more serious. "*Nuestra Señora de los Dolore*s, Our Lady of Sorrows is one unhappy *chica*."

To my inquiring look, he explained, "Two years ago, Dolores was on the Ph.D. track subsidized by her parents when they were killed in a car crash. They didn't leave her much money, but she did inherit a younger brother afflicted with MS who needs constant care."

The coffees arrived, and after sipping the steaming brew, Eddy continued. "The department took on Dolores as a senior instructor to ease her economic burden, but she barely makes ends meet. She believes the whole world is conspiring against her."

I felt my cheeks color with shame for having misjudged the woman. "I don't blame her," I said while stirring my usual four packets of sugar into the tiny espresso cup. One day I'd have to drop that bad habit, but today I needed the energy. "Do you know what she has against me?"

Eddy's eyes widened like two buckeyes. "I thought you knew. She applied for your position in Medieval Iberian Literature, even though she knew she didn't have a chance."

I took a sharp intake of breath. "No wonder she acts so hostile toward me!"

He toyed with his spoon, then said, "I think Suzanne Selos eggs Dolores on.

And I suppose I've contributed, too, by way of encouraging her to get out there and make something of her talents. Despite my advice to the contrary, she applied for a tenure track position here, the same school where she's studying, which is a no-no in Academia. The truth is she'll never teach here on a higher level." He raised both palms in a gesture of helplessness.

I frowned. "But isn't your encouragement prolonging her agony?"

He put down his cup, and his spice-nut eyes became hard black walnuts. "As her thesis advisor, I can say that Dolores' translation of the Vicente play we're staging is nothing short of brilliant. I can't stomach seeing such a fine talent go to waste."

I had nothing to add to that, so our conversation died. A soft breeze shimmered across the deck, and I watched it lift the edges of the tablecloth. Perhaps I'd been too hasty confiding in Enigma Eddy. Something was simmering beneath the surface in him. Something unpleasant.

I sipped my breeze-cooled coffee and turned my eyes toward the traffic floating along the road. What had I gotten myself into? Not the perfect teaching position where I could communicate my hard-earned knowledge to eager students and pursue beloved scholarly research. Tensions, jealousies, and out-and-out animosities hadn't been in my grand plan. If this was part and parcel of all of Academia, why hadn't I noticed it back East? Because I was a student then, that's why.

Eddy calmed quickly. "You seem miles away."

"Uh…I was wondering how rehearsals are going?"

"They're coming along, but as usual, I've a million details to work out, not least of which includes shaping up some of my actors."

"Like getting Michael Kent to show for rehearsals?" I said with raised eyebrows. "He rarely graces my class with his presence either. When he does, it's like he and Javier are engaging in a proverbial Mexican standoff."

"No love's lost between those two. They've got a history that goes way back," Eddy said with a shake of his head. "But since they both need Medieval Lit to graduate, they won't get up to any real tricks in your classroom."

"Speaking of tricks, I hope you can get those platforms to work. I love the way they highlight the play's symbolism."

Eddy smiled in satisfaction. "Thanks, it was my idea. What I like better, though, is Olivia's concept for the finale."

"What's that?"

"Have you ever seen *The Little Shop of Horrors?*"

"Are you kidding? It was one of my favorite movies when I was a kid. I still have an Audrey Two piggy bank that eats up coins."

"At the play's finale—at least the way it's usually staged—the mushrooming plant Audrey Two ranges out of control and gobbles up everybody. Onstage, and in the first several audience rows, soft ropes of fake foliage drop from the rafters and hit the spectators."

"*Chévere!*

"Yep, it always gets squeals of delight from the small fry." He sipped his coffee. "Anyway, Olivia wants to hang muslin bags to look like clouds from the top of the stage and fill them with dried rose petals. She can get tons of spent petals for free from a couple of florists in town who are happy for her to sweep them from the floor. She plans to dry them and spray on inexpensive rose cologne to enhance the fragrance. She knows an aromatherapist in town who will help her."

I drained my cup. "I approve. Roses were an important medieval symbol of love, devotion, and high aspirations."

Eddy finished his coffee and wiped his mouth with his napkin. "In our finale, when Dona Inés and the White Knight rise to Heaven, the clouds will open and release the petals. The idea is for the audience to experience both the vision and fragrance of the godly realms."

"*Formidable!* Can you get it to work?"

"The technicians think they may be able to—"

At that moment, a silver Porsche Carrera with its top down came careening along the highway at a speed that far exceeded tourist pace. We looked to see Michael Kent, AKA Miguel de la Madrid, screech by. He wasn't decked out in his accustomed Preppy style, but in old gray sweats. He also sported a distinct five o'clock shadow, and his hair looked like an exploded shaving brush from driving in the wind.

Eddy whistled. "*Híjole!* I wonder what Michael's doing here instead of at rehearsal."

"Looks like he spent the night in the rough. Sure is a fancy car, though."

"I'm sure it was a present from his daddy." The corners of Eddy's mouth turned down in a wry look, but his eyes were dancing. "Wouldn't it be nice to be rich—"

"Instead of so good-looking," I finished his sentence, and we both dissolved in laughter. "First, you think you see a colleague, and now a graduate student flies by. Next, it'll be a reunion of the entire department."

"Let's hope not." His eyes still held their amused look. "Speaking of which, are you coming to the department party tomorrow afternoon?"

"I haven't been invited to any party."

"It's at Baldo's house. He wants to kick off the summer semester and get everyone enthusiastic about the fundraiser. I'm sure you're invited; we all got e-mailed."

"Ah, that explains it. The computer system was down briefly at work, so my e-mail account won't be completely set up until later today." I put down my empty cup. "I usually have Sunday dinner at my parents', but I'd like to go to the party instead. I don't know where Professor Vigil lives, though."

"No problema." He grinned. "Why don't you come with me?"

Chapter Seven

"No hay tal cosa como diversión para toda la familia."
"There's no such thing as fun for the whole family." — Spanish Proverb

I awoke Sunday morning to a cold, forbidding sky and a white mist that obliterated the usually spectacular view of the Flatirons. The air felt damp and clammy, so unlike Colorado's usual crispness. I clicked my tongue like my mother in a gesture of disgust. As they say, if you don't like the weather in Boulder, wait fifteen minutes, and it will change.

I tucked my hands and feet under the covers to warm them and tried to piece together the strange dream I'd had of *alebrijes*, those brightly colored Native American fantasy animals. In my dream, the painted wooden figurines reminded me of the department faculty, smirking as they paraded across a blood-red background. A skeleton resembling Eddy, bone white in contrast to the vermillion backdrop and leering like a coyote, led the procession in a sort of macabre medieval dance of death.

I shivered. Why had I cast Eddy as the skeletal leader? He, Mrs. Webber, and Olivia Oakes were about the nicest people I'd met in the department so far. To be fair, I also had my classes. Most of the students appeared eager and bright,. And thank heavens I was left on my own to teach the way I wanted.

Pounding on my front door roused me from my reverie.

"No need to break the door down. I'm coming."

I shrugged into my red flannel bathrobe and stumbled from the bedroom. On my way past the kitchen, I squinted at the espresso machine's clock. 7:03

AM. *"Jesús!"*

I cracked open the door with the chain attached, and immediately closed it, unhooked the chain, and opened.

"Angela! What brings you here so early? It's not even a school day. Want an espresso?"

My fourteen-year-old sister trailed me into the kitchen. "Some of us have important things to do *every* day," the girl said in her isn't-it-all-too-boring? monotone.

But her face was flushed, and her blond hair, the legacy of some Galician ancestor and the bane of her existence because it made her look so so Angla, frizzed around her head like a halo askew. Bad sign. Who was yanking her chain now?

Yawning, I felt for the button on the espresso machine. As I prepared the coffee, I said, "*Some* of us had to stay up late to prepare our classes. Contrary to popular belief, a professor's job doesn't end when class is out." I could pout, too, especially at this outlandish hour.

"*Ay,* that explains it." Angela dumped her backpack on the floor and dropped onto a kitchen chair.

"Explains what?" I narrowed my eyes, bloodshot from the restless night I'd had.

"I guess I don't exactly mean 'explain.'"

I set two little black steaming cups in their saucers on the table. I took a seat opposite my sister and sipped the reviving brew. "Then you should say what you mean."

The Devil made me say it. I know that provoking Angela when she's in a snit never results in anything good. The teen stared at me with her deeply set eyes so dark they were almost black. Worse sign: they were flashing.

Angela took a gulp of coffee. "I *mean,* that's the excuse you'll use for why you didn't join us in the march for Lupita González yesterday afternoon."

I thumped my forehead. "Must be going senile."

Lupita, a young woman from the barrio in Denver, had married an out-of-work macho man. He beat on her whenever he felt life was cutting him a raw deal, which was half the time, or when he got drunk, which was the other half. One fine day, Lupita got fed up and struck back. With an onyx paperweight from Chihuahua, the closest object at hand. The blow killed the worthless *frijol* and landed Lupita in jail.

As far as the police were concerned, it was one more barrio domestic dispute turned violent. Without money for a hotshot legal team to prove self-defense, Lupita was on her way to getting peeled, stuffed, and fried like a plump Anaheim pepper.

The Aztec Liberation Front (acronym FLA), along with feminists and human rights activists, rallied behind her. They organized a march to the state capitol to broadcast her plight and raise money for her defense. I'd meant to attend, but the rehearsal and my whirlwind date had sent thoughts of Lupita González flying out the window.

"Sorry," I apologized. "Had to go to a play rehearsal at the college."

"Not that *estúpida* medieval play?" Angela drummed her magenta-colored acrylic nails on the tabletop.

"The play is not *estúpida*. It's a good play."

Angela stuck out her chin. "Juventino Guerrero and the FLA say it's *estúpida*."

So, my pugnacious colleague was mixed up with the FLA. Not to mention my little sister. A thought struck me. "The FLA doesn't plan to picket the play, do they?"

"Why do you care? 'Fraid we'll poke a dent in your precious ivory tower?"

"Angela," I tried to explain nicely, but somehow it came out sounding condescending, "the play is being staged for the entire community, not just the university crowd."

"So why don't they stage something that takes on real issues like immigration and workers' rights, huh?"

I felt the all-too-familiar solid wall, thicker than any our current national administration could build, rise up between us. I defaulted to teacher mode, partly for protection and partly because I knew it annoyed Angela. "I'm sure the play's theme gives valuable insights into contemporary society or Professor Calderón wouldn't have selected it. I've heard some of the roles are quite thought-provoking."

"Don't talk to me about roles!" Angela pushed away the half-drunk coffee and made a face. "You're supposed to be a role model for me, but all I see you doing is buying into the Anglo establishment. You don't even have time for your family."

"Pero, Angela—"

"Don't come down on me with that per-persnickety *'pero, Angela'* tone. What makes you so superior, huh?"

"Angela, I'm not—"

"What do you know about life to tell me what to do, huh?" Tears of frustration brimmed in her Madonna eyes. "You've never even had a boyfriend!"

She pushed away from the table, tipping the cup and spilling the coffee. Then she jumped up, grabbed her pack, and stomped out the door.

I stared at the rich chocolaty liquid as it streamed to the end of the table and dripped like black blood on the cream-colored tile floor. Persnickety? A realist, for sure. And if truth be told, sometimes a tad bossy. But persnickety? Where did my sister learn a word like that? Too much social media, undoubtedly. My throat tightened.

What makes Angela such an angry person? We both come from the same background. My sister even grew up in more comfortable circumstances because Papi had a successful restaurant by the time she came along. That my little sister is young, earnest, and naïve, with all those hormones throbbing through her blood, is to be expected. But the vitriolic outbursts—I don't understand them.

Angela's virulent comment about my personal life hit the mark. True, as yet I've not had a serious love interest. Not that I've never dated. For instance, there was the Latino grad student who'd taken me out when I was a senior. He spent half of the evening telling me what courses I should take and how he knew everything there was to know about the Generation of '98 in Spain, his thesis topic. I never learned how the second half of the evening would have panned out because I asked him to take me home before we made it to the art film theater.

Then there was the gawky Anglo-Spanish major with the thinning hair who crowed about how he knew what kind of housekeeper his dates would make because he could see the dust bunnies on top of their refrigerators. *Vaya!*

Maybe I'm too much into this career thing. My gaze wandered around my kitchen. What am I doing anyway with a deluxe espresso machine and a two-bedroom condo with its cream-tiled kitchen, eco-smart wood-burning fireplace, and scenic view if I have no friends to invite over and no one to share it with?

I felt my eyes water. Grabbing a sponge from the sink, I furiously wiped up the mess. No use crying over spilled milk. Or, in this case, coffee.

I brewed another espresso to take to the bathroom, where I began my ablutions. My runt sister wasn't going to ruin my day. Today I was going on a picnic with my colleagues. Strange as these people seemed, they shared my love of literature, teaching, and research. I belonged with them. The memory of Eddy's herbal-musky scent and the pressure of his hand on mine stirred a long-buried thrill of excitement. Perhaps later today I would prove Angela wrong.

Chapter Eight

"No hay camino tan plano que no tenga algún tropezón."
"There is no road so level as to have no rough places." — *Miguel de Cervantes*

The chairman lived in a big, blocky hacienda-style ranch in the Freemont Vegas subdivision. The houses were all new, so the land around them was pretty much devoid of foliage except for a few struggling aspen saplings and low-growing junipers. In the spitting spring rain, the only season in which we can generally count on moisture in this semi-arid region, the neighborhood looked abandoned and forlorn. The kind of landscape around here that, as the season progresses, succumbs to ragweed, bindweed, and wild lettuce.

Where the front lawn should have been, masses of pebbles tinted black, brown, tan, brick, and white, arranged in geometrical patterns, glistened with drizzle. They reminded me of pictures I'd seen of mosaic floors of an ancient Roman villa. Taking a deep breath, I commanded myself to remember I was here to get to know my colleagues better, enjoy myself, and forget about the hurtful things my sister had said.

I stepped up to the portico with Eddy. The massive mahogany door, carved with unidentifiable animals and the predominant initials B V, was flanked by two Doric columns. Vigil's wife answered the bell and welcomed us into a Romanesque atrium crowded with succulents, mostly cacti. Penelope Vigil was a gangly woman with big feet, a beaky nose, and skin stretched taut around anxious eyes. With a rough, work-worn hand, she plucked at the sleeve of her oversized white linen hostess dress, which had wrinkled in the unaccustomed humidity.

"No need to show us to the party if you have goodies to prepare in the kitchen, Penny," Eddy said after making introductions and offering his hostess a colorful bouquet and a dazzling smile. "We'll follow our noses."

We left our umbrellas in the hall, dripping in harmony with several companions. Turned out it was the only harmonious resonance I would experience all afternoon. Stepping around a renegade cactus that threatened to impale me, I followed Eddy and a trail of barbecue smoke to the screened back porch.

The grill, the source of the smoke, had been moved there because of the rain. It crouched in the center of the room like an ill-tempered dragon, belching out puffs of gray smudge at frequent intervals. Most of the faculty hunkered nearby on folding chairs set in a semi-circle around the grill to avoid sitting too close to the room's edges because of the rain filtering in through the screens. To me, the group looked more like they were waiting out a siege than enjoying an afternoon picnic.

The squat, bald man with the Hitleresque mustache, whom I took to be Chairman Vigil, was vigorously tending the grill. He cruelly stabbed the bratwursts, piercing and flipping over the sausages as they browned. The gesture and the gusto with which he executed the grilling reminded me of how an Inquisitor might rake a suspected infidel over the coals.

Noticing my glance, Eddy whispered in my ear, "As St. Lawrence, while being roasted, was claimed to have said, 'I'm done on this side. You can turn me over now.'"

I suppressed a giggle but shivered nonetheless. I wrapped the cotton scarf that matched my blue-and-white cornflower sundress around my shoulders. I had nobody to blame but myself for being so vain as to wear the flimsy summer outfit on such a dismal day.

Eddy brought me a glass of white wine and a Dos Equis for himself and we joined the others nursing their drinks.

Since I hadn't yet met the chairman, I was surprised that when he saw me, he smiled unctuously and announced, "Has everyone met Isabel Castillo, our new Medievalist?"

For a man of such short stature, Baldomero Vigil's voice carried across the room like that of a Shakespearean actor who needed to be heard at the back of the auditorium. The subdued conversations ceased, and all eyes turned toward the Chair.

The odd thing about Vigil, something nobody could fail to notice right away, were his eyes. While his right eye homed in on its objective with imperious precision, the left one tended to orbit around of its own accord, not quite fixing on a specific target. In the old days, the superstitious would have claimed Vigil was plagued with the *mal de ojo,* the Evil Eye.

I pasted on my face what I hoped was a pleasant smile. If my colleagues didn't beam back, most acknowledged me. Georgina Rampage sat bolt upright in her folding chair without touching her back to it. She looked as disdainful as if she'd found herself perched in a rowboat surrounded by leeches. I recognized the steel-gray pantsuit from the day before, with the added festive adornment of a chrome necklace that looked like it would feel more comfortable gracing an automobile grille than Georgina's Modigliani neck.

The modern literature professor had been listening to Carrot Top Clive, who was waxing on the theme of clocks in the works of Julio Cortázar, punctuating his points with large gestures. When he saw me, he leaped up, rushed over, and squeezed my hand.

"Lovely to see you again, dear lady." He grabbed my wrist. "Let's take a peek at what you're wearing today." His turquoise orbs sparkled. "Oh, my whiskers! If it isn't a Pink Panther watch!" He eyeballed the watch I sometimes wear to dress up a bit. "You've outdone yourself."

"Strange!" the chairman snapped, and Clive dropped my arm like it was a hot tamal. He retired to a chair but continued to direct furtive glances my way.

Suzanne and Dolores hunched together on their folding chairs like a pair of conspirators. Suzanne waved the sleeve of her electric pink muumuu at me like she was swatting flies, but Dolores averted her eyes.

A smooth-faced, dark-complexioned man in jeans and a red and black wide plaid lumberjack shirt open at the collar stood in a relaxed stance behind Suzanne's chair. "I'm Joe Selos," he introduced himself. "I don't work at the college, but I'm married to Suzanne." He leaned over and gave his wife a toothy grin, which she ignored.

Vigil, who had just speared a sausage, volunteered another introduction with a wave of his fork. "You may not have met Juventino Guerrero, our Caribbean and Mexico specialist."

El Señor FLA—Aztec Liberation Front Guy—stood next to a woman at a screened window, his back to the ensemble, legs apart, fists clasped behind his back. He barely turned to acknowledge me with eyes that looked like he spent way too much time indulging at Starbucks. When he noticed Eddy, he stiffened and swung back to the window. His companion was more forthcoming. Uma Clone Bibi Pomodoro turned at an angle. Placing her weight on one foot, she stuck out a provocative hip, lowered her eyelids at Eddy, but spoke to me. "Hello, Isabel. Baldomero didn't introduce me because he knows I'm in your class."

I wish that girl would quit using first names. And what's a student doing at a faculty party, anyway?

Penelope, Olivia, and Mrs. Webber arrived from the kitchen, weighted down with serving bowls of potato salad, coleslaw, baked beans, and other picnic food, sadly unsuitable for the dreary weather.

"Glad you could make it, Issy," Olivia greeted me. "Are the brats ready, Baldomero?" She eyed the grill. "Why, you've scorched those poor weenies within an inch of their lives."

The women set the bowls on a long table covered with a red and white checked vinyl cloth, and everybody shuffled over to fill their dishes. With plates in hand, most people ate and conversed while milling around. I joined Vigil, Georgina, and Olivia.

Vigil was saying, "—graphics artist we commissioned last winter has finished the new design for the department letterhead."

Georgina pursed her lips like she was sucking a lemon.

He said, "If we all approve, we'll order the stationery right away so we can use it to invite alums to the fundraiser for the book collection. Our elegant letterhead will help persuade potential donors to part with some of their money."

I hoped that the merits of the collection and the desire to improve students' education at the alums' alma mater would count for more than the appearance of the paper on which the requests were written, but this wasn't the time or place to voice my opinion.

I left Vigil to talk to Mrs. Webber and Penelope, but the chairman's voice surged over the others' conversations. I heard him say to Eddy and Suzanne, "We also need to present our request to the dean as soon as possible so he can resolve the Portuguese program issue before the fall semester begins."

On the other side of the grill, Dolores straightened as if she'd been stuck with a hot poker, but kept her eyes riveted on her plate.

"Oh, not that again!" Clive, who was returning from the drinks table, rolled his eyes and nudged me. "The perennial topic of conversation around here is whether to give old Dolores the boot."

Then to the group, "This, when we have *so* many more critical matters to discuss, such as how to synchronize the clocks in the classrooms. It's scandalous how some show as much as twelve minutes difference. How are we expected to time our lectures? And why in blazes doesn't the college invest in some of those inexpensive atomic clocks? With all due respect, Chairman Vigil, I suggest you bring this up with the dean."

Vigil's mustache twitched as he ignored Clive and addressed the entire gathering with a commanding voice and eye. "Our stationery states that we are 'The Department of Spanish and Portuguese,' but we don't offer much beyond Dolores's occasional 101 class and Portuguese for Spanish speakers. When she leaves, we can eliminate the word from our letterhead and also save money." His smile looked as satisfied as if he'd discovered a way to pay off the national debt.

Dolores dropped into a chair, and on seeing her bleached pallor, I feared she might faint. Instead, she placed her plate on a nearby chair and stared at the floor.

Suzanne plunked down next to her friend and threw a protective arm around her back. "I'm sure Dol is short on numbers because it's the summer session," she told us. "Many of the grad students, who confide in me like their sister, intend to take her class in the fall."

At this, Dolores raised her purple-rimmed eyes and pleaded, "Suzanne, don't."

Juventino had been staring out the screened window at the rain, throwing back occasional shots of Scotch provided by the thoughtful Bibi. Now, he turned his bulging eyes on the chairman. "My independent studies student wants to include the Brazilian MPB Movement in his paper on Latin American songs of protest." He spoke as if everyone knew about the MPB and was awestruck by its importance.

Eddy's eyes glowed as he reminded the group, "Don't forget I'm producing a play by a Portuguese dramatist. If I can convince the dean to let me take it on the road, we're sure to draw many new students to the program."

Georgina's baritone grumble made her words sound contentious. "Speaking of the dean, I think it's time to approach him again about my offering a class in feminist lit—"

Olivia broke in. "In the first place, Baldomero, I hope you're not suggesting we ax the Portuguese program just to make our letterhead look tidier. And since I don't recall we've ever bothered to poll our students to see whether they want to pursue Luso-Brazilian studies, how can we assume they're not interested? Let Dolores offer a fall class on Brazilian Literature and Culture and see what happens."

"We need the dean's approval for any new classes." Vigil's right eye glared at her.

Even though Dolores had given me no reason to defend her, my heart went out to the beleaguered instructor for being blistered like one of the brats. I felt the color rise in my face and balked about making my views known in this disquieting forum. But if I didn't speak up now, it would only get harder to do so in the future.

"Um." I cleared my throat. All heads swiveled in my direction. "I'm teaching Medieval Galego-Portuguese Literature, and my class roster is full. So, I think there may be enough interest in Portuguese and Brazilian literature and language, at least, initially, to warrant continuing to teach it."

I smiled at Dolores. Instead of the positive response I expected, I found myself warding off a look that made me feel like I'd stumbled on a nasty cold spot in a haunted house.

Vigil, who I wasn't sure had heard me since he hadn't responded to me with either eye, shrugged and said, "We'll take up this issue formally at a faculty meeting."

The tense moment passed, and the conversations turned toward less controversial topics.

After a while, Eddy wandered over, and, with a comical arch of an eyebrow, asked, "Enjoying the party, are we?"

"Immensely." I arched both my eyebrows in kind.

"You may find that some of our little ways take time getting used to, but I assure you we're harmless. Most of the time." He glanced at Juventino's back. "Of course, not everyone is here during the summer session. For example, Bill Long, our linguistics specialist, whom you met at your MLA interview, is in Chile gathering data for a paper on 'Araucanian Vestiges in the Dialect of the Montaña.' Such a fun guy—keeps us in stitches."

I had to laugh at that one. "I'm sure everything will make sense once I settle into the routine."

I'd become so absorbed in our conversation that I hadn't noticed Dolores, Suzanne, and her husband getting ready to leave. As they passed by, Suzanne chirped, "Tweet, tweet, tweet. Have fun, you two lovebirds!"

She flounced off. Her husband, smiling an apology, trotted after her. Dolores, her emaciated frame dwarfed by a black raincoat, ghosted along in their wake.

I turned as pink as Suzanne's muumuu. The end of my first week at work and I'd already managed to become the topic of gossip. *Híjole!* To cover my embarrassment, I said to Eddy, "You mentioned yesterday that you grew up in Santa Fe. My family is originally from New Mexico."

"We have something in common then."

"Did you really live in a haunted house?"

"Absolutely! In an old house in the same neighborhood as the oldest home in the United States. So many spirits appeared and disappeared through nonexistent doorways that I got covered with bumps and bruises, trying to follow them through the walls. The American Psychical Research Society even came out and recorded the apparitions."

My eyes widened. *"De veras?* Real live ghost hunters?"

"De veras. I swear. Live bodies in search of spirits of the dead."

"I'd love to live in a haunted house."

"Say, I've got a photo of it squirreled away somewhere in a drawer in my office. Want to drop by there when we leave here?"

"Why not?" *The sooner we dematerialize from this place, the better.*

* * *

"Bien. I can understand Dolores," I said as Eddy negotiated the murky, rain-slicked streets on our way to the department, "but what's Suzanne's problem? I mean, she's talkative enough, but almost every word she says seems laced with venom."

By the time we escaped the party, dusk was looming, and a dense fog had settled over the town along with persistent rain. Eddy, to whom I was grateful for taking his Subaru instead of the Harley, slogged his car through a big puddle, then said, "La Celosa is another story altogether."

"La Celosa? Ah, I get it. *Celos* means 'jealousy' in Spanish."

"Yup. Selos by name, *celosa* by nature. I think she's jealous of anybody whom she perceives has a better life than hers."

We ground to a halt at a red light, and Eddy explained, "She got seduced by a handsome face and *piropos,* you know, the pretty compliments we Latinos throw at anyone wearing a skirt. Suzanne, who, because of her large girth and even larger personality, had probably never enjoyed such attention. She fell hook, line, and sinker for Joe, the high school football star. They took the plunge, and now she feels marooned with him in the deep end."

He turned onto University Drive, negotiating a trickling stream that had sprung up from nowhere. "Much to her chagrin, he prefers climbing trees for Joe's Landscaping and Tree Service instead of jetting around the world like she yearns for."

"If their marriage is such a disaster, why doesn't she ask for a divorce?"

We streamed into the almost empty faculty lot, and Eddy parked. We got out, raised our umbrellas against the rain, and continued our conversation.

"It's complicated," said Eddy. "Joe seems smitten with Suzanne, and he gives her a lot of latitude. Plus, he owns that landscaping business and has acquired several commercial customers to go along with it. He keeps Suzanne independent from her parents, whom she hates."

We followed the fog-misted walkway, almost obscured by bowed, water-laden maple and oak branches. "If you ask me," Eddy mused, "I think she's looking for something exciting to occupy her fertile mind. I can't blame her for not wanting to languish in the basement, subduing a bunch of unruly TAs. She told me she once dreamed of going onstage, but her parents wouldn't foot the bill for acting school. That's why I've given her the female lead in the play."

"Aw, that's sweet of you!"

We were traversing the crosswalk over a narrow drive that snaked through campus and by the department. Eddy's eyes widened in alarm.

"Watch out!"

He grabbed my arm and catapulted us both to the other side of the crosswalk as a big gray van barreled down the drive past where we'd been walking. Our umbrellas flew out of our grasp and skidded across the grass.

The driver halted the van several feet away, rolled down his window, and called in a laconic voice, "Didn't see you."

"Watch where you're going, Guerrero," yelled Eddy. "You almost killed us!"

"I said I didn't see you." With that, Juventino rolled up his window and vaporized into the gloom.

"*Idiota!*" Eddy huffed across the lawn to rescue the umbrellas.

I'd been stunned into silence by the narrow escape, but now found my voice. "You've got sharp eyes, Eddy. Thanks for pushing me out of the way."

He returned with the umbrellas and his composure intact. "I'm here to serve." He peered down the dark drive toward where the van had been swallowed up. "Funny, I could have sworn Juventino was aiming for you."

I gulped. "It looked to me like he was aiming for *you.*"

He shrugged and turned back to me. "That *tipo* doesn't know what he's aiming at in more ways than one."

We scurried to the department in what had turned into a downpour. Panting to a stop at the lighted portico by the main door, we shook out our umbrellas. I noticed the stain on the sidewalk that had dripped from Michael Kent's bloody nose had washed away.

Eddy opened the door for me, and Clive Strange burst out.

"Ah!" he exclaimed and stopped short. For a moment, his bright eyes stared us up and down. Then he blurted, "Scorpio and Scorpio. You two were destined to forge an alliance."

"An alliance?" I echoed. "What alliance?"

"An alliance, and more, but what more is not yet clear."

"Isn't it time you toddled home, Strange?" Eddy said with a raised eyebrow.

"Time," pronounced Clive. "Time may be running out for one among us." He cast a dark look toward the blackened sky. "It's written in the stars, and the stars never lie." With that, he shot off across campus like a UFO that had just discovered it had landed on the wrong planet.

We entered the department and trudged to the second floor, our wet shoes squelching over the varnished wood.

"How did Clive manage to get here before we did?" I wondered. "And what was all that about Scorpios and the stars?"

Eddy laughed and shook his head. "Clive's everywhere and nowhere. He's a slippery fish. I've no idea why he's so obsessed with clocks and astrology."

"He may see astrology as some sort of corollary to the time and clock theme," I mused. "Perhaps he feels he exerts little control over his own life except for what he can measure with timepieces and the stars."

"I've never looked at it that way, but you may be right."

We reached Eddy's office and he unlocked and opened the door. Following him in, I shut it behind us. I hung my damp scarf to dry on one of the pegs on the back of the door, sank down on the loveseat, and rubbed my calf. It felt like I'd pulled a muscle in my leg sprinting across the drive, and I ached all over. It felt good to sit placidly within this sanctuary, listening to the rain pattering like a soft chorus of friendly voices against the windowpanes while Eddy poked around in drawers.

I stared at the Native American rug. It was woven with figures of turtles, eagles, bears, and other symbolic animals rendered in bright greens, blues, and yellows on a dark red background. Somehow, it looked familiar, probably because I'd seen it the day I broke my heel.

"Nice rug," I commented.

"Thanks." Eddy's mind was still on Clive. "I'm afraid Strange takes both astrology and clocks a bit too seriously." He continued to comb through his desk drawers. "He refuses to talk to me because he claims his and my signs clash. And that's about to create a big problem."

"Why?"

He banged one drawer shut and opened another. "Mark Allen, the guy you replaced, called me last week from Montana, where he retired, to tell me he's missing a clock since he moved. Not just any clock, either. It's a Louis XVI mantelpiece worth a small fortune that he kept in his office."

"You think Clive took it?"

Eddy paused in his search. "It seems so. As you can imagine, he's always drooled over that clock. When Mark was moving out, Clive offered to help pack the U-Haul. I watched him carry the clock down the hall and out the door. That was the last time anybody saw it." He went back to opening and closing drawers.

I clicked my tongue. "Doesn't look good for Clive."

"It gets worse." He looked at me with expressive eyes that for a moment, made it seem like he was probing the depths of my soul. "Issy, can I confide in you?"

I felt little beads of perspiration forming under my armpits. This guy was starting to share TMI too soon. But I said, "Of course."

"When we were in Nederland the other day, I hadn't spotted a colleague in that alley. I was checking out a clock repair store. The owner, who's known in the region as an expert in timepieces, also deals in rare clocks."

My eyes widened. "What did you find out?"

"The owner was at an antiques fair in Denver and the assistant didn't know zip." He sighed and went back to his search. "I must have a man-to-man with Clive soon, no matter how much our signs clash. I think he'd rather deal with me than with Baldo."

I remembered Vigil's accusatory eye. "If Clive publicly admits to the theft," I said, "won't that put a black mark on his record?"

"Oh, it will do more than that. He'll probably lose his job. I've tried to catch him all week, but the party wasn't the right place to—*Epa!* Here it is!" From the back of a drawer, he extracted an old black-and-white framed photograph.

Photo in hand, he got up and came to sit beside me. As I bent to better see, we almost touched heads. With a grin showing a missing front tooth, a young boy posed next to a little girl on the sidewalk in front of an old adobe-style house.

"She's my sister," he said. "I'm the runt with the skinny legs. Sorry, I've never been able to snap a photo of the ghost."

I admired the photo and listened to Eddy spin several yarns of spirit visitations until I stifled a yawn.

"Looks like somebody needs to get to bed," he remarked.

"I guess I'm tired from the week's activities," I admitted. "Besides school and moving into my condo, I've had a few family issues to deal with."

"Let's pack you off to your place."

I stood and gathered my purse. As Eddy opened the door, he moved close. Again, I caught his indefinable musky scent. "You know, Issy," he said in a husky voice, "you've brought a ray of much-needed sunshine into the dark corridors of this department."

I started to deny it, but he pressed his index finger to my lips. "Really, you have. I hope you'll be very happy here." With that, he lifted my chin and kissed me.

Chapter Nine

"La vida es sueño."
"Life is a dream." — Pedro Calderón de la Barca, 1600-1681, Spanish Dramatist

Even at this stage I hadn't an inkling of the horror about to unfold. I thought the alarm bells had to do with dating, not murder. *Híjole,* was I wrong!

It took me a while to fall asleep. What to make of Eddy Calderón? As flattered as I was by his attentions, I couldn't help thinking this was a case of too much too soon. Not to mention, I had no idea about university rules regarding faculty fraternization. I needed to know a lot more about Enigma Eddy before I'd consider getting intimate. That he often didn't answer my questions directly and didn't always look me in the eye puzzled me. Was he serious or joking with some of his off-the-wall comments, such as the one about Boulder being a good place to hide one's identity? Or how faculty members were harmless "most of the time."?

Also, he seemed to want to control people and situations, including Dolores, Suzanne, Clive, and, to some degree, Javier and even Georgina. He carried a chip on his shoulder about the chairman. For that, I didn't blame him. But what was up between him and Juventino? Something to do with Uma Clone? Bibi was with Juventino at the party but kept stealing glances at Eddy. Were the two men rivals for her attentions? The attentions of an undergraduate? Where were the morals there?

I punched my pillow and rolled onto my side. I was making a mountain out of a molehill; worse, seeing wedding bells from one little kiss.

I lay on my back and stared at the ceiling. My poor attitude isn't all my fault. With Mami going on about my high school friends who are married with kids, and Papi, the "Build the Wall" Trump man, hinting that he hopes his daughter hasn't been infected by what he considers the Ivy League diseases—Lesbianism and promiscuity—I've been feeling more pressure than ever to find a mate. But I refuse to be pushed into marriage so I can settle down and conform to the dictates of the conservative branch of Latino society. Despite Enigma Eddy's attractions, I'll go into this dating thing with caution.

The last image I registered before falling asleep was the picture of the New Mexico pueblo I'd taken from the living room and rehung on the wall opposite my bed. It reminded me of Eddy's conversation about living in a haunted house in Santa Fe.

* * *

I must be having another bad dream because something is terribly wrong. I feel paralyzed, unable to move or cry out. I'm wrapped tight as a mummy in a threadbare orange blanket, hunched immobile over the long-extinguished ashes of my kiva. The icy wind from a sudden spring storm is dumping heavy snow on my pueblo to the depth of a third of a full-grown pine tree and is moaning outside. Little fingers of frost are creeping down the walls from cracks in the closed ladder opening in the roof.

Except for the wailing wind, everything, including me, lies still, both inside and out. Not a crow, jay, or magpie, let alone a human being, is foolish enough to venture forth in this blizzard. Mountain Lion waits out the storm with her pride. Black Bear, snug in his cave home, has not yet awakened from winter's slumber.

I clutched at my sheet. Where was this place? So familiar, yet so alien to me. Besides, I don't have a kiva.

The bleak afternoon has changed to night and plunged my little adobe into darkness. Neither the blanket nor the gray ashes warm my body, which, by now, looks purplish-brown and wrinkled like a dried-up plum. I still can't move, but no longer care because I know I'm dead. That's right! Dead as the flies that hatched around the remains of my last meal, only to be frozen by the abrupt drop in temperature.

Dead? I can't be dead! I'm home in bed, tangled in the covers. Why can't I move?

Now, I'm hovering near the ceiling, observing the scene with an eerie air of detachment. I no longer feel involved with my withered, contorted shell. Nor am I engaged with the oddly familiar dwelling and its hard-packed dirt floor that smells of Mother Earth. Even the pueblo and its brown-faced people, who I've known so well, have ceased to engage me. The fabric of emotional attachments has separated from my essence along with my life like cottonwood fluff. Without a body, I no longer experience pain, only lightness and buoyancy. If I had a mouth I would giggle like when my mother tickled me.

Yet I'm aware of an uncomfortable thought persisting somewhere in the depths of my being. I remain suspended over the scene instead of moving on, as I know I should. Slowly, the pattern of my life is coming into focus.

Whose life? Am I really not asleep in bed in my condo but instead, hovering somewhere in the sky?

Life in the pueblo, where I lived as a child of Earth, has been good. I know every plant, animal, and particle of soil, from the red clay of the riverbanks to the smoky candle-gray rocks of the canyon walls and the yellow dirt of the cornfields. My mother, also an herbalist, taught me the basic properties of botanicals—what can cure and what can harm. Always inquisitive, I've made many experiments and soon became adept at healing my people of their physical and emotional ills. Over time, I've also contemplated the larger questions of life, death, and the role humanity plays in the world.

It doesn't surprise me that I've lived most of my life as a hermit except for my animals and clientele. Yet I also have known love—the love of my parents who died too soon, and the brief but passionate love of a man—a stranger and a Spaniard, who long ago passed through the region searching for gold. From our union was born my daughter, whom I adored beyond all else and to whom I expected to pass my accumulated herbal wisdom.

No, no! It's all wrong! Mami and Papi are alive and well. I barely know Eddy. And I know for a fact that I've never had a baby. I struggled to free myself from this state of suspended animation and wake up, but lethargy took over, and I plunged back into the depths.

The atmosphere around me is trembling almost imperceptibly now. I find myself outside my adobe, above the red-tiled roofs, eye-to-eye with the foam-capped mountains. Below, the rutted mud path that surrounds the pueblo and the stream that separates the north and south halves of the settlement glitter under a pale moon traveling across the midnight sky. Nearby, I sense the subtle rustlings of another world urging me to merge with it.

But the niggling thought still shimmers in my mind like too much sparkling snow on a sunny day. I need to tidy this loose end before I can leave.

Leave for where? What have I been thinking?

Oh yes. My daughter showed no interest or aptitude in the healing arts. She grew up, married, and moved away. Not even to a neighboring pueblo, no, but far away to a place called Colorado, where her family sought work.

I remained in the pueblo, isolated by the reverence of my people. They always held me aloft with respect like the statues of the saints they parade in front of the church on festival days. Without anyone on whom to confer my knowledge and continue the healing, my bloodline will die out.

"Isabella," the stars are twinkling a message, "it is time to come with us."

If I had a chin, I would stick it out stubbornly. "No, it is not ended. I must stay!

What? I'm Isabel—Issy, not Isabella. Stay where? Here in Colorado? I fought even harder against the all-consuming light, feeling myself reel from side to side.

One of the stars is glimmering bigger and brighter than the others, and I'm aware of a voice pulsating from its glow.

"Isabella, you who so often have witnessed the flux and reflux of life, know that the time has come for transformation. This does not mean that all is finished, for in our endings, we find beginnings."

The light is swelling, pushing away the black night from the sky. "Listen to us, Isabella. All is not over. You still have an important mission to accomplish. Your inheritor needs you. Have faith! You will see!"

* * *

A bright flash and a loud crack made me sit bolt-upright in bed. Sweat was pouring down my face, and I was staring straight ahead at the picture of the pueblo I'd hung on the opposite wall. My heart raced, and I trembled from the dream, or vision, or whatever it was. It took me five minutes to quiet down and reengage with this time and this place. I realized that the flash was from the lights of a police car that had stopped a car on the road above my street, and the crack was the closing of a car door.

When I was able to move, I staggered out of bed, flung open the curtain, and stared out my bedroom window. Even though my feet were still tingling, I knew I was alive and in Boulder. It was the twenty-first century, as I could tell from the streetlights and the police stopping a motorist for a traffic violation.

Hombre, either you've been drinking way too many espressos, or the glass of wine you had at the chairman's party disagreed with you. You'd better cut down on both.

I stood in front of the open fridge and extracted a bottle of milk. Warm milk, that's what I needed to put that terrifying nightmare behind me. And that picture of the pueblo, as intriguing as it was, had better go back into the living room. Or maybe I'd donate it. I'd think about that and the dream tomorrow. Right now, I needed to get some rest.

Chapter Ten

"Un buen amigo es mejor que una relación cercana."
"A good friend is better than a near relation." — *Spanish Proverb*
"What about a doppelganger?" — *Issy Castillo*

After last night's excitement, I slept poorly, obsessing over what it all meant and coming up with no explanation. So I faced Monday morning with nervous tension rattling around in my head like the coffee beans in my espresso machine. Nevertheless, I took a deep breath of the musty air emanating from the department basement and marched downstairs to begin my workday. When I approached my office door, I noticed something tacked under my nameplate. In the dim light, I bent close to identify it. Reeling back, I hit the wall on the opposite side of the hall and let out a shriek. Impaled on the door like specimens in a butterfly exhibit were two scorpion corpses. And this was no dream.

The office door across the hall groaned open, and Dolores Lopes stuck out a sour face. "I thought I heard a commotion." She spoke in a tired voice like an ancient Victrola winding down.

I felt like the little girl who, on opening her desk during third period, screamed at the sight of the rubber spider a boy had flopped there. "It's only me. Sorry to disturb you. Somebody left two dead scorpions on my door, and they startled me."

Having recovered from my momentary jolt, I decided Dolores had offered me the ghost of an opportunity. If I ever wanted to get on this senior instructor's good side, now was the time. Acting more breathless than I was,

I panted, "M-may I come in and sit for a minute?"

Dolores deadpanned from me to her office interior and back to me again. She shrugged and cracked her door a smidgen wider. I followed her in and sank into an easy chair.

"Sorry to be such a pansy," I apologized. "I need to catch my breath."

Dolores shuffled over to her desk and slumped in her chair, facing me.

"It was probably students," she said in a monotone. "They can be quite cruel." Hers sounded like the voice of experience.

Speaking of pansies it dawned on me that her chair had a cushion with a slipcover of cheerful violet printed chintz, and that drapes of the same material with dainty, scalloped edges hung at the window. Taking the throw pillow with its contrasting nightshade-purple floral design, I wedged it behind my back.

"What a pretty office!" I commented. "It looks fresh as a spring morning."

The shadow of a smile skittered across the instructor's lips. "I don't have much money to spend on decoration. I pick up things at thrift stores and do my own sewing."

I smiled in encouragement. "Maybe you can give me some ideas on how to redo my own office. It's a real dungeon."

"I'm sure you don't need help in that department." Dolores' voice now held a curt edge. She picked up a red marking pen and poised it over a pile of papers on her desk. She may have opened her physical door but letting me into her personal life wasn't going to be so easy.

"I see you're busy grading papers," I said and stood to leave. "Thanks for letting me rest here a minute."

Frowning at the stack of papers as if she were obliged to discover the key to the Rosetta Stone hidden somewhere in the pile, Dolorous Dolores nodded. And so, I was dismissed.

I went to the bathroom for paper towels so I wouldn't have to touch the offensive little carcasses. Returning to the door, with trembling fingers, I removed the scorpions and tacks, then walked back to the bathroom and dropped the mess into the wastebasket.

***

After teaching my morning classes, I felt too spooked to go back to my office. Finding myself at a dead end in more ways than one, I left the university and wandered home. During the night, the rain had stopped. Now, the sun shone bright in the newly washed blue sky, exuding with its warmth the promise of summer around the corner. I drank in the sharp, piney scent of the Foothills forest to help chase away the stink from the department. Unlocking my front door, I tossed my keys and briefcase on a side table and flopped down on my living room sofa, another thrift store purchase.

I'm not a doom-and-gloom type by nature. Really, I'm not. But with a couple of notable exceptions, the picture painted so far by the department and its inhabitants would have challenged both Coco and Cantinflas to put on a happy face. The more I thought about the fusty reception I'd received from some of my colleagues, the near collision with Juventino's van, and now the scorpion incident, the more edgy I got.

Had Juventino meant to run me down, as Eddy implied? Had he learned that Angela was my sister and that I'd object to the impressionable teen taking too active a part in FLA activities? Would that provide enough motive for Juventino to want to kill me? Scare me, maybe. But kill me? I couldn't fathom that.

Whose nose had I put out of joint enough to pull the scorpion prank? Surely not a student. None of them knew me very well, and I hadn't had time yet to dole out any failing grades. How about Clive? He'd babbled on about Eddy and me being Scorpios, the sign of the scorpion. Could Carrot Top hold that against me? Eddy might know in the same way he knew that Dolores resented my presence.

Dolores could have done it, although I didn't see her as the type to play such a trick—it would sap too much of her strength. There *was* La Celosa Suzanne. She appeared to brim with what, in a kinder mood, I might have termed "misdirected energy." Jealousy could be her motive, but again, jealous of what? It wasn't as if I were climbing into the sack every night hot and heavy with Eddy.

Eddy. Hmm. He might possess the makings of a good friend and provide an island of protection in a stormy sea of envious women, subversives, and thieves. But I hesitated to express my concerns to a man. What I needed was a female friend to confide in. And no way was I going to discuss this with my family. They'd insist I quit teaching, move in with them, go to work at the restaurant, and marry some nice Latino businessman. Olivia seemed a good sort, but our friendship was still in the bud phase. I found myself rubbing my sore neck muscles.

Struggling to my feet, I went to the window and pulled open the drapes. Buttercup-yellow sunshine cascaded into the room along with a Chamber of Commerce view of the Flatirons thrusting up against the sapphire sky. Essences of mountain sage, lavender, and wild geranium released from their leaves a warmth that wafted through the screened window like fragrant smoke from Aladdin's lamp. The Foothills, as mysterious and iconic as the Great Pyramids, beckoned. Maybe a change of scenery would kickstart my flagging intuition.

I scrounged around for my backpack, threw in a bottle of water, a chocolate bar—a promiscuity substitute, I told myself—and my journal. I exchanged my teaching clothes for cutoff jeans and a red tank top and added socks and running shoes. As I passed from the bedroom to the bathroom, I paused to glance at the picture of the pueblo. Such a bizarre dream I'd had. At the time, I felt I was two people: myself and some ancient Indian herbalist with a very strong personality. I shivered at the thought, then shook my head and brushed it off. In the bathroom, I wound my hair into a thick black braid to keep the curls out of my face, scooped up my pack, blanket, keys, and wallet, and sped out the door.

My second brother Germán, the used car salesman, had sold me my aging VW. After subjecting it to some major bodywork, I had it painted a wild iris color, my favorite hue. Now it sat waiting in the parking lot, looking more like a patient purple grazing cow than a wild iris. I put everything into the backseat and coaxed my girl into action. Off we went, and if we didn't breeze up the canyon, we chugged along at a dignified pace, giving us both the opportunity to admire the scenery.

After driving a few miles up Boulder Canyon like I'd done with Eddy, I turned right and headed up the less traveled Four-Mile Canyon Road toward the former mining town of Gold Hill. Here, the creek ran high from recent rains, and in the narrow, shady canyon, everything smelled more of earth than grass. The odor of old smoke still lingered from the massive fire that almost destroyed this canyon a few years ago. But new grasses, wildflowers, junipers, fir trees, and aspen were poking out from the ash-fertilized ground, reaffirming the indomitable life force that is Nature. Enough conifers had remained unscathed along the roadside that they loomed over the road like sentinels monitoring the Beetle's intrusion into their territory.

I maneuvered the VW around several switchbacks and halted alongside one. Taking my pack and blanket from the backseat, I locked the car and hiked up a sketchy trail that wound through the forest toward my hideaway.

My brothers Tony and Germán and I had discovered the place one weekend when the family drove to Gold Hill to visit friends. I must have been eight or nine because Angelita hadn't been born yet. Rambling around some abandoned mines, we'd spied an old wagon track that dead-ended in a clearing bounded by a sheer cliff. It was only a ten-minute walk, but straight up through fir, pine, hawthorn, grape holly, kinnikinic, dog rose, and wild geraniums. I arrived at the clearing, panting in the 8,000-foot thin air.

Everything looked the same as always. Snow laced the shady hollows at this higher altitude, and the temperature was much cooler than in town. Rocks that my brothers and I had dragged into a circle to create a fire pit were still set in place.

Wiping a trickle of sweat from my forehead, I stood facing east, and through a gap between the hills and trees gazed twenty miles back to Boulder blinking in the sunlight. I took a deep, cleansing breath and drank in the symphony of fragrances that emitted from the damp forest floor. It was so quiet that only after a while, did I distinguish a soft, persistent buzzing in the background. City sounds. *To think, we live in that noise pollution every day!*

I spread my blanket to sit next to the little pile of kindling I'd gathered to build a fire. Lighting a few pine needles, I blew on the glowing embers and coaxed them to life. Now seated cross-legged by the fire, I contemplated my decision to return to Boulder.

Accepting a job back home had meant missing out on promising opportunities for career advancement on the East Coast. Yet, despite the recent upsets, I wanted to stay. My family was here, and my roots were here, not back East. And every so often, a vague feeling that something even more significant was drawing me back home landed like a wisp of cottonwood fluff on my conscious mind. Did it have something to do with my dream? Perhaps some knowledge I needed to acquire to further expand my horizons waited around the corner. But what?

As I stared at the fire, the buzzing in the forest grew louder. Instead of drifting up from town, it emanated from the trees, rising from the fragrant needles and sighing through the boughs. The sound made my heart beat faster. I wasn't concerned about being alone in the woods among chipmunks, birds, and deer, and yet...

I closed my eyes and concentrated on the flames crackling and sizzling with heat. It was probably the bees. Accustomed to my presence, they were once again going about their business, attacking the wood hyacinths. I willed my breathing to become deep and regular. After a while, my eyelids began to feel pleasantly heavy, and I let my head drop forward.

Suddenly, an intense vibration assaulted my brain and penetrated the center of my being. My eyes snapped open, and I sat bolt upright. A hummingbird had buzzed me like a miniature fighter plane. Now, it hovered in front of my face, furiously beating its wings. To my amazement, in a high, tremulous voice, the bird squeaked,

"Buenas tardes, Isabel. I am your ancestor, Doña Isabella. I've flown up from Taos to help save your bacon from almost certain disaster. Aren't you going to offer your six-times-great-grandmother any refreshment?"

Chapter Eleven

"Most elegantly finished in all parts, (the hummingbird) is a miniature work of our Great Parent, who seems to have formed it the smallest, and at the same time the most beautiful of the winged species." —J. Hector St. John de Crèvecoeur (1735-1813), French Writer and Diplomat

"What? Who?" My heart beat as fast as the little hummer's. I glanced around. Except for the bird, I was alone. It sang to me in a language that sounded like Spanish, but with some unknown tongue mixed in. More startling, I understood it.

The bird's chatter took on an irascible timbre. "How can you expect to take advantage of my words of wisdom, *Chica*, when you don't listen, *eh*? I already told you, I'm your ancestor, Doña Isabella. We share a name; well, almost. I flew up from the Pueblo of the Red Willow People outside of Taos just to see you. You should have intuited this from the dream I sent you."

The shiny little eyes regarded me as if the bird suspected I had bananas for brains. "I must say you took your time getting here," it tweeted. "If I weren't already a spirit, I'd have wasted away. You know, the flower season arrives late in the High Country. Hint, hint!"

The hummingbird flew three circles around the fire and hovered above it. It emitted a strange, high-pitched sound that, if it had been from a human, I would have interpreted as a cackle. "I guess I'm gonna have to spell it out for you. Don't you carry any honey in that backpack of yours?"

It dove close to investigate my pack, and I swore I discerned in its face the features of a wizened Indian woman, the same woman from my dream. I shook my head to banish the hallucination.

The hummer warbled, "Do not disbelieve, my dear descendant. You're here to learn, for I've chosen you as my successor."

"Go away!" I shouted into the fire, then thrust a stick at the burning kindling, sending sparks flying.

If a bird could scowl, this one did. "Trust your famous intuition for a change," it shrilled. "It's telling you I'm real."

I dropped the stick and stared at the avian aberration that now flitted around a wood hyacinth. It poised seemingly motionless in the air, evidently waiting for her "dear descendant's" intuition to kick in. Then it pointed its long, narrow beak at me and trilled, "If you'd brought along a little sugar water, this transformation would've been easier. It takes a lot of energy to pull it off, you know."

I blinked, and in an instant, the bird turned into a skinny, wrinkled Indian woman dwarfed in a tattered skirt and blouse, the color of Concord grapes. With gnarled fingers, she pulled a dirty, burnt copper-colored blanket around her shoulders and lowered herself stiffly to sit on the ground on the other side of the fire. For a moment, she looked exhausted. Then, her eyes brightened into two onyx-colored beads. She stared me up and down.

"*Chica*, you look tired."

"That's because I *am* tired." Maybe this hummer in human form *was* my relative because she was beginning to sound like Mami.

"Know what's wrong with you?" the old lady said. "You're afflicted with the twenty-first-century disease: stress! You need to chill, girl. How can you expect to absorb important information, avert danger, and expand your horizons if you're stewing over your job and personal life?"

I bristled. This so-called spirit I'd somehow conjured was starting to aggravate me. And what did she mean by danger? "I can't kick back on a fluffy pink cloud and float off into infinity like you presumably can."

Doña Isabella's bird-like pupils grew smaller and brighter. She coughed. "Ech! Ech! Testy, testy! I must've pushed the stress button. True, you're not esoterically advanced enough yet to float on clouds, let alone foresee events in your life, but you can use aromatherapy to soothe your frazzled nerves and more."

"Aromatherapy?" I squinted. "If you lived so long ago, how do you know about aromatherapy?"

The ancient face, as wrinkled as a walnut, frowned. *"Ay, m'hijita,* my dear child, I see you've a lot to learn. Aromatherapy isn't a fad from your time, no. People throughout history have taken advantage of the healing properties of scents because aromatics belong to the natural world and are available to everyone.

"Odors played a key role in more primitive societies, like where I came from. In my time, hunters tracked their prey using their noses. Healers diagnose disease by giving patients an olfactory once-over. Some even claimed they could sniff out murderers and other evil-doers and tell people's social status by smelling the kinds of food they ate. Which, if you don't mind me saying so, was a lot more accurate than checking out labels on clothes like folks do today. If you get adept enough at distinguishing scents, soon you might identify a killer that way."

I couldn't believe what I was hearing. What killer? I didn't have time to ask because Doña Isabella was speeding on.

"Then there's the scent of sexual attraction your hoity-toity scientists didn't run across until the end of the twentieth century. They named their so-called discovery 'pheromones.'" She snorted. "I guess they thought if they gave it a mighty enough sounding name, people would believe they'd invented it. *Cruz!*" She blew on an ember and sent sparks flying. "We knew all about pheromones back in the Pueblo. How do you suppose you came to be born?"

My ancestor glared at the dancing flames, and her face seemed to pull a veil down over itself in the way peculiar to Native people when they are being either stubborn or introspective. I sat stock-still, fearing any movement on my part would dissolve the illusion. I could feel myself getting sucked in, curious about what would happen next. After a few moments, Doña Isabella roused herself from her reverie and fixed her black-eyed gaze on me.

"I wish you'd quit resisting me. I'm only here to help because you called me."

My eyes widened.

The old lady arched her thick, matted eyebrows. "Yes, you summoned me with your subconscious mind. I couldn't manifest until then. Those are the rules Up There." She cast a pious glance skyward.

"I suggest you first get this stress thing under control. After that, you can work on your family, your job, keeping out of trouble, and finding that Prince Charming, whose pheromones turn you on." She winked.

The nerve! How dare she stick her nose into my private affairs! Aloud, I said, "How dare you stick your nose into my private affairs!"

Doña Isabella grimaced. "I heard you the first time when you thought it. I may be dead, but I'm not deaf."

I felt my jaw jut out. "As to your advice," I told the spirit, "they say, 'There's a big distance between saying and doing.'"

Doña Isabella's jaw jutted out even farther. "Let me tell you something that may come in handy sooner than you think. If you can't alter a situation, you can change your physical and emotional responses to it. Remember that next time you find yourself in a really tight spot." Having thrown down the gauntlet, she folded her arms and waited for my response.

Cruz! If I was dialoguing with myself, this took the cake. I waited for the vision of my ancestor to dissipate, but when it didn't, I said, "Okay, I've no idea about the trouble you're referring to; then again, I'm no psychic. I admit I'm under a lot of stress. So how do you suggest I get rid of it?"

My ancestor unfolded her arms, straightened her blanket around her shoulders, and flashed a gummy grin that made her look like Jimmy Durante, the vaudeville star of decades gone by. "I thought you'd never ask. Meditation, path workings, yoga, and physical exercise all help. But you need to put a little zest into your life. Why don't you take a class in aromatherapy?"

I clicked my tongue. Swell suggestion—a professor going back to school. Just what I couldn't wait to do after having studied and worked so long and hard for my doctorate. Not to mention how becoming a student again couldn't fail to impress my colleagues.

Doña Isabella read my thoughts again. "It won't do your reputation any harm," she said. "Besides, you never know when what you learn about aromatherapy may save your little behind."

"Save my little behind?"

My ancestor lowered her gaze to the fire and whispered, "I can say no more on that subject for now."

"More Rules Up There?"

"You betcha! In case you're interested, I happen to know that a competent teacher is giving an aromatherapy workshop at an herb store downtown."

"Hmm," I muttered. "Aromatherapy can't have anything to do with my professional life."

"You'd be surprised." The old lady drew her blanket around her like a Sherlock Holmes cloak.

It was my turn to raise my eyebrows. "Have it your way, but isn't aromatherapy a complicated subject to learn, and won't the class cost a lot in materials? I'm on a strict budget."

"Not necessarily and not necessarily. There are lots of simple recipes that anyone able to boil a cup of water can whip up. They don't need to cost a sheep and three blankets either."

She must have noticed my confusion, for she clarified, "Sorry, it's an old expression from the Pueblo. I think you people would say, 'an arm and a leg,' though frankly, that sounds pretty bloodthirsty."

I laughed despite myself. "Okay. How do I begin?"

Doña Isabella rubbed her hairy chin with a gnarled forefinger and said, "Get out the journal you squirreled away in that miserable pack instead of the honey you *should* have brought and take notes."

How did she know these things? If she were a spirit from the Other Side, she might have considerable knowledge. If my imagination was playing tricks on me, I'd remember I brought the journal. But I couldn't have anticipated the aromatherapy workshop. I fumbled in my pack, pulled out my notebook, and realized I'd forgotten my pen. *Típico!*

"Don't be so hard on yourself, *Chica*," the spirit clucked. "Relax, calm your breathing, and listen. You'll remember."

I took a few deep breaths as instructed. "Okay, I'm ready."

As she talked, Doña Isabella got up and walked behind a fir tree. When she came around, she'd turned back into a hummingbird, but still spoke in a high-pitched human voice like Janis Joplin on helium.

She said, "A simple, soothing bath in sea salts and water every night will do you a world of good. Sea salt is chock full of minerals that remove toxins from your body, strengthen your immune system, and help you relax.

"Pour a pound of coarse ground salt into a big jar. If it's an old honey jar, you don't even have to clean it because honey, besides tasting good to hummingbirds and others—" she cast me a meaningful glance—"it soothes your body. Add ten drops each of eucalyptus, lavender, Siberian fir, and neroli, and five drops of bergamot essential oils. With that, you're on your way to a good night's sleep."

Suddenly, the bird did something I'd never seen. She flipped over on her back and poised mid-air. Her wings beat so fast she looked like she was lying still. From this position, she continued to hold forth.

"Cap the jar and shake it well. You'll have enough for many baths, as you only need two tablespoons each time."

I addressed the supine bird with suspicion. "How do you know about the benefits of sea salt if you lived your whole life inland?"

In a maneuver as smooth as a Cirque du Soleil acrobat, the hummer flipped right-side-up again. "Because, *Chica,* now that I'm of Another World, I can access the accumulated knowledge of the universe, including the Akashic Records, which register all human thoughts and deeds that have ever occurred on the face of the Earth. You might call me a cosmic computer." She twittered at her joke. "That's how I peeked into *your* future."

I raised an eyebrow. "My future that you won't tell me about?"

"As they said in the Sixties, one of my favorite decades, 'Right on, baby!' Ready for the next recipe?"

I shrugged. "Why not?"

"Before going to bed, drink a cup of Sleep Tight herbal tea. You can make a small amount, or for convenience, buy the botanicals in larger quantities, mix them together, and store them in a big, wide-mouthed jar. Fill a tea strainer with the blend for each cup of tea. Combine equal parts of chamomile and lemon balm. Add a few rose petals and crushed rosehips for taste and to fortify you with vitamin C, and maybe some dried, finely chopped orange peels."

"Sounds yummy."

"It's even better if you add a teaspoonful of honey." My feathered friend blinked and then said, "There's probably not enough room between all that linguistics and literature you're toting around in your noggin to remember more now. But I'll give you one more tip anyway. Buy a candle scented with essential oils and burn it for twenty minutes before going to bed. Get one fragranced with rose, frankincense, hyssop, elemi, sage, or any of those essential oils in combination—"

"Pardon my ignorance," I interrupted, "but what exactly is an essential oil? I mean, how does it differ from colognes and perfumes?"

My ancestor zoomed around a tree. From behind the trunk, she called, "You'll discover that when you take the class. Gotta fly. Can't hold these manifestations for long. As a spirit, I'm not allowed to interfere with the normal course of events. However, as your blood relative, I can, and will give you some advice about the dangers that threaten you and your associates."

Despite the blazing fire, I felt cold, and shivers skittered through my body. "Dangers?"

Instead of responding directly, my ancestor said, "As I'm visiting you today in my hummingbird form, I'm reminded of the adage often spoken by some of my feathered friends. "Two sparrows upon one ear of corn cannot agree.'"

"Huh? What do you mean?"

"If that one's too tough for you, I'll tell you another of my favorites," she said. "'The slanderer kills a thousand times; the assassin but once.'"

I stood to walk around the tree. "I don't understand. Do you have to speak in proverbs?"

The answer came, but from farther away in the forest. "'Proverbs in conversation are torches in darkness.'"

I hurried around the tree, but the hummingbird had vanished into the proverbial thin air. From somewhere above the canopy of trees, I heard my ancestor's faint singsong voice call, "And most importantly for you, Isabel, remember that 'The throat must pay for what the tongue may say!'" Then, the voice was swallowed by the wind.

* * *

I made sure the fire was out and cold before I packed my things. On the way down into town, I tried to make sense of my experience. Had I received a visitation from the spirit of my six-times-great-grandmother? Had the spirit spouted those aromatherapy tips for stress relief, or had I fallen asleep by the fire and dreamt it? Was this a continuation of last night's dream?

And what about all those crazy proverbs? Granted, Latinos, me included, are fond of peppering our conversations with aphorisms to throw light, and often, humor on difficult situations. But the ones my ancestor chose mystified me. Who were the slanderers? What did the old lady mean about sparrows on corn and throats paying for what tongues said? And what dangers could I face teaching at a small university in Colorado? It was all too absurd.

As often happens when I venture into the mountains, on the way up, the cares of my mundane existence lifted like a veil. For a brief time, I lived in a world where reality was carved from the bright blue sky and fresh green forest, with the addition, this time, of a celestial visitation. And as also often occurs, on the way down, my mundane concerns crept up on me. By the time I arrived home, the experience with Doña Isabella had dissipated like morning fog.

After dumping my pack on the sofa and flicking on the TV, I was startled to see the educational channel airing a program on hummingbirds. Later, on the way to the trash, I noticed a neighbor nailing a hummingbird feeder to the wall by her tiny garden. Another odd coincidence! The wind was rising and blowing papers around the dumpster. I dropped in my eco-approved paper garbage bag, and as I turned around, a discarded flyer flew up and stuck to my neck and shoulder. I peeled it off and read:

The Fragrant Veil Presents
Aromatherapy Workshop
By Certified Herbalist
Elsbeth MacLeod
Register by phone, text, or in person.

Again, prickles ran up my spine. I folded the paper and secured it in my pocket. That night, I tossed and turned in bed. When I dropped off, I had another eerie dream. Doña Isabella came and sat at the foot of my bed so close I smelled the smoke from the campfire still clinging to my ancestor's clothes.

The spirit said, "You're a stubborn person, *Chica*, and convincing you of my existence is taxing my resources. I, too, am stubborn and will rise to the challenge." She rubbed her hands together as if in gleeful anticipation of a duel. "Like the hummingbird assaulting a trumpet vine in full flower, I'll bombard you with a mountain of evidence until you capitulate."

The next morning, when I emptied my backpack, I took out my journal. It fell open to what should have been a blank page. Instead, set down in tiny, precise, old-fashioned handwriting were the recipes Doña Isabella had spoken to me. I shuddered and felt as if a shadow had passed over my grave.

The handwriting wasn't mine. Besides, I'd forgotten my pen. Had I fallen into a trance and somehow contacted a reservoir of knowledge hidden deep within the recesses of my mind? Had I then recorded the formulas and convinced myself I hadn't brought a pen? That had to be the answer. What about the coincidences and the dream? Both dreams! I had to get a grip.

On my way to school, I headed to a local diner. When under duress, a hearty breakfast helps clear my head. I perched on a cherry-red vinyl counter stool, sandwiched between a couple in love and a hulk of a guy wearing leather and a Peace Frog T-shirt, who probably owned the Triumph motorcycle parked outside. The waitress sauntered over to take my order.

"What's the special?" I asked.

"Hummingbird wing on toast," the waitress quipped, snapping her gum. When she saw my face blanch, she quickly added, "Just kidding. It's the

Denver omelet."

"Give me the huevos rancheros!" I demanded, too rattled to be courteous.

While waiting for my meal, I tried to lose myself in a newspaper, but couldn't help overhearing the lovers' conversation.

The woman was saying, "—didn't realize when I bought the hanging fuchsia for the patio that it attracts hummingbirds. Yesterday I spent an hour reading outside, and as long as I kept quiet, the hummers buzzed the plant."

That was the last straw! For lack of anywhere else to look, I turned my eyes to the ceiling and mouthed, "You can quit now. I'll stop by The Fragrant Veil today and check out that aromatherapy class."

And on many levels I'm sure glad I did.

Chapter Twelve

"Perfume would seem to be one of the elements, one of the original secrets of the universe...it belongs to those invisible powers whose influence is incalculable, and as yet unknowable." —Richard le Gallienne (1866-1947), The Romance of Perfume

Late as usual!

I puffed through the door to the workshop at The Fragrant Veil, breathless from my sprint to arrive on time. The lecture was already in progress.

I swear it wasn't my lack of self-organization that made me late. Javier Malecón kept me forever in my office, bending my ear about his theory that some medieval *cantiga* poetry may have been written by homosexual knights. He'd extrapolated this idea from possible double meanings in some poems. A clever deduction, but difficult to prove, and which would necessitate trips to libraries in Spain and Portugal. He mentioned he might choose this as his thesis topic, in which case I would end up being his advisor. Lots of fun.

I registered for the aromatherapy workshop on the day after my mystical and mystifying encounter with my avian ancestor. I felt that somehow this class would prove useful. I didn't know how useful until much later.

The workshop started the next evening in a little Craftsman-style house-turned-gift-shop a block off the downtown mall not far from campus. A pot of fragrant water steaming on the gas fireplace emanated a rich, warm aroma that conjured visions of creamy, dark chocolate drops with hints of vanilla and cinnamon. When I inquired, the owner told me she calls her signature blend Angelaroma because she believes it draws the love and protection of the heavenly realms. Not to mention that the subtle fragrance also attracts customers. Might I be able to call on Doña Isabella this way, that is, if my ephemeral relative really existed?

I scanned the room for a seat and noticed Olivia Oakes in the back row. She looked up, smiled, and patted the empty chair beside her. Panting, I slid into it. It didn't surprise me that Olivia was here because Eddy told me she wanted to use rose petals in the play's finale. Maybe she got the idea from the instructor.

Speaking of whom, I finally caught my breath enough to concentrate on her. Elsbeth MacLeod looked to be in her early thirties. Long auburn hair with bangs cut straight and even swayed whenever she turned her head to take in the entire class. Her lacy sleeveless blouse and long emerald-green velvet skirt that matched her eyes lent her an air of someone between a pioneer schoolteacher from a Laura Ingalls Wilder novel and a New Age hippie. Standing beside a long table covered with a black cloth, she nodded at me in acknowledgment and passed over some handouts while talking.

"—questionnaires you filled out when you enrolled in this course," she was saying in a Scottish lilt, "you gave many reasons for your interest in aromatherapy. Some of you seek a holistic approach to the study of health and healing, of which aromatherapy forms an integral part. You realize that many illnesses originate in the mind and that scents profoundly affect our mental, emotional, and physical bodies."

Several participants nodded.

"Others have seen or experienced the dangerous side effects of so-called wonder drugs chemically concocted in laboratories, and you prefer to stick to gentler, more natural remedies that may reach for the spiritual levels that aromatherapy offers."

She surveyed the group of twenty eager faces. "You're a knowledgeable lot. I feel privileged to work with you and share my garden of magical delights. Ta! Da!"

With that, she extended her pale arms across the table like a magician executing a conjuring trick. Drawing away the cloth, she revealed scores of amber bottles of different sizes and shapes glistening in the overhead lights. The class caught its collective breath.

"Odors affect the emotions as well as body and mind," Elsbeth explained. "They can calm a restless child, create a congenial environment for a party, or encourage an athlete to achieve peak performance. Who knows?" Her sea-green eyes seemed to reflect a faraway future. "One day, enormous bowls of soothing aromatics may, as a matter of course, grace the conference tables where world powers negotiate peace."

Olivia covered the side of her face with her hand and whispered to me, "We could use some soothing aromatics to bring peace and tranquility to the department."

I smiled and nodded as my mind wandered to my family. I envisioned myself putting together colorful little baskets of spicy potpourris to regale the tables at my parents' restaurant. The piquant fragrances would help stimulate the diners' digestive juices and generate a welcoming environment. Not to mention festooning the family dinner table with a little basket or two. What was I thinking? Papi would never go for such a progressive idea.

This was hot stuff, but after my interrupted conversation with Doña Isabella about essential oils, I needed to get something straight. I raised my hand.

"Sorry, Miss, you are….?" Elsbeth asked.

"Issy Castillo, and I'm a bit confused about terminology. When you refer to fragrances and oils, I don't know whether you're talking about essential oils or perfumes and the difference between them."

"How would *you* define essential oils?" Elsbeth asked, arching China doll eyebrows so perfectly shaped they could have been painted on.

I could see this lady was a fan of the Socratic teaching method of asking a question to answer one because I use the same ploy with my students. Now, the professor-turned-student was on the receiving end. I ventured, "Aren't essential oils produced by plants, and don't they have complex chemical structures?" All heads swiveled toward me.

"You're right, Issy. Many essences, which are derived from plants, contain more than one hundred components. Scientists haven't come near to discovering them all, let alone reproducing them in a lab. The old Renaissance alchemists, always searching for the key to immortality, believed essential oils comprised the soul of a plant and embodied the elixir of life."

She appraised the table laden with bottles. "The alchemists weren't far off the mark in their assumptions. Science has since proven that essential oils possess measurable energies. These, along with their complex chemical structures, offer clues to why essences make such valuable healing agents for equally complex human organisms. It's also why they add special warmth and verve to perfume blends unattainable using synthetics."

I still wasn't clear. "Are perfumes, then, blends of pure essential oils?"

"Due to the high price of essential oils, perfumes are often made from a combination of synthetics, and if you're in luck, the perfumier trickles in a few drops of essence to round out the formula." She noticed my crestfallen face. "I fear the art of perfumery gets complicated fast. We'll discuss essences and synthetics more as the course progresses."

She switched topics. "One way to understand the psychological impact of fragrances is to learn something about perfume lore. The history of fragrances shows how people around the world and over time have perceived and used scents.

"For example, wearing gardenia essence was once believed to keep a lover from straying. Geranium was alleged to throw back on the perpetrator's vicious gossip spawned by jealousy. Lotus was thought to lengthen the lifespan, increase fertility, and drive a man wild with passion for a woman. Something akin to an ancient version of Viagra."

Now, there was a handy idea. Perhaps I could learn to concoct a blend to attract and hold a Prince Charming. But would reeling in a guy that way be fair to him?

Moving on, Elsbeth said, "I invite you all to the table to uncap bottles and start sniffing. But fair warning: your sense of smell will probably be inundated fast unless you take a short rest and breathe some fresh air."

Chairs scraped as the class rose in unison. We made our way to the bottles, murmuring our eagerness for an evening of experimentation. I tested fragrances and contemplated ways I could use aromatherapy to help others. I could encourage students to enjoy studying language and literature, help create a cooperative environment in the department, energize Mami, who works too hard in the restaurant. Maybe I'd even find a fragrance to persuade Angela to behave more like a human being. That would be a miracle "heaven-scent!"

I refocused on the instructor, who was saying, "—ancestors were no slouches when it came to understanding how substances from nature connect with mind and body. They helped make their findings readily understandable by associating various odors with their deities, who, in turn, stood for certain concepts and ideals. For example, neroli was sacred to Zeus's wife, Hera, the mother goddess, who also represented marriage." She held up a bottle. "This is hyacinth oil, which in the ancient Roman world was thought to enhance the attractiveness of homosexuals and hermaphrodites. Some people still wear this scent in the belief that the aroma will boost their sex appeal. The sweetly perfumed hyacinth also marks the first full flowering of spring."

She replaced the bottle on the table. I took it up and inhaled the heady floral fragrance with its tangy afterbite. I could sense its appeal, but the sweet odor was a bit cloying for me.

Elsbeth continued. "Speaking of the Romans reminds me of their special affinity for roses." She looked around the table. "Now, where did that bottle of otto of rose go?"

"Here it is." Olivia handed her a tiny vial.

"Thank you, Olivia." She uncapped the bottle, took a sniff, and sent it around the group.

She said, "True otto of rose is so expensive because it takes over a thousand petals to extract a mere ounce of essence. The Romans may have suffered from something of a 'keeping up with the Joneses' complex when it came to roses. They covered their floors with petals at dinner parties, weddings, and other special occasions. Stepping on the petals released the delightful aroma. One emperor, at his coronation, ordered rose petals to shower his guests from the ceiling. So many thousands of petals piled up that some celebrants suffocated and died."

"Death by rose petals," commented a middle-aged woman wearing jeans, a hand-knitted sweater, and thick glasses. "Sweet!"

Olivia, who was standing next to me holding a four-ounce bottle of cinnamon oil, asked, "If even pleasant scents like rose can be lethal, are there any noxious fragrances that can kill?"

"Good heavens, yes!" Elsbeth said. "Certain essences, like datura, will poison you if you ingest them, which can happen even if you get some of the oil on your fingers. Even that cinnamon leaf oil you're holding is caustic if you apply it to your skin without diluting it in a carrier oil like sweet almond or grapeseed. The odors that emanate from some essential oils can make a person dizzy or even faint if disseminated in a closed environment.

"We've been talking about pleasant-smelling scents that might harm, but this leaves out an entire class of olfactory stimuli not associated with fragrances that bombard us daily. For example, everybody is aware of the dangers to the environment from the stinking chemicals and gases that factories spew from their chimneys."

She paused, as if to gather her thoughts then said, "And speaking of noxious gases, one of the most common deadly ones is carbon monoxide. It's dangerous because it's odorless."

I saw Olivia's face turn ashen, and she swayed. Slowly, she replaced the bottle of cinnamon oil on the table. The woman in the glasses distracted Elsbeth's attention with a question, so the instructor didn't notice the reaction.

"Are you okay?" I whispered.

Olivia swallowed hard. "All these smells must have gone to my head. I think I'll take Elsbeth's suggestion and step to the window for some fresh air."

After a few minutes, she returned and continued sampling, but her face looked pasty, and her eyes hooded. At the end of the session, I tried to ask her about it, but she said, "I need to get home. I've a stack of quizzes to correct," and hurried out the door.

Turning my attention back to the classroom, I watched the instructor. This long-limbed woman with high cheekbones, straight hair, and peaches and cream complexion couldn't be more different from me, at least on the outside. My face looks a little like a dusky full moon. And every morning, I have to beat back my runaway curls with a collection of hair tamers that would be the envy of any sadist. But somehow, I intuited a kind of empathy between us.

After class, I waited until everybody who had clustered around with questions left before approaching Elsbeth.

"I hope you didn't mind my questions," I said. "I'm so interested in the subject."

"I appreciated your questions," said Elsbeth. "They helped guide me in the direction I wanted to go." She started collecting oils, placing them in boxes.

"Here, let me help."

When we finished packing, I got up from the floor and dusted off my jeans. "Do you have time to go for coffee? The Zeus Café up the block is still open."

"Sounds delightful! I love their Chai, and I always get thirsty after teaching."

"Now there's something I can relate to!"

* * *

Reflecting on the evening, I concluded that I'd stepped through a fragrant veil on my journey of discovery into the world of aromatherapy and also made a friend. Elsbeth is a Scottish herbalist with little formal education, while I, a Latina through and through, have earned a doctorate in literature. Elsbeth is a divorced single mom with two small children, and I have yet to meet the love of my life. At least as far as I know. Still, we share a love of beautiful aromas and the natural world of herbs and flowers, and we have similar attitudes toward life.

As I fell asleep, I wondered what the aromatherapy information that Doña Isabella was so insistent I find out about had to do with anything important in my life. *Ay!* I would soon find out. And not in a pleasant way.

Chapter Thirteen

"Caras vemos, corazones no sabemos."
"Appearances can be deceiving." — Spanish Proverb

Over the weekend, I bought ingredients at The Fragrant Veil to make the stress relief recipes that either were given to me by my ancestor or were the result of my own intuition. I still wasn't sure if I believed in this entity. While I worked at the kitchen table, I thought about my other new friend, Olivia Oakes. I hadn't bought her story that the aromas overwhelmed her, but the opportunity never arose to ask about her reaction. And I didn't want to look like a snoop.

Eddy invited me to Saturday's rehearsal again, and Olivia joined us afterwards for lunch. As we were leaving for the restaurant, I got a feeling like pinpricks running up and down my spine. Turning around, I saw Suzanne and Dolores huddled together in a back row of the auditorium, casting veiled glances in my direction. Before I could invite them to join us, they got up and left.

At the Italian restaurant on The Mound, a shopping area across from campus that caters to students and faculty, we took a front booth, and Eddy sat next to me. When I asked Olivia about her interest in aromatherapy, she made the vague reply that taking night classes helped pass the time, and she wanted to learn about roses because of the play. What a puzzle Olivia is. She's usually open and friendly, but sometimes seems remote, as if preoccupied with deep thoughts. Well, she's half-Angla, which may account for her occasional standoffishness. Still, it seems there are hidden depths to her, as to everyone, that will only be revealed in time.

While we sipped our coffees, I found myself rubbing the stress knot at the back of my neck that by now, had become a permanent feature of my anatomy.

"Allow me," said Eddy, and extended his hand to rub my neck.

Then I noticed Suzanne and Dolores seated in a back booth, their faces averted from us. *They sure got here quick!* Giving into Eddy's soothing fingers, I soon forgot about them.

The mini massage was energizing, but not in the way it may have been meant. Eddy's touch, rather than relaxing me, sent electric shivers through my body. I was glad I wore a bra.

While Eddy worked on me, Olivia stared across at us for a long moment. The poker-faced look in her reflective gray eyes was impossible to decipher. She didn't mention anything to me about the neck massage, not even when Eddy left us for the theater and we returned together to the department. As a Latina, I'm not afflicted with the phobia that seems to curse Anglos about touching and being touched; to me, it's a natural part of human interaction. But I wondered if, in this rarefied academic environment, I should behave more circumspect, at least in public.

Sunday morning, Elsbeth, her children, and I took a walk in the sparkling sunshine on an easy nearby mountain trail. The kids looked so sweet running around discovering bugs, pretty stones, and flowers that I wished I had two of my own. *Come on. That's a bit like building the house, beginning with the roof. Or, as Anglos might say, "putting the cart before the horse."*

Later that day, I made sure to redeem myself with my family by dining with them at their little blond brick suburban ranch built in the 1950s. Lately, the vintage design of homes like theirs have come back into vogue. I hope this style will still be popular when my parents choose to sell and downsize so their investment makes them a packet of money for retirement. After inhaling Mami's home-cooked taquitos, enchiladas, guacamole, and refried pinto beans, I was glad for the earlier walk.

During the meal, Papi remarked how he'd fired a kitchen employee because the fellow was openly gay. He worried the guy might be HIV positive and contaminate the food. Germán, Angela, and I jumped all over him, insisting that being gay doesn't equate with disease or moral turpitude. And that gay, trans, or straight people are people.

Later, after I'd calmed down, I realized Papi was merely expressing one of the prevailing beliefs among some conservative Latinos and others. Coming home meant I was going to have to understand and deal with such attitudes without rushing to judgment. The bright spot in all of this was that it showed one point, at least, on which my siblings and I agreed.

* * *

I kept so busy at work on Monday that when I glanced at my wall clock, which I'd fixed to mark the correct time for Carrot Top Clive's benefit in case he ever visited my office, I couldn't believe it was already past four. I hustled up to the main office before it closed to ask Mrs. Webber to give me information on a student who requested I write a recommendation.

The head administrative assistant regarded me over her tortoise shell-framed glasses; her voice tinged with motherly concern. "How are you getting on, Issy?"

"I've more or less settled in, although some things around here have me baffled."

"Like what?"

Our conversation stopped when Michael Kent ambled into the office to check his mail at the graduate student boxes. Mrs. Webber readjusted her glasses against her nose and resumed clicking the computer keyboard. I studied the page of student information she'd given me but was also observing Michael. His white shorts, pink Lacoste shirt, and powder-white tennis shoes, this time worn *with* socks, made him look more like he was on his way to a golf or tennis lesson than to class. Which may have been the case.

His dreamy eyes took a moment to recognize me. *"Ah, Cómo estás, Issy?"*

Not another student using my first name. Cielos! "Can't complain, *Michael*," I said, paying him back in kind by using his English-given name. I eyed his tan. "Looks like you've been enjoying our fine weather."

"*Sí, sí*. Beautiful Boulder. So many warm sunny days." He stifled a yawn. "I…uh…I wanted to explain about the last test."

"It was pretty lame."

He shifted back and forth on his feet and gave me a look that he may have meant as sheepish, but which ended up appearing puckish. I imagined this was the same expression he used with his parents when, as a little boy, he got in trouble, but was always forgiven because he looked too cute for words.

"I know," he said. "I've been going through a rough patch. Other commitments, you know. Maybe I could see you…you know…about doing some…um…extra credit or something to make up for it?"

His contrite but hopeful expression reminded me so much of my brother Germán trying to wheedle money out of our father. Papi almost always gave in, and this time, so did I. "Why don't you come see me during my office hours?"

He grinned like a happy monkey. "Gotcha!"

As he spoke, Dolores materialized at the door, almost dwarfed under an armload of books. When she saw Michael and me, she glowered at us like a thwarted vampire, turned on her heels, and slinked off.

Michael's eyes became hooded like a snake's, and he sent a half-smile in the direction of the Portuguese instructor's retreating, rounded shoulders. "Must run," he said. "Got books to hit. See you soon." He waved at me and Mrs. Webber and slithered out the door.

I turned to Mrs. Webber and, with a wry smile, said, "Judging by Michael's less-than-stellar performance in class, the only thing he's likely to hit his books with is a Lacrosse stick. The essay he wrote on his last test was so disjointed it sounded like he'd written it while high."

Mrs. Webber laughed, and at the same time, the inner door to the chairman's office opened. Vigil and Eddy emerged together, both looking tight-lipped and stiff.

When Eddy saw me, his face brightened. "*Qué pasa, calabaza?*"

"The usual. Busywork."

"Me, too." He indicated the thick file folder he carried. "You going back to your office?"

"I am."

"I'll walk with you."

Eddy's gait lightened with every step that led him away from the office.

"Something up between you and the Chair?" I asked.

"You know I'm up for tenure at the end of the summer."

"Is there a problem?"

He gave a short laugh. "That's an understatement. I'd like to talk to you about tenure and our chairman. What are you doing later this evening?"

I made a face. "I've got to come back to work here for a while. I've recommendations to write and a lot of other stuff that's piled up in this short Maymester."

We reached the staircase to the basement and paused. I tried to ignore the evil, musty smells emanating from the stairwell.

"Excellent!" he said. "I've got rehearsal again tonight and would love for you to join me afterwards over pizza and beer."

"Pizza sounds yummy after a hard night slaving away at my desk."

"Can you wait until around nine or nine-thirty to eat?"

To my nod of assent, he said, "I'll call you from my office after rehearsal."

Chapter Fourteen

"Nuestras vidas son los ríos
que van a dar en la mar, que es el morir."
"Our lives are like the streams
That flow into the sea and die."
—*Jorge Manrique (c. 1440-1479),* Coplas a la muerte de su padre

And so, the fateful evening arrived. If I had paid better attention to Doña Isabella's warnings and the incidents that occurred prior to the murder, I might have saved Eddy, not to mention myself. But no, I walked into the situation as blind as a newborn kitten.

It was one of those clear, mild June evenings when magic seemed to thrum along just beneath the surface of mundane events. Even the floral-scented breeze bore on its wings the magic of Shakespeare's Puck, Titania, and Lysander.

I left the university to amble downtown amid honking E-bikes and pedestrians. Those bikes are becoming quite popular here with the physical fitness minded. But I prefer to stroll and take in my surroundings. Besides, an electric bicycle is a tad beyond my budget right now.

At The Fragrant Veil, which was still open, I bought a book on aromatherapy that Elsbeth had recommended in her workshop. While I was at it, I stopped by The Zeus for a quick double espresso and a *pain au chocolate* to tide me over until pizza time. Not diet food, but I was in too good a humor to fret about my waistline.

Although it was not yet dark when I ambled back to campus, a big full moon had already risen. It brightened the Sistine-blue sky in the east with its bright white light. To the west, the sky over the mountains had turned a deep valentine rose color with the setting sun, tinting the peaks with a sensual red glow.

By now, most students had left campus for the night. I made my way along almost empty sidewalks with only the padding of my footsteps and stirrings of nature in the shrubbery to keep me company. A crow cawed, and I glanced up to the canopy of great old oaks that spread like a mantle above me. I wondered how many generations of students, faculty, and staff those trees have seen pass beneath their boughs. How fleeting our individual lives and concerns are considered against the backdrop of history.

The air was redolent with the intermingled fragrances of damp earth and conifers. As I sauntered past the botanical gardens, I drank in the aromas of night-scented phlox and spicy musk roses. In the workshop, Elsbeth told us that the rose is considered the queen of the flower kingdom, and jasmine, the king. Tonight, the queen was holding court.

I stepped under the old-fashioned, electrified lantern that illumined the staircase to the Charles B. Kent Theater as it lit up. The building's front doors stood wide open to let in fresh air during rehearsal. Suzanne's voice rang out clear and strong, carrying all the way to the sidewalk where I stood. Perhaps this woman with big aspirations *had* missed her calling as an actress. I wondered whether the stage crew had figured out the problems of the platforms and rose petals.

Turning away from the theater, I meandered along a tree-lined walk toward the department, the moon lighting my path. I recalled that American Colonists had aptly named the June full moon the Rose Moon after the quintessential flower of love. What would I discover on this enchanted evening? Would I, at last, find love?

As I approached the department, I noticed several lighted office windows, including Juventino's, whose office was the first near the entrance. Evidently, my colleagues, like me, had procrastinated and were now hastening to finish their paperwork before Maymester ended.

From a distance, I recognized Vigil and Strange conversing under the portico. Clive's shadowy form gesticulated like a scarecrow flapping at birds in contrast to Vigil's stolid fireplug outline. By the time I reached the entrance, both had disappeared.

I descended the stairs through the stale air of the empty TA den and headed to my office. I didn't expect to see any grad students hammering away at schoolwork on such a beautiful evening. In the dark hall by my office, I felt for the keyhole and fit my key into the lock. As I stepped in and snapped on the overhead light, my foot squished something soft that had been left against my door.

I bent to pick it up and saw it was a kind of poppet. Made from dark purple material with a floral pattern, it was fashioned into the likeness of a female with a wax head and black curly yarn for hair. A big ebony hatpin pierced the figure's heart. A Voodoo doll!

I dropped the disgusting effigy on the floor like it was a piece of burnt toast. From its mop of black hair, I understood the doll was meant to represent me.

Collapsing into my chair, I stared at the poppet. It stared back with sightless, brown button eyes and a red-beaded mouth that sloped down in a grimace. I'd passed off the scorpions as a student prank, but this doll was a whole different ball of wax. Literally. Growing up Latina, I've seen the results of black spells too many times not to take the dark side of magic seriously. Someone bore me a tremendous grudge. I shuddered, not so much out of fear, as from determination to block any negativity that might leak from the fetish and enter my body.

Not wanting to touch the poppet again, I took two pens from the pencil holder on my desk and gingerly lifted the doll. I was about to take it to the bathroom trashcan but hesitated. Something about the figure besides its resemblance to me looked familiar, but I couldn't think what. I carried the abomination to my filing cabinet. Prying open the empty bottom drawer with the toe of my shoe, I shoved it in and slid the drawer closed as if it were a body drawer in the morgue. Then I fled to the bathroom and washed my hands with plenty of antibacterial soap and water to remove the dank odor of patchouli that had emanated from the doll and soiled my hands.

Back in my office, I tried to work on the letter of recommendation, but the words didn't flow. Little creaks, rustlings, clanking pipes, imagined or real footsteps above my head disturbed my concentration, and my mind kept wandering to the file cabinet drawer. I heard creaking again, louder this time, sounding like somebody in the hall.

I jumped up and flung open my door in time to see Bibi's black-clad size two behind disappear up the back stairs. Nobody ever uses that staircase. It's narrow, only leads outside, and doesn't have a light. I swung around to my door and examined it and the floor for unsavory donations. Nothing! Maybe the light under my door had warned off the girl. Or maybe her business wasn't with me at all.

I was about to go back into my office when I noticed something white and crumpled on the lowest step where Bibi had been. I sprang on it, fearing another poppet, but it turned out to be a scrap of paper. Bibi must have dropped it. I picked up the paper and on examining it, saw that it showed four horizontal columns of numbers. Each line was preceded by a letter, which when read from top to bottom, spelled W-I-N-K. I returned to my office, stuffed the paper into my purse, and dashed off the letter of recommendation. It wasn't purple prose, but would have to do.

When the phone rang, I almost jumped out of my skin. Little did I know my life was about to whoosh downhill faster than an Olympic skier on a very icy course. Only I was no expert at maneuvering on this kind of ice and was completely blindsided by the events that were about to occur.

* * *

In an interview room at the police station, while waiting for Chief Mondragón to come interview me, I obsessed over what I could have done differently to have anticipated this disaster and avoided it or somehow intervened to keep Eddy's death from happening. But really, I had no clue. So, events unfolded pretty much as earlier described. I was released into Papi's care without being charged after being advised to stick around in case detectives had questions for me and was driven to my parents' house, where

I remained for three days.

* * *

"How could you have done something so—so—*feo*—so ugly?"

"Need I remind you that I did not kill him?" I retorted to my sister as I tore off a piece of tortilla with vigor. "Eddy Calderón was my *friend*."

Angela's face flushed to the roots of her burnt-gold corkscrew curls. "You might as well have for all the shame it's brought on our family." She slammed down her fork.

"*Hija!*" Mami snapped from the end of the table. "Any more of that talk, and you are going to your room." Under the vigilant eye of parental authority, the teen settled into a silent, long-term sulk. As unfair as Angela's heated words were, with a heavy heart, I realized I'd better get used to hearing them. They looked to be a harbinger of things to come at the college.

I was still staying at my parents' house the next day and enduring dinner with the family. I'd expected this from Angela and also from Papi, who ranted about how if I'd moved in with them instead of insisting on an independent lifestyle, I wouldn't have gotten into this mess. For once, Papi's faulty logic and ludicrous assumptions didn't bother me. In fact, I found this predictability comforting. But now, a dark cloud hung over the entire family. I could just imagine the rumors and gossip flying around the Latino community.

Mami, in her apron and huaraches, pushed aside a graying curl from an eye and worried aloud about the long-term effects on my psyche for discovering a murder victim. I was thankful she hadn't made the connection that Eddy and I had started dating. Not knowing how else to comfort me, she prepared my favorite food, blue corn chicken enchiladas with green salsa, to coax me to eat. Everything tasted like sawdust.

After dinner, two detectives, neither of them Mondragón nor the others I'd seen at the jail, came to the house to interview me once again. Again, they advised me to stay in town in case they required more information. What more information could I give? With Papi pacing in the kitchen, I went over my story—not a story, but the truth! —several more times before the detectives left.

When I wasn't at the dinner table, I lay on my back in my twin bed, staring dull-eyed at the popcorn-textured ceiling, struggling to make sense of it all to no avail. By Wednesday, I'd emerged from my lethargy, impatient to get back to my condo and prepare to face my colleagues and students. Might as well not prolong the agony. But since Wednesdays were family dinner nights at the Castillo household, I reluctantly stayed over. Germán, his wife Juana, and their little pink bundle named Sarita joined us.

"I can't imagine who would want to kill Professor Calderón," I said for the twentieth time that day. "He was so popular."

"Apparently not with everybody," said Papi the Realist as he dug into his chalupa.

Mami the Diplomat passed me the Fiesta ware bowlful of frijoles and asked, "Did you see anybody suspicious in the building, *hija*?"

I took a spoonful of beans and passed the bowl on to Miss *Cara-de-Vinagre*, Sourpuss Angela. "Nobody suspicious, but a lot of people were milling around that night. Besides the cast and crew of the play, Chairman Vigil and Professor Strange were discussing something at the department entrance and then went inside. At least, I think they did." My intuition told me to hold off for the moment about spotting Bibi.

"Surely you don't suspect the chairman," said Juana. She'd been holding Sarita in her lap. Now she lay the baby in her basket on a neighboring chair and reached for the pitcher of *agua de Jamaica* with a thin, sallow arm and work-worn hand. In this, my sister-in-law reminded me of Dolores. I wondered, not for the first time, how my used car salesman brother treated Juana in private. And this also made me wonder how Dolores was holding up.

"Chairman Vigil is not a suspect," I said with more conviction than I felt. "But Professor Strange is stranger than an *alebrije*. Now that I think of it, Professor Guerrero's light was on when I entered the building. He must've been in his office at least part of the time."

Angela bristled. "Juventino Guerrero would never stoop to killing

Calderón. He's involved in so many more important things!"

I took my time slathering guacamole on a homemade tortilla before saying, "Oh? Like what things?"

My sister rose to the bait. "Like fighting for legal status of undocumented workers! He's too busy to pay attention to *tontos* like Eddy Calderón, who are against La Raza's cause."

I felt my cheeks blaze at the unfair remark about Eddy, but for once, kept my mouth shut.

Germán had been occupied, as usual, shoveling in food nonstop. Now, he raised his narrow-eyed gaze that always made him look like he was peering through Venetian blind slats. He smoothed his John-Travolta-As-Pulp-Fiction-Hood hairstyle from his brow. "You mentioned that some people were at a play rehearsal before the murder happened. Do you know who?"

"Let's see." I stared out the dining room window and watched the last rays of sun disappear behind the Flatirons while I pulled together my thoughts. "Dolores Lopes, Suzanne Selos, and Javier Malecón were there for sure. And probably also Professors Rampage and Oakes, Michael Kent—"

My brother snorted. "You mean Miguel de la Madrid?"

"You know him?"

"Who doesn't? If I were making a list, he'd be my Number One Suspect."

Suddenly, Sarita broke into a wail. Everyone rushed to calm her, and the conversation thread got lost in the commotion. Soon after, Germán and his family left for home.

Chapter Fifteen

"Si la amistad es un tesoro, gracias por ser parte de mi fortuna."
"If friendship is a treasure, thank you for being part of my fortune."
— *Spanish Proverb*

Work proved every bit as foul as I'd dreaded. Clive Strange, the first person I ran across, bug-eyed me as if I were the timing mechanism on a bomb about to detonate. Then Chairman Vigil, whom I rarely see roaming the halls, bustled by like the White Rabbit in *Alice in Wonderland,* perpetually late for an important date. The minute he saw me, he managed to avert both eyes more or less in tandem and shook his head mournfully. In the TA bullpen, the graduate students glued their eyes to their computers. As soon as I passed through, they started whispering.

I escaped to my office and inserted the key in the lock. Suzanne opened her door and swiveled her head into the hall. Her hoary hairdo looked even more disheveled than usual. Dark red blotches on her cheeks warned that she was working herself into a very foul humor.

"I'm amazed you have the guts to show your face around here today," she jeered.

After all I'd endured, this was the limit! I strode to Suzanne's doorway and, with fists clenched at my sides, stared straight into my accuser's piggy eyes. "I am as devastated as you and resent your insinuation that I had anything to do with Eddy's death. You *will* stop insulting me right now."

Suzanne's blotches turned poison hemlock-purple, and she backed up a step. Dolores' door cracked open, but she didn't come into the hall.

Suzanne thrust her arms akimbo and fixed me with the malevolent stare of a basilisk poised to strike. "I doubt very much that *you* could feel as aggrieved as *I* do. *I* was about to become Eduardo Calderón's wife!"

Dolores' door creaked open another inch.

Rarely am I at a loss for words, but this was one of those occasions. I opened and closed my mouth like a gasping fish, then opened it again and said, "What makes you think Eddy wanted to marry *you*? You're already married."

Suzanne's words erupted in a torrent. "Because, Miss Latina Hot Pants, he took a personal interest in me and nurtured my career. Long before you tottered on the scene with your big hair and little princess sandal heels, he was encouraging me to give up teaching for acting. I was going to divorce Joe, and we would blow this joint. I could've been a shooting star with Eddy by my side."

With that, Suzanne, steaming with rage, slammed her door shut and pushed past me. She rumbled down the hall, more like a bulldozer preparing to wreak havoc than a starlet treading the boards. Dolores' door clicked shut.

* * *

Although nobody mentioned the murder in class, I felt the students ogling me with covert curiosity. Bibi was a palpable exception. Her saccharine smile and smooth brow made an unsettling contrast to her laser beam gaze. I couldn't tell whether the girl looked triumphant, angry, or fascinated. When the bell rang, Javier slipped out as quietly as a shadow, which I took as an indication of his embarrassment at my situation. Michael, on the other hand, made a point of staying after class. He expressed sorrow over the school losing such a fine professor and sympathy for me having discovered the body.

His moist eyes held an almost doe-like quality when he patted my arm and said, "You're so brave to continue teaching after such a shock."

Maybe I'd rushed to judgment about Michael. Under his polished Preppy façade, he was a good-hearted kid after all.

* * *

I couldn't muster the energy to go anywhere off campus for lunch, so I opted for the faculty dining hall. Leaving the cash register with my tray, I scanned the spacious lunchroom with its warm sandstone walls, wood-beamed ceiling, and bank of divided light-paned windows, searching for an unoccupied seat. I spied Olivia and Georgina at a table for four in a corner.

"May I join you?" I asked, arriving with my tray.

"Take a seat," Olivia offered with a warm smile. "I tried calling you at your office to invite you to lunch, but you must've been in class."

Georgina was seated facing away toward the window, so I didn't see her from the front until after I sat. Her pinched, washed-out face looked like it had lost a quart of blood. In one bony hand, she crushed a sopping shredded napkin. Reaching out with the other clammy hand, she clutched my arm.

"What a loss! What a loss!" Her voice was hoarse from crying. "He was writing a play about me, you know."

To my astonished look, she jerked her head and said, "Yes, it's true. The drama was going to be about a girl who, like me, grows up poor on a dairy farm in Minnesota. Through hard work and determination, she becomes a world-renowned authority on Cervantes and helps the Spanish police crack the famous case of the Don Quixote Murders."

She unclenched her hand from my arm and fingered the metal pieces of her chrome necklace as if they were rosary beads. Her ashen face colored. "The part about the Don Quixote Murders is fiction, but he was basing the main character on me."

"We all feel very sad about Eddy," I said, patting her on the sleeve. "Such a life force."

"We'll miss him terribly," Olivia agreed. In the light streaming in from the window, I noticed that her eyes were also red-rimmed.

Georgina squinted at the wall clock and gave a mighty sniff. "It's time for me to teach. I don't know how I'm going to keep it together."

101

Olivia smiled in encouragement. "You will, Georgie, you will. You know Eddy. He would have told us that the show must go on."

After Georgina drooped out the door, I nibbled at my salad, then said, "I wouldn't have thought a tough feminist like Georgina would take Eddy's death so hard."

Olivia finished her iced tea. "Once you get to know her, you'll find that Georgie's an old softie. And Eddy did have a winning personality."

"I ran into Suzanne this morning, and she's convinced he was going to marry her."

Olivia folded her napkin neatly on the table and sat back. "I'm not surprised. You know, Issy, Eddy was one of my dearest friends, an enthusiastic people-person who encouraged everyone to be the best they could be. But sometimes that passion was misunderstood."

I toyed with a cucumber slice. "You mean he led people on?"

"Not that he meant to, but please understand that, first and foremost, Eddy was both an actor and a director. When he was in the moment, as they say in the theater, he sometimes got carried away. I think there's an old Spanish proverb that goes something like, 'He who assists everybody assists nobody.'"

With a pang, I thought of my day in the mountains with Eddy and, later, the kiss.

Olivia was saying, "…had a real…zeal, I guess you might call it…to do the right thing. He stood up against those whom he judged were carrying out unfair practices, and this conviction made him enemies."

"Like Juventino?"

"Like him and others."

The lunchroom was clearing out. The noise level escalated as faculty diners rose and headed for the door, clattering silverware, plates, and trays into the designated bins.

I decided I'd had enough of my half-eaten salad and put down my fork. "I'd love to chat more about this," I said. "I need to find out who killed Eddy. He was the first person to befriend me here. Besides, I don't like being the hot topic of gossip."

"Eddy was also my friend," Olivia reminded me. "He was there for me during a difficult time in my life. I'll help you any way I can."

We rose with our trays and joined the end of the exit line.

I said, "Elsbeth MacLeod and I have become friends outside the aromatherapy classroom. She's invited me over after work today for tea and sympathy and to help create a list of suspects. If you're not busy later, I'd be grateful if you'd stop by, too."

"I'd love to join you," said Olivia. "After all, three heads are better than two."

"As soon as we leave here, I'll call Elsbeth and ask if she minds entertaining both of us."

Chapter Sixteen

"Six eyes see more than two." — Spanish Proverb modified by Issy Castillo

Four o'clock found Olivia and me ensconced at the knotty pine farmhouse table in the kitchen of Elsbeth's little Victorian house perched on a bluff overlooking the town in the historic Whitman neighborhood. A light breeze ruffled the red-and-white chintz curtains and stirred the air with the rich smell of freshly baked chocolate chip cookies. We sipped an iced herbal drink from tall glasses while Elsbeth's children sat cross-legged on the colorful braided rug that hugged the golden fir floor, snacking on cookies.

After contemplating the view of the Flatirons thrusting dagger-like from the mass of blackish-green conifers that carpeted the hills below, I broke the silence. "This drink is delicious, Elsbeth. What's in it?"

She looked pleased. "It's my special restorative. I conjured up the recipe to ease my pain after Fergus and I divorced. It's made from rosehips and petals, fresh lavender buds, dried hibiscus flowers, and hops."

Today, Elsbeth wore a summery red and blue peasant skirt and turquoise blouse that highlighted the golden strands in her auburn hair. Watching her open a board game for her children, I wished some of my friend's innate serenity and poise would rub off on me. My nascent romance, nipped in the bud, the uncomfortable department environment, topped off by murder all had combined to rock my inner balance. I needed to get back in tune.

As if reading my mind, Elsbeth said, "The ingredients in this tea are thought to restore balance to body, mind, and spirit."

I drank in the refreshing intermingled aromas along with the brew. "It's doing its job because I feel better already." Then I remembered how, on one such sunny afternoon less than a week before, without a care in the world, Eddy and I had laughed and gossiped over lunch at a log cabin restaurant in the mountains. My throat tightened, and I blinked back tears.

"It's okay to cry," Elsbeth comforted. "Sometimes, after you think you've put everything out of your mind, you sit still for a moment, and the memories come flooding back. Grief has a way of sneaking up on you like that."

"I'll be all right in a minute." I glanced at Olivia, who looked stricken, too. Straightening in my chair, I smoothed the skirt of my navy business suit that I hadn't time to change. I assumed a brisk tone. "*Bien*. The best way to begin to heal is to find Eddy's killer. And I'm afraid the list of suspects may be long."

"Oh?" Elsbeth arched her pale amber, pencil-thin eyebrows. "I only know about Eddy through you, Issy. Did he have many enemies?"

"A few," Olivia replied for me, "and perhaps a few complicated relationships as well."

Interesting. As I watched Olivia, I got distracted, wondering how she'd found time after class to change from work clothes to khaki shorts and a crisp, spring green short-sleeved linen shirt. And her athletic legs were so slim. I pulled the hem of my skirt to cover my knobby knees.

Elsbeth reached behind Olivia to open a drawer in a pinewood hutch and produced paper and pens. "Shall we begin by making a list of suspects? I assume we can eliminate both you, Olivia, and you, Issy."

"Absolutely," we chorused.

The cookies smelled tempting, and my stomach, to my surprise, rumbled despite my heartache. I slipped a cookie the size of a saucer from the plate on the table to my napkin. Why was I so easily distracted? *Focus, Issy*, my inner critic chided. "You mentioned complicated relationships, Olivia. Did Eddy have any with anyone outside the department?"

Before answering, she took a smaller cookie from the plate and nibbled it. "I don't think so. His work kept him occupied because he was up for tenure."

The memory of Eddy emerging from Vigil's office flitted through my brain. "I remember him saying something about having trouble with that."

"Everybody has trouble getting tenure," Elsbeth put in. "My ex didn't get it. That's one reason he scarpered back to Scotland." For a moment, her gaze drifted to her children, who were absorbed in their game.

Olivia blanched as she had that night in the aromatherapy class, and her gray eyes took on a flat expression.

Until that moment, I'd concentrated on my own loneliness and need for friendship. Now, I realized that my circumstances paled beside those of my friends. I had experienced the loss of a new friend through death, but Elsbeth had suffered the greater loss of a mate through abandonment, and Olivia's loss was of a long-term friend.

"Are you alright?" I asked Olivia.

She sipped her tea, and the color flowed back into her cheeks. "I'm fine. It's that whenever anyone brings up the tenure issue, I think back to my husband and how he died."

To our surprised expressions, she explained. As she spoke, I saw her shoulders tense. "Roger and I both taught at St. Mary's in Denver. I already had tenure, and he came up for it, but was denied. Neither of us saw the blow coming, and it shocked us."

She cleared her throat and continued. "I guess the shame of my getting tenure, but not Roger was too much for him. He didn't even give us a chance to talk it out. The next day, when I arrived home from work, I found him dead in the garage of carbon monoxide poisoning."

So that was why she turned ghost-white that night in aromatherapy class when Elsbeth referred to that deadly gas! I leaned over and hugged her, and Elsbeth refilled her drink.

Olivia's eyes glistened with tears. She blew her nose and sipped her iced tea. "I'm okay now." She took a ragged breath. "I left St. Mary's because of too many bad memories and applied to GMU, where I got this tenured position. It was Eddy's first semester here, too. With his sympathy, good humor, and friendship, he helped me get over the worst part."

She drained her glass, and her shoulders relaxed. "Anyway, that's all in the past. What's important now is solving Eddy's murder. I can tell you that

Vigil didn't support Eddy for tenure because he wanted to bring in one of his Bolivian cronies." To my mute inquiry, she said, "Yes, Baldomero is from Bolivia. I guess he'll have the opportunity now to hire whomever he wants."

I said, "I saw the Chair at the door to the department the night Eddy died." After noshing at my cookie, I set the rest of it on my napkin and wrote Baldomero Vigil's name as Number One on the suspect list. The others followed suit. "He had opportunity, but would wanting to bring a friend into the department be a strong enough motive for murder?"

"People have killed for less," said Elsbeth, "particularly in Academia, where, according to Fergus, the stakes are so low."

Olivia and I chuckled for the first time that afternoon.

"What about Juventino Guerrero?" I asked. "I swear he tried to run over Eddy and me in the crosswalk by the department after Vigil's party, and he had that altercation with Eddy at the theater. Olivia, do you know what the flap was about?"

She shrugged. "Something to do with politics, but what, I don't know. Let's put his name on the list, too." Everyone wrote down Juventino as the Number Two suspect.

I took another bite of cookie while contemplating other possibilities. "Clive Strange was also prowling around. Eddy wanted to question him about the disappearance of a valuable antique clock that belonged to my predecessor, Mark Allen." Strange's name went on the list. "The only other professor around this summer is Georgina Rampage."

"She was at the rehearsal, but I can't imagine Georgie harming Eddy," said Olivia as she daintily dabbed cookie crumbs from the corner of her mouth with her napkin. "She thought the world of him and was bawling her eyes out today." She considered. "It is odd, though, that she talked about him using her life story in a play. I had no idea he was writing about her."

"I don't know her," said Elsbeth, who was refilling our glasses and passing the plate of cookies to her children. "Could Eddy have written something unflattering about her because he wanted to publish a sensational play that would get him tenure, and her show of grief is an act? That sounds like the sort of thing that would get up an academic's nose."

Olivia and I gave her doubtful looks, but Olivia said, "I can check into it. Now that Eddy's gone, lucky me, I've been promoted to play director. Maybe he left notes on his office computer."

Elsbeth asked, "What about the others in the play?"

"Let's see," I mused. "Dolores spends a lot of time in the theater helping behind the scenes. Suzanne, Javier, and Michael are the principal actors in the play, so they're around after hours more than the rest of the cast. Suzanne claims Eddy wanted to marry her, although he told me he only gave her a starring role to occupy her idle mind."

"Javier hung out a lot in Eddy's office," said Olivia, "so I assume they were friendly. But I don't think Eddy and Michael had much to do with each other outside class. Nevertheless, all four were on campus that night, and each had opportunity."

Four names were added to the list.

"There's another person associated with the play," I said. I'd hesitated to mention Bibi because, to my chagrin, I felt an odd kind of jealousy toward the blond Amazon for trying to capture Eddy's attention. This made me doubt my own judgment of the girl. But Eddy was dead, and a person couldn't be jealous of a relationship where one of the parties was no longer alive.

"After I hung up with Eddy that night," I continued, "I heard a noise in the hall outside my office. When I went to look, I saw Bibi Pomodoro—she's a senior majoring in Spanish, Elsbeth—disappear up the back stairs."

"That staircase only leads outside," said Olivia. "Whatever was Bibi doing there?"

Elsbeth stifled a laugh. "Sorry, but so many members of your department have such funny names." She read off her suspect list. "You've got Vigil, whose name in Spanish, I presume, is the same as in English. By your description of him, he seems to keep watch with at least one commanding eye over his department."

"I never thought of that before," Olivia said with a twinkle in her voice, "but some other names are descriptive, too. Like, Guerrero, which means warrior."

"And Selos," I broke in, "which, as Eddy himself pointed out, sounds like *celos,* meaning 'jealousy.' And then there's Dolores, whose name translates as 'pains.'"

"Don't forget Strange," said Elsbeth. "He sounds hinky, and Rampage, whose manner as you describe her, resembles someone perpetually on the rampage. Then there's this Pomodoro student. Doesn't the word *pomodoro* mean 'tomato' in some language?"

"Italian!" I piped.

"Perfect description," said Olivia, laughing now. "Although she's not acting in the play, she assists me with prompting and other tasks. And as her name implies, almost anybody in pants is hot for that ripe tomato's bod."

"Including Eddy?" asked Elsbeth.

"The jury's still out on that one," I said. "Even though I can't think up a motive for Bibi killing Eddy, she was in the right place at the right time, so we should put her name on the list."

After everybody added Bibi's name, Elsbeth asked, "So how are we going to handle the investigation?"

I reviewed the names. "Olivia, you offered to look into Georgina. And because my brother told me that Michael Kent would head his suspect list, I'll talk to Germán about him. I'll also catch Javier after class and interview him."

"What about the chairman?" Elsbeth asked while bending to wipe chocolate onto her napkin from her little boy Jamie's fingers.

"Eddy wanted to tell me something about Baldomero," I said, "but never got the chance. I had the impression it was something other than the tenure issue, but I may be wrong." I turned to Olivia. "Didn't Vigil get his Ph.D. at Brownell in Boston?"

"That he did."

"A friend of mine from grad school teaches there now. I'll call her tomorrow and see if she knows anything about our esteemed Chair."

"What can I do to help?" asked Elsbeth as she held the plate of cookies for little Ginger to choose another one.

I considered. "The other day my sister let slip that she's involved with

Juventino's FLA organization. I won't be able to drag anything out of her, but perhaps you, because of your experience with children, can help interview her."

"I'll be delighted to meet Angela."

"Checking on the Internet to see if any antique clocks matching Professor Allen's have turned up on eBay or elsewhere on the market would get us started with Clive."

"Which reminds me," said Olivia, "I haven't called Mark yet to tell him about Eddy. When I do, I can say we're looking for his clock, get a description, and give it to you, Elsbeth. As to the rest of the names on the list, other than their odd behaviors and involvement with Eddy, there doesn't seem to be a concrete reason to link them to the murder. We'll have to keep our eyes and ears open."

I regarded my friends. "You know, guys, I think we have the makings of a pretty good detective team. We should go into business."

"Since 'The Number One Ladies' Detective Agency's name has already been taken, we could take a name that celebrates our town with a punny twist," suggested Elsbeth. "How about The Bolder Women Detective Team?"

"Perfect!" we chorused and clinked glasses.

Chapter Seventeen

"No conviene mostrar la verdad desnuda, sino en su camisa."
"Never show the truth naked—just in its shirt." — *Francisco de Quevedo*
(1580-1645), Spanish Poet and Diplomat of the Baroque Age

"Che! Qué pasa?" Ana Torres answered on the first ring. "How's life treating you in The Wild West?"

I visualized my highflier friend from graduate school days poured into one of her many power suits, probably a red and black ensemble, sitting straight as a stick at a polished metal desk in a sleek, high-rise Boston university office. Ana would be patting her trim new hairdo, jet black eyes gleaming at a very important conference paper that required her immediate attention. She never understood why I'd applied for a job at a smaller college in the boonies when I could have sprung for a champion academic career in the Big Leagues.

"You know me," I drawled. "Pokin' along, enjoyin' the bright blue skies and cool, high-altitude temperatures. How's summer in the asphalt jungle?"

"Hot, humid, and rainy, as if I had to tell you," Ana twanged in her New Jersey-Cuban accent. "I'm leaving tomorrow for a conference in London." No matter how often I ribbed her about it, Ana couldn't help pronouncing the "g's" at the end of "-i-n-g" words.

"Giving a paper on Rosalia de Castro?" I asked, citing Ana's area of expertise.

"Workshop. A precursor to a bigger presentation I'm doing in Spain at the Celebrate Galicia conference in the fall. Are you going?"

"Don't know yet. I'm working on a paper. Life's been conspiring against me lately, and I haven't found time to finish it." I gave a light laugh but drummed the end of my pen on my desk. "Listen, Ana, I called because I want to check on somebody here who got his degree from Brownell. I thought you might be persuaded to snoop around for me."

"Oooh!" Ana's voice took on a throaty, conspiratorial tone. "Is he jumping your bones or stealing your work?"

"Neither. It's the department Chair Baldomero Vigil, formerly from Bolivia. He's a bit of a pontificator, not easy to get to know. I want to understand whom I'm dealing with."

I imagined Ana nodding her head knowingly. "Gotcha. You always were one to dot the 'i's' and cross the 't's,' *Che*. That's what made you such a worthy competitor at school." She paused, and I figured she was checking her phone's calendar. "As I said, I'm leaving tomorrow, but when I get back, I'll see what I can dig up. Not in any rush, are you?"

"No rush at all," I lied. "Thanks, Ana Banana. Have fun in London. And don't come back with a British accent, or I'll never speak to you again."

I replaced the receiver in its cradle. If anyone could dig up dirt on Baldomero Vigil, my friend and bulldog researcher Ana Torres would.

On my way out of the department, I reached the top of the stairs at the same time Suzanne was clumping down, and Dolores was wafting toward the main hall. To my surprise, they both made a point of greeting me, but passed each other with no acknowledgment whatsoever. Things on campus were getting freaky.

* * *

By Saturday, I was feeling antsier than a picnic table on the Fourth of July. Neither Olivia nor Elsbeth had found time to begin their inquiries. I had to bite my tongue; after all, they weren't the ones laboring under a black cloud of suspicion.

Besides, I'd struck out with my own investigations, too. I knew I'd have to cool my heels for a while concerning the chairman, but when I called my brother to question him, he was too occupied closing "an important deal" to talk. For Juana's and Sarita's sakes, I hoped the deal had to do with selling cars, not with betting on the fights. And I hadn't come up with a creative way to approach my sister about Juventino either.

The detectives' insistence when they interviewed me at my parents' that I stick close to home sounded like the police suspected me of criminal activity in spite of the Chief having known me all my life. Did they mean, like they say in old Westerns, that I shouldn't leave town? It was all too *ridículo*!

Feeling constricted made me yearn to get away. If I went up into the mountains, the clear air might chase the cobwebs from my brain, and maybe I'd think of something. And to be frank with myself, I was desperate to talk to my ancestor again. Even if Doña Isabella was a figment of my imagination and not an assistant from The Great Beyond, at least that part of my brain might activate itself at the stone circle. To heck with staying in town!

I shot furtive glances around the parking lot, looking for plainclothes cops before starting my car. I needn't have worried. On that postcard-perfect Saturday morning, the entire complex, street, and neighborhood were deserted. Many people move to Boulder because of the generally dry, sunny, pleasantly warm weather so conducive to athletics and other outdoor activities. So, those who could were probably enjoying recreational activities on such a lovely day.

The Purple Grape didn't zoom up the road to my retreat; it wheezed and putzed. I caressed the dashboard with my free hand. Maybe my girl was feeling stressed, too.

Once at the stone circle, I built a fire like the time before, figuring it might act as a beacon to call my ancestor. Sweating from my exertions, I threw a handful of frankincense and myrrh on the flames that I'd bought at The Fragrant Veil. Those heavenly aromatic resins have been used for centuries to invoke spirits and deities of every pantheon imaginable, so they just might work here. I sat and tried to empty my mind by tuning in to the morning stillness.

"Doña Isabella?" I whispered. The vast forest swallowed my words. "Are you there?"

Balsamic smoke rose from the kindling and resins drifted through the trees, and, so I hoped, into the cosmos. I squeezed my eyes shut and held my breath. Nothing! In the distance, a crow cawed. I prayed aloud. "Please come, Doña Isabella. I need you!"

* * *

The fire heaved, and my eyes snapped open. Through rings of smoke, I distinguished my ancestor standing on the other side of the fire pit, her shawl hanging over one shoulder.

"I told you, *Chica*, just call me, and I'll come to you," she said in her raspy voice.

The spirit regarded my offering with a jaundiced eye. "I gotta tell you, though, since I'm an Indian, tobacco, and salt would've made a more appropriate offering." She sniffed the air. "But I appreciate the gesture of frankincense and myrrh. It gives your invocation an eclectic touch." She readjusted her shawl. "What can I do for you today, Miss Worry Wart?"

It was going to be difficult to talk without breaking down. I swallowed hard. "You probably know that my colleague…friend…Eddy Calderón…h-has…"

"Passed through to this side of The Veil? Yep, I know," she said in a matter-of-fact tone.

My eyes clouded, and I croaked, "Is he alright?"

"Sure, he's hunky dory." She shot me a sidelong glance. "Other than the fact he's *dead*. He's resting up over in Cabana Number 256, where it's real comfy. The dying process can be pretty tough on the old constitution, but we all survive it, so to speak."

I swallowed again. "Does he know how he died and who killed him?"

The old lady plucked a few stray pine needles stuck to her shawl. "Natch, and so do I."

She removed her shawl, set it on the ground, and eased herself into a cross-legged position by the fire. Sighing with pleasure, she said, "Ah! It's good to take a load off the old dogs. I've told you before that nobody on The

Other Side can interfere directly with what goes on where you are. But as your elder relative, I can tell you that Eddy and you were not a match made in Heaven, if you pardon the pun. Ha!"

It was my turn to sigh. "I've thought of that, and the more I learn about Eddy, the less I feel I knew him. It seems he may have gotten too mixed up in other people's lives."

"Eddy was a righteous dude, but he tended to tell all he knew and judge all he saw. 'He who tells the truth doesn't sin but causes many inconveniences.' In this case, the inconvenience was his own demise."

I threw dried twigs into the fire and watched them spark. "I'm glad to hear that in his ending, Eddy is finding a new beginning. But with his death, my own terrestrial problems have shifted into high gear." As I talked, I felt the tension knot in my neck growing. Somehow, I'd have to make my ancestor understand I was in deep trouble. I dove in.

"Since I discovered the body and because my scarf was the murder weapon, I'm now probably Police Suspect Number One. Not to mention my new status in the department as a pariah. I must find out why Eddy died and who killed him to clear my name." I puckered my forehead. "Even though you can't tell me outright, I'd appreciate any hints you might pass along."

"Hints?" The old lady scoffed. "I already gave you hints, *Chica*, and you chose to ignore them. I thought that 'The throat must pay for what the tongue may say' was a pretty nifty use of a proverb to warn you that your boyfriend might be offed by strangulation."

I felt my chin jut out. "I understand now what you meant, but at the time, I assumed you were referring to department gossip."

"Well, you assumed wrong." The spirit cocked her head toward a looming fir. "And right, come to think of it. What about the two birds on the same ear of corn? You haven't addressed that one yet."

"I'm thinking about it, but I'm still reeling from Eddy's death."

Doña Isabella was occupying herself by extracting little nuts from several piñon pinecones she'd pulled from a pocket of her capacious skirt. Through a mouthful of nuts, she muttered, "I know you won't believe me, but aromatherapy is crucial to solving this mystery. For the moment, though, I think it's best you back off. Put yourself in balance again so you can move forward, make better judgments, and use your noodle to find and interpret clues. Aromatherapy can help you with that, too." She offered me a toothless grin.

For a moment, I closed my eyes that were stinging from the fire smoke, then opened them, and looked my ancestor in the eye. "*Abuelita,* you know I love learning about aromatherapy and enjoy taking the class you suggested; I've even made friends there. But my life has taken such a sudden and serious downturn. At the moment, I'm not in the mood to absorb any more teachings."

"Tough rocks!" Doña Isabella dismissed the excuse with a wave of a bony hand. "I'm going to give you a couple of recipes anyway. You'll thank me later."

Por el amor de Dios! I shrugged, resigned to the inevitable.

The old lady busily ate the nuts she'd collected like a squirrel, savoring each one, while I waited impatiently.

"In case you're interested, I'm not really eating these," my ancestor explained. "I'm merely enjoying the memory of their taste. You'll find them all in a neat pile on the ground when I leave."

She rubbed her hands together, presumably to brush away nonexistent nut crumbs. "All right. First of all, you need to 'Calm the Troubled Spirit.' By that, I mean your own spirit, not me. Ha! Ha!" She hooted. "I'm as serene as a fluffy white cloud. Here's how to go about it:

"In a dram vial, blend twelve drops of rose, six drops of vanilla, three drops of cinnamon, and three drops of angelica oils. Angelica is a precious essence, one reason you only use three drops." She gave me a sly look. "You can substitute clary sage or narcissus, if angelica is too pricey for your puny budget."

Despite my troubles, this spirit had managed to capture my interest. So, I ignored the not-so-veiled reference to my tendency to overspend. "How do I use this concoction?"

"In my day, we sprinkled it over hot rocks in the sweat lodge, but you can put it in a room diffuser, on a light bulb ring, even in an inhaler. Or to use it as a perfume, fill the rest of the vial with sweet almond oil, shake well, and dab it on your pulse points."

She finished off the last nut and licked her fingers. "I call the next formula 'Balancing Act' because it helps balance the emotions. Use fifteen drops each of amber and neroli. Add a few drops of any combination of allspice, bitter almond, lavender, or spruce. Use it in the same way as the previous formula."

She paused, then fixed a jet-eyed stare on me. "I'll give you yet another recipe in case you sniff out that someone has it in for you. Like maybe they left a Voodoo poppet by your office door, or something like that. It'll protect you from the brunt of that person's wrath."

I stared at her but kept quiet.

"Mix together twenty-four drops of red rose and six drops each of cinnamon, marjoram, basil, and juniper. Add this mixture to a four-ounce bottle of aloe vera carrier oil, and you'll have created a protective massage oil." She gave me a sideways glance. "Of course, you're gonna need to find someone to rub it on your back."

I flashed back to Eddy lying stone cold on the rug, and a lump caught in my throat. I looked down at my notebook and coughed. "These formulas look great, *Abuela*. I think they'll help keep me going."

Doña Isabella tossed the empty pinecones on the fire and pinned me with a penetrating look. "I'll tell you something else, my six-times-great-granddaughter. Whenever you see one side of a coin, you can assume that the other side also exists." She paused to let the words sink in, then continued.

"I don't need to tell you, being a literary genius and all, that in every story between the beginning and the end is the middle. And you're in the middle of this one up to your eyeballs."

My spirit granny had managed to divert my attention with the recipes. Now all the pain and uncertainty came flooding back.

"Don't you think I know that?" I snapped. "I've tried to make sense of it all, but I have a list of suspects longer than a Latin American constitutional document. Everyone's on it, from Baldomero Vigil to Clive Strange."

My ancestor cackled and waved a gnarled hand. "As to many of your suspects, I say, 'If every fool carried a stick, firewood would be scarce.' If you want my advice, pay attention to what everyone says. As the proverb goes, 'Each word might have three explanations and three interpretations.'"

I started to reply, but my relative cocked her head toward the sky. "Hear that?"

I shook my head. Not a sound disturbed The High Country summer serenity.

"I guess it doesn't penetrate through the ether to this world. It's the Holy Bells calling us to choir practice with the angels. The longest day of the year is coming up later this month. Up There, the angels put on a fancy celestial celebration to welcome in the summer season."

"You sing in the choir?" I couldn't believe the angels would let my *abuelita* sing with her raspy voice.

"With my raspy voice? I don't think so."

Doña Isabella stood stiffly and bent to retrieve her shawl. "I pump the celestial aroma diffuser. It's something like an ethereal organ, only it plays fragrances instead of music. My guardian angel, though, has a divine voice and is chief soloist." She turned to go.

"Wait! You have a guardian angel?"

"Of course, and so do you. Your guardian's quite a personality. We play skittles together and joke a lot, even sometimes about you. You should visit with your guardian and have a chat about The Love Department."

"But I want to know—"

Doña Isabella cackled. "You want to know many things, but Heaven waits for no one. *Hasta la vista, Chica.* Happy scenting!"

With that, she spread her arms wide with her shawl and disappeared into the ether. From somewhere high above the trees, I thought I heard a hummingbird twitter the message, "Oh yeah, I almost forgot. Remember the maxim, 'One misfortune calls another.'"

Chapter Eighteen

"Al que no quiere caldo, dos tazas."
"It never rains but it pours." — *Spanish Proverb*

On Sunday, I struggled to fit into my favorite pair of jeans and failed. Standing in front of my full-length closet mirror with the pants barely over my knees and looking like I'd just dismounted from a horse after a hundred-mile ride, I clicked my tongue in disgust. Why hadn't I asked Doña Isabella for something useful when we visited, like some extreme weight loss recipes? Between dinner at my parents' twice a week, the calorie-loaded, institutional food at the faculty dining hall, and the even worse fare at Taco Loco, my default fast food restaurant for when I don't feel like cooking, which is almost always, not to mention my mounting stress level, the pounds were creeping on.

My parents were on a weekend fishing and camping trip, one of the few respites they allow themselves from the daily grind at the restaurant. So, I wasn't eating at their house tonight. Time to take swift action. Armed with my credit card, I hopped into The Purple Grape and plowed over to Regal Foods with visions of cauliflower and celery dancing in my head.

The supermarket always teemed with shoppers on the weekend, so I parked in front of the adjacent strip mall. As I checked out store display windows on my way to the market, I noticed a hole-in-the-wall that sold clocks, watches, and small electronic devices. Maybe they also carried antique clocks or at least knew about them. It was worth a try.

The attendant was a pimply, gum-chewing college-age kid. He wore black shorts that did nothing for his knobby knees and a black and chartreuse day-glow T-shirt emblazoned with the logo "Lager Heads Beer." He seemed more interested in fooling with his phone than attending to his lone, over-18-year-old customer.

"We only sell hot new stuff here." He shot down my question about antique clocks with a roll of his wrist that implied he didn't get why anyone would want to buy old junk anyway.

On my way out the door, my gaze lit on a sleek-looking silver pen in a display case. "What an attractive pen," I said. "Can you tell me about it?"

The boy drifted over to the case. With more enthusiasm than he'd shown previously, he told me that they'd just gotten this in. "It's a pen and then some. Cool, i'n'it?"

"What's cool about it?" I asked with forced patience.

The boy took it from the case and demonstrated by scribbling on a scrap of paper. "It's a real pen, alright, but it's also a voice-activated mini recorder."

"But can't a phone do that?"

The youth fixed me with a pitying look. "You don't get it, do ya', lady? Spies use this when they don't want their targets to know they're being recorded. This baby doesn't make a sound." He snapped his gum for emphasis.

I was intrigued. "So, how does it work? "

"See this clip thingy? You attach it to your purse, your belt, or your pocket. Jus' move the clip forward to record and back to stop recording. An' see." He unscrewed the pen at the center. "You got here an 18 GB USB flash drive. This li'l puppy's got MP3, 512 Kbps audio quality, and 142 hours of digital recording time. All in a pen. And this pinhole microphone near the clip records up to 20 feet. Sweet, huh?" He twirled the pen around like a miniature baton, chomped his gum, and grinned like Alfred E. Newman.

I took the pen and weighed it in my hand. For now, it might be useful to record ideas related to the murder as they popped into my head. My enthusiasm was building as I thought that, like an international spy, I might record interviews with suspects without them knowing. I could also use it to record ideas for papers I was writing, or classes I was teaching whenever the spirit moved me. I grinned to myself. I could record Angela when she's complaining about me and play it back to her. I might even record a session with Doña Isabella to see if her voice was real or in my head. Then again, I might not be eager to find that out.

Five minutes later and having spent more than I should, but believing the investment worth it, I trolled the produce aisle at the supermarket with "Lady Spymistress" attached by its "clip thingy" to the inside of my purse. After an hour, I emerged victorious with a grocery cart that looked like I'd bought a truck garden.

I tucked the bags as gently as babies into the back seat of The Grape so as not to bruise the pristine greenery. But when I went to start the car, the engine made clickety-click noises like a bicycle with a card in the spokes.

"What's happened to you, girl?" I lifted the hood and stared at the car's innards.

"Something up with your car, Issy?" A voice from behind startled me.

"Oh, hello, Michael. It seems my Bug's gone belly-up."

Michael Kent surveyed the car through eyes so hazy I wondered whether he'd just rolled out of bed despite the fact it was mid-afternoon. Then again, his eyes often held a drowsy look. "Try starting it up again," he suggested.

I attempted to, but only got the clickety-click.

"You can stop now," he called. "I know what's wrong."

He closed the lid and came around to my side. "The solenoid on your starter motor's not working right. You'll have to get it towed, or we can give it a push."

"Oh dear, that's serious!" I exclaimed with conviction, even though I hadn't a clue what a solenoid was. "Thanks for offering, but I'll call my brother. He's got a friend with a tow truck." I stared at the bags of produce in the back seat and wrinkled my forehead. "It'll take them a while to get here. Meanwhile, what am I going to do with all these groceries?" I moaned.

Michael followed my gaze. "No worries. It'll all fit in my car. I'll drive you home."

"Would you, Miguel? That's sweet of you."

Michael, or Miguel, as I thought I'd better start calling him now that he was playing Good Samaritan, moseyed off. I called Germán, who said that he and his friend Al Benavides, who owns an auto repair shop, would be over to pick it up in an hour or so. Michael—I mean Miguel—returned a few minutes later with his Porsche convertible. After we stuffed everything into the jump seat, we climbed into the car and lurched into traffic.

"Hope you don't mind if I stop by my place to get something," he said without asking me where I lived. "Won't take a minute."

"No problem," I shouted over the engine's roar as he lead-footed it through a yellow light. How could I object? He was doing me a favor.

After a rollicking ride through most of Boulder, we screeched to a halt at Miguel's place on the northern edge of town. My mind was on the unprotected produce languishing in the sun, but I acquiesced with a polite nod to his invitation to come in and take a look around.

Squeezed between a run-down motel and a facility for the homeless, the sagging single row of apartments looked like they'd been slapped together from former storage units. The double garage-like space that Miguel called home was divided in half by cheap wallboard. The front area had been converted into a living room and kitchenette. A doorway crudely cut into the wall revealed the bedroom and bathroom beyond.

"I fell in love with it the minute I saw it," Miguel said, his eyes now looking opaque. "This is where the real, down-home people hang, not the boring college crowd up on The Mound." He led me from the main room toward the bedroom. "Wadjda think?"

I paused in the doorway, leaning my hand on the molding, and peeked into the bedroom. The only furniture was a king-size waterbed covered with a black velvety spread, a dresser that looked like it came from Goodwill, and a full-length mirror opposite the bed. "Hmm. Unique."

I turned back to the living room and ogled the posters plastered on the walls advertising heavy metal and redneck metal bands. I never would have guessed this aspect of Michael Kent, given his Preppy attire and demeanor at school. "Looks like you're into hard rock."

He leaned lazily against the doorway to the bedroom and, in a slurred voice, said, "Yeah. I go to every conshirt I can. Hey, wanna drink? It'll relash you."

"No thanks." Obviously, he'd already indulged in one too many. Funny, I hadn't smelled any alcohol. Maybe he drank vodka, but didn't vodka also smell? I shifted my weight from one foot to the other My shoes were starting to pinch. "I've got to get going. Put away the groceries and all. Didn't you say you wanted to pick something up here?"

He gave me a bleary-eyed smile and raised his hand with the thumb and forefinger almost touching. "Jus' hol' on a liddle minute. Now don't you go dishappearin' on me."

And how could I do that with my groceries expiring in his car? Yet in his current condition I doubted I wanted a ride home from him anymore.

Michael vanished into the bedroom and closed the door. Standing awkwardly in the middle of the living area, I tapped the toe of my sandal on the dirt-brown shag carpet. Glancing around, I took in the heaps of magazines burying the coffee table, greasy automobile parts piled in a corner, a stack of unwashed dishes in the sink, and a thick layer of dust coating everything. The apartment reeked of stale cigarettes and beer. *Caray! Qué lío!* How to get out of this mess?

Before I could decide, the bedroom door swung open. I was stunned to see my student appear wrapped in a burgundy-colored plush bathrobe, balancing two joints between his fingers.

"One for the profeshor and one for the shtudent," he said with a lopsided grin.

My heart started pounding, and I backed up all the way to the front door. "No, Michael." My voice came out, sounding strangled. "You have the wrong idea."

"Oh, come on, Ishy. Don't fool around. You knew what this wash about when you…ah… accepted the ride."

I raised a palm in protest. "No, Michael, *te lo juro*, I swear this was not my intention." I scrambled to assume a professorial tone. "Now my groceries are spoiling in your car, and I need to get going right now."

With a slow and careful movement, he set one joint in an ashtray on a nearby table and lit the other one with a lighter he took from his robe pocket. All the while, my mind was calculating that if I turned and ran, could I get to the main road before he chased me down? He looked unsteady, but my wobbly sandal heels were not the ideal footwear for quick escapes. *Cursed heels! Whatever possessed me to wear spiky heels to the grocery? Vanity, that's what. If I ever get out of this pickle, I swear I'll only shop in sweats and sneakers for the rest of my life.*

Another problem surfaced as I thought that if I ran, Michael would know he'd frightened me, and things could get awkward in the classroom. On the other hand, if I waited for him to make a move toward me, I'd be forced to kick him in a tender spot, and I'd get arrested for assaulting a student. Wouldn't that look *bonito* alongside a murder rap? Then again, it was better than the possible alternative—rape! The appalling thought sent shivers up my spine worse than any horror flick had ever done.

Michael took a long drag on his joint and semi-focused on me. Only then did it dawn on me that he'd been high in the grocery store parking lot, too. And half the time in class. Why hadn't I associated the dreamy look in his eyes with drug use before?

"Whatta tight-assed bitch you are," he drawled. "Almost as bad as that freakin' Dolores I boinked."

"Michael, I don't want to hear about your love life," I said, groping in my shoulder purse for my cellphone.

"Love life? With Dolores? *Mierda!* You jump that sorry bitch's scrawny bones once or twice, and she thinks you're headed for the altar. Her name tells it all. Dolores is a real pain in the ass. Ha! Ha! Ha!" He laughed and slid down the doorframe, landing seated on the floor.

I seized my opportunity and bolted into the parking lot.

Who to call? Not Papi. Not Germán. Not anybody at work. I didn't want my family or colleagues to ever find out about this embarrassment. Frantic, I punched in a number. *Mary, Jesus, Joseph! Let Elsbeth be home.*

Boulder is a compact town. Twelve minutes later, Elsbeth's Toyota scooted into the parking lot, her kids staring wide-eyed out the backseat window. As we shoveled the groceries into Elsbeth's trunk, Michael pulled open his front door, propped himself against the frame, and giggled at our frenzied maneuvers. In two minutes flat, all that was left of my presence was the cloud of dust that the car's skidding wheels raised in the dirt.

Chapter Nineteen

"Hijole!" I exclaimed as we pulled onto the main road and turned toward town. "You're a lifesaver, Elsbeth."

"What happened? Who was that Ned, I mean, ruffian?" Elsbeth asked as she maneuvered adroitly through traffic.

I took a tissue from my purse and pressed it to my forehead, realizing I was so nervous I'd worked up a sweat. "I never saw it coming, or believe me, I wouldn't have gotten myself into the situation to begin with."

"We've got a couple of bottles of water on the floor of the back seat. Want one?"

"Yes, please."

Elsbeth glanced in her rearview mirror and spoke to her daughter. "Ginger, can you hand Auntie Issy a bottle of water?"

Gratefully, I accepted the bottle, opened it, and took a long pull. *"Ay,* that's better. As you can tell, I was at Regal Foods when my car broke down. Michael, or Miguel, is one of the graduate students we were talking about the other day."

"One of the actors in the play?"

"Right. He appeared out of nowhere and offered me a ride home, but said he needed to stop by his place first."

I lowered my voice so the children wouldn't overhear. "Elsbeth, I swear he's never been anything but Preppy polite to me. When we got to his apartment, he disappeared for a couple of minutes and returned in a bathrobe with two funny cigarettes. It was like Jekyll and Hyde."

"How off-putting! He never came on to you before?"

I leaned closer to Elsbeth and whispered, "He's always been affable to the point of obsequiousness, but I assumed he was brown-nosing to get a better grade. I never dreamt he'd try to get me into you-know-where. He got unpleasant when I refused his advances and bragged about how he'd been with Dolores and what a bad you-know-what she was."

"Hmm. I wonder who else knows about that."

I leaned back in my seat. "From the way he talked, he's probably blabbed to everybody." The light dawned. "Now that I think of it, this must've been the reason for the quarrel between him and Javier that occurred the day I arrived here. Javier seems tight with Dolores. I remember that before he punched Michael in front of the department, he made some reference to how Michael had ruined somebody's reputation."

"Sounds like your student is a nasty piece of work," Elsbeth commented while checking on her children in her rearview mirror. Luckily, they were engrossed in their tablets.

I said, "When Eddy and I were up in Nederland we saw Michael speed by in his car. He didn't look his usual Brahman self that day, either. He was probably high, like today. Oh!" I wailed. "Why didn't I see this before?"

"Because you weren't looking for it. Smells like you have a skunk of a student with a substance abuse problem."

Elsbeth turned off the main road and wound through the side streets of my neighborhood. She changed the subject. "Speaking of Nederland reminds me that since yesterday, I've made a teeny bit of progress on the clock."

My eyes widened. "You have?"

"Don't get too excited. I rang up all the area pawnshops and nobody's received an item that fits its description."

"You call that progress?"

"Hang on a tick. One helpful shop assistant suggested I contact a man who runs a repair place in Nederland. He's an expert on eighteenth-century clocks. He buys, sells, and repairs them. If anyone in the region knows anything about Mark Allen's mantle clock, he's your man."

"He's got to be the same guy Eddy tried to visit." I remembered Chief Mondragón's strong suggestion to stay around in case the police had more questions for me. I shrugged. I'd left town once; I might as well do it again. Besides, nobody need know I was away.

"Since today's Sunday," I continued, "I suppose the Nederland shop is closed. If you have time later next week, maybe we could go there together and interview him."

"I'd love to if you don't mind me bringing the children."

"Of course not."

We pulled into my parking lot. Elsbeth helped me unload the now soggy and shriveled produce, then left.

The Anti-Diet Fairies might have been tempting me back down the slippery slope to Taco Loco, but at least I'd snagged a couple of leads for the Bolder Women Detective Team's murder investigation. Michael had slept with Dolores and gossiped about it, thereby angering Javier. Information about the clock might soon be forthcoming as well. What all this had to do with Eddy's death escaped me for the moment. What I did know was I'd better get on my cell to Germán right away. While my brother worked on my car, I'd work on him about what he meant when he said that Miguel would head his suspect list.

* * *

I called my brother from home. He and his auto mechanic buddy had already hustled to Regal Foods and hauled my ailing girl back to Al's shop. They'd scorched over in record time because Germán knew he'd sold his sister a car with problems and that his responsibility was to fix them. Throughout the rest of the evening, one of Doña Isabella's proverbs, "One misfortune calls another," kept repeating in my brain. Had the spirit been trying to warn me about Michael or about my car? Or both? In bed, I shivered and pulled the blanket up to my chin.

On Monday, I taught only morning classes, none with Michael in them, *gracias a Dios*. As I was soon to find out, the fact that he wasn't in my class didn't prevent him from making a nuisance of himself.

I decided that after lunch, I'd catch a bus over to Al's shop to see how the repairs were coming along. Maybe Germán would be there, and I could grill him about Michael. On my way out of the department, I stopped in the women's room. As soon as I entered, I heard muffled sobs emitting from one of the old shower stalls. In days gone by, the building housed female faculty, so the bathrooms were outfitted with tubs and showers that no longer functioned. Curious, I entered the shower alcove and pried open the frosted glass door.

"Georgina!" I cried. "What's happened?"

My colleague crouched against the far corner of the cold, cobweb-infested stall like a whimpering animal. She clutched a handkerchief, dabbing at swollen eyes.

"It's nothing. Nothing at all," she said in a quavering voice.

I reached out and touched Georgina's heaving shoulder. "It's all right to still be grieving over Eddy. Every so often, I'm overcome, too."

Georgina blew her nose vigorously. "It's not about Eddy. Or maybe it is because I shouldn't have gotten upset over something so inane."

Her words didn't convince. "It can't be inane if it upset you so much," I soothed and guided her out of the stall and into the main part of the bathroom. "Tell me what happened."

Georgina blinked and peered around. "There's nobody else in here, is there?"

I knew we were alone but checked under the stalls to be certain. "The coast is clear. Now, what's up?"

Georgina dropped her voice an octave and growled, "That damned Michael Kent!"

Always gruff sounding, her vehemence still took me by surprise. "Did he assault you?"

"Not physically." The professor's face flushed dark red, and her eyes ignited with anger. Her usual dry academic demeanor had transformed her. In her charcoal gray suit and repressed rage, Georgina Rampage reminded me of a figure in a Greek tragedy. She paced up and down the small room like it was a jail cell. Her large feet, encased in stolid orthopedic shoes, slapped the linoleum as she trod.

"He said something unforgivable to me at the wrong time and in the wrong place. In front of my seminar students, no less."

"What did he say?"

Georgina stared at the floor and seemed to talk aloud to herself. "Michael came up after class to tell me he had a family crisis and couldn't finish his term paper. He wanted me to give him two more weeks. I told him I'd already given him two extra weeks in the post-Franco literature seminar last semester. That time, he also claimed family trouble, and he still hasn't turned in the paper. 'No, Michael,' I said," and she bobbed her head from side to side. "'You can't fool me again with that excuse.'"

She stopped pacing and turned to me. Her face was drained of blood, and her eyes held an expression as steely as a convicted murderer on death row. At that moment, I believed Georgina capable of anything and was exceedingly glad we were on friendly terms.

"The students were still gathering their books and chatting," said Georgina. "That's when he said it."

"Said *what*?"

Her face contorted, and she trembled. "He called me a dried-up old Lesbo witch, a fossil better off behind a glass case in a museum than behind a podium teaching. *Everybody* heard him, and they scuttled out of the room like a bunch of spiders being chased by a can of Raid."

"*Caramba!* How disgusting!"

Georgina stopped shaking and narrowed her eyes. "That's not the worst part. He said Eddy told him that when he was researching for the play he was writing, he found out my parents weren't married, and my father was an alcoholic who couldn't hold down a job. Lies! A pack of vicious lies! Eddy would never write such trash."

I started to protest that Eddy wouldn't blab an untruth, especially not to a graduate student, but Georgina's deadly stare silenced me.

"Michael said that if I didn't give him an 'A' in his class, he would make sure everybody learned everything about my background."

She grabbed my arm so tight it hurt. "Isabel, you can't imagine how many years it's taken for me to forge a new life and image. I don't want certain elements of my past for which I'm not accountable to dog me. Just because I teach feminist literature doesn't mean I'm a Lesbian. I'm more of a Betty Friedan liberal, married to my job." Mercifully, she let go of my arm and strode to the sink.

Now wasn't the moment to ask my colleague whether the other allegations were true. I needed to say something to assuage her. "Both you and I know Eddy wasn't the sort to spread malicious gossip."

Georgina didn't appear to have heard. With puffy eyes, she hiccuped once and stared into the mirror at her white, tear-stained face, which, at the moment, bore an unfortunate resemblance to Raymond Massey as the murderous brother Jonathan in the Hitchcock mystery-comedy *Arsenic and Old Lace*.

I pulled some paper towels from the dispenser, ran the faucet for a minute, and wet them. "Here, press these to your eyes. The cold water will help bring down the swelling."

The water did its trick, and Georgina revived.

As the woman repaired her face, I said, "You know, Georgina, in the end, you have the power. No matter what Michael says about you, if he doesn't meet your academic expectations, you can fail him. And that makes him fear *you*. I'm sure it's why he lashed out."

Georgina patted her face dry, reapplied her signature carmine-colored lipstick, and gave me a crooked smile in the mirror. The storm had passed, and lightning hadn't struck anybody dead—yet.

"Of course, you're right. I don't know what's come over me since Eddy's death. It must have affected me more than I realized." She let out a horse-whinny sniff.

"It seems that as time passes, life moves in increasingly complex patterns. Some days, I feel overwhelmed. Then, when a student like Michael Kent, and many Michaels have preceded him, says something callous, it sets me off. I guess I'm getting old." She stared ruefully at her reflection.

"No, Georgina," I countered, "you're like what the proverb says, 'Cheese, wine, and a friend must be old to be good.' While you and I are new friends, you have a longstanding relationship with Olivia, and you're highly regarded in the academic community for your many achievements."

She flushed and looked almost chipper. "Thank you for that."

Soon after, rubbing my pinched arm, I left and caught my bus to Longmont and Al's.

Chapter Twenty

"Cada uno es como Dios lo hizo, y aún peor muchas veces."
"Everyone is as God made him and often worse." — *Miguel de Cervantes*

*A*y, what a powerful motivating force guilt is! Germán was at Al's garage, and like a surgeon's assistant, he was poised by the engine, handing over tools as Al asked for them.

"Quihubole, 'mano! Alberto!" I greeted them. "What's the diagnosis?"

"Your friend was right," said Al. "The solenoid was shot, so I'm replacing it and the starter motor."

"That *tipo* is no friend of mine!" To their startled expressions, I looked past them and toned down my voice. "Just one of my graduate students who happened to pass by in the parking lot at the right moment."

"Your car will be ready in a half hour if you wanna wait around," said Al. With a grease-coated hand, he waved toward a corner. "There's soda and chairs over there."

The refreshment machine stood against an Army-green-painted wall behind a couple of aluminum folding chairs and a magazine-littered coffee table. I picked my way past scattered auto parts and tires to the waiting area that reeked of gasoline, motor oil, and stale cigarettes. I bought a soda and settled in amid the chaos of the auto mechanic's garage. After leafing through a couple of *Popular Mechanics* and *Muscle and Fitness* magazines, my eyes grew heavy in the blinking and buzzing overhead fluorescent lights.

I awoke with a start when Germán plunked down in the other chair.

"Is The Purple Grape ready yet?" I asked, stifling a yawn.

"Almost."

I regarded my brother. His white shirt, that Juana always washes and presses so neatly, was rumpled, and perspiration showed through. *How does Germán manage to make ends meet selling used cars?*

"So, Germán, how come you're not at work today?"

His gaze swiveled to the girlie calendar on the wall, to the clock, then over to the posted list of employees' rights, and back to me. "You know good old Vargas. When I told him there was a family crisis involving you, he let me take the afternoon off."

Muy bien! Now I'm a family crisis! But I clamped my mouth shut.

Germán, who I know hates silences, kept talking. "*Oye 'mana*, I'm really sorry about your VW. If anything else goes wrong with it, tell me, and I'll fix it right away. You bought it from me when I really needed the *lana*, some dough, so I wanna make it cool with you."

"*Gracias, 'mano*, I appreciate that." I sipped my half-drunk, flat soda. "I've been meaning to ask you about something you said the other night at dinner. You told me that Michael Kent—Miguel de la Madrid—would head your suspect list for Eddy Calderon's murder. Why?"

He gave me one of his easy, open smiles, the smile that came over him when he was relaxed and enjoying himself, the smile that must have attracted Juana because it was so appealing. "*Ay, ese Miguel.* Everyone knows that *naco* is bad news."

To my questioning look, he clarified, "You know, *perico, porro, besuco.* Drugs."

"Is he dealing?"

Germán gave a short, low laugh. "No way, Ray. That's all controlled by Big Carlos and The Low Riders."

Carlos Machado was always big for his age, even back in kindergarten when we were in the same class. And mean. One day, when we were all choosing blocks to play with from a big bin, Carlos started to harass little Lenny Pérez, a skinny boy with a constant cough and permanent dark circles under his eyes. When Carlos pushed Lenny aside, I tapped him on the shoulder. He turned around and as my older brother had taught me to protect myself, I punched the bully in the stomach,. First, with my left fist, and then with the right. Of course, I was sent home from school, but Carlos always treated me with respect after that. And I could see that Papi, although he warned me I should never do anything like that again, expanded his chest a bit, possibly with pride.

I straightened on my chair. "You mean that old gang from high school is still operating?"

"*Ay, 'mana.* They're not just operating; they're thriving. Big Carlos has got himself quite a spread up around Nederland. He deals in Boulder, Lafayette, Longmont, Denver, Fort Collins, and even as far south as The Springs and Pueblo." He shook his head, looking serious. "The Latino Mafia, mon, they're never goin' away."

The smile reappeared as he returned to the topic of Miguel de la Madrid. "*Sí, ese* Miguel, he's one of Carlos' best customers. Keeps the big guy in Havanas."

That explained why Eddy and I had seen Michael driving near Nederland. From personal experience, I already knew Michael was into drugs, but hadn't realized how far. However, what my brother told me didn't explain why he knew so much about the inner workings of the Low Riders. I figured I'd better concentrate on one mystery at a time, at least for now.

"I suppose that being from an affluent family, Miguel's got plenty of money to throw away on drugs," I commented.

Germán shook his head. "I think you're wrong there, *'mana.* The swanky clothes and fancy car, sure, they come from his Papi. But I don't think he can hit them up for the money he's blowing up his nose, at least not without making them suspicious. That's why he lives in a dump outside the city limits. He has to economize." He drew out the vowels of the last word.

I finished my soda and tossed the empty can into the nearby recycling bin. "*Cielos!* Who would've guessed? I wonder how he gets the money to pay for his habit."

"*Ay,* that's where things get funky. Being Miguel's so connected, he has ways of finding things out about people *Chismes,* gossip, that sort of thing." Germán shifted his skinny body closer to me in his chair. "Word on the street is that when he comes up with a juicy tidbit on someone, he threatens to go public unless the mark pays him to keep his mouth shut."

Michael Kent, a blackmailer! It made sense, though. He was just getting started on Georgina. I said, "Do you think he could've been blackmailing Eddy, and when Eddy refused to pony up, he killed him? What could he have been blackmailing Eddy about?"

My brother, the Man of the World, shrugged. "Maybe about Calderón's relationships with women. According to *chismes,* that theater prof was a real ladies' man. Joe Selos' woman was over the moon about him. That Dolores Lopes *chica,* too, and who knows who else?"

Who else, indeed! Georgina, Bibi, probably Olivia, me—well, almost me. That pretty much covered every female in the department except Mrs. Webber.

"If the prof was fooling around with a married woman *and* with a student," Germán said, "I don't think he'd like his *jefe* finding out about it. Maybe Miguel had proof and was blackmailing the teacher. Or, could be the professor found out about Miguel's habit and threatened to expose him to his parents unless Miguel anted up."

"You mean a blackmailer blackmailing the blackmailer?" I shook my head, bewildered. "Somehow, I don't think Eddy was the sort to extort money from anybody."

Again, my brother, the Answer Man, shrugged. "Since Miguel's parents give lotsa dough to your college, maybe your prof wanted Miguel to influence them to support him for some prestige thing like a medal or something."

I raised an eyebrow. "Something like tenure?"

"*Mira,* I don't know what is this tenure thing. What I do know is there are lotsa *tíos raros* at that college. I hear about one scandal after another up there, so it makes me wonder."

"What do you mean?"

"Take that, Dolores. She sleeps with Miguel, and him, thinking he's God's gift to women, spreads it around that he's given her a mercy fuck."

"No!"

My brother saw my face turn lobster red. "Sorry to sound crude, but those were his words, not mine. As they say, 'A woman's honor consists of the good opinion the world has of her.' That's probably why Javier Malecón got so bent out of shape and punched out Miguel."

"Then are Javier and Dolores dating?" I remembered the affection with which they treated each other at rehearsal.

"Who knows?" Germán said with a lift of a hand. "That Malecón is another *tío raro*."

I raised my eyebrows and shifted in the folding chair. "What's so strange about Javier? He's a bit quiet in class, but he's smart, polite, and turns in his work on time."

Germán shook his head. "Are other teachers up at the college as innocent as you?"

If I hadn't been hanging on every word, I would have taken exception to the remark, but I didn't want to interrupt the flow.

He said, "You know Malecón used to be a boxer and was even a Golden Gloves champ?"

I nodded, recalling my conversation with Eddy about Javier on the day of the punch-out.

"And do you also remember Sonny Vasconcelos from high school?"

"The boxer who married my childhood friend Marirosa? He won the State Junior Boxing Championship my senior year."

"Sonny and a bunch of other ex-boxers still train at a gym in Longmont. Malecón goes there, too, but doesn't have anything to do with them. Won't even go for a *pisto* after a workout. *Fíjate!* Everybody thinks something's up with him, but no one can figure him out."

Al came over to us. "She's all fixed and ready to go!" he said with a broad grin.

"*Excelente!*" I stood, picked up my purse, and began fishing in it for my phone with my credit card app. "How much do I owe you?"

Germán stood, exchanged glances with Al, and put his hand on my arm. "It's cool, 'mana. I'll take care of it."

"Well, thanks guys. And Germán, thank you for the information."

* * *

On the road home, my brain spun with thoughts about what my brother had told me. Could Eddy have been a blackmailer blackmailing a blackmailer so he could get tenure? Or maybe he found out about Michael's machinations. In an effort to reform him, Eddy could have threatened to tell the parents unless Michael cleaned up his act. Then Michael killed him to shut him up. I sighed. I consider myself a good judge of character, and Eddy didn't seem like a tattletale.

What a menace Michael was! Not only did he go around kissing and telling and practically assaulting women, but he was also a blackmailer and a drug addict. If he was blackmailing Eddy, what did he know about others in the department? Who else had something to hide? I recalled the faces of Baldomero Vigil, Juventino Guerrero, Clive Strange, and the dagger-eyed Bibi Pomodoro. Then there was the so-called *tío raro*, the "weirdo Javier." I'd have to find out how he fit into the puzzle. I couldn't wait to mull over the information with Olivia and Elsbeth.

I raced home, and as soon as I got inside, my cell rang. It was Olivia.

"I'm glad you called," I said as I set my purse on the kitchen table and went around opening windows to let in fresh air. "Wait until you hear what my brother told me."

"I've got news for you, too." Olivia's voice held repressed excitement.

"Since you called me, your news first."

"I found Eddy's journal, and as our students might say, it's huge."

Chapter Twenty-One

"Donde no piensan, salta la liebre."
"Things often happen when you least expect them to." — *Miguel de Cervantes*

Despite our excitement, Olivia and I decided to wait to share our discoveries with Elsbeth. After a round-robin of texting, we settled on meeting at Elsbeth's after dinner when her kids were in bed.

Mindful of my diet, I prepared and ate a dinner salad from what vegetables were still edible after their romp in Michael's car and washed everything down with sparkling mineral water. Afterwards, I zipped around my bedroom, getting ready to go. I flipped on the remote, and my pint-size flat screen sprang to life, warming the room with its cheery glow. A television in the bedroom—what luxury!

I recalled how my hardworking parents endured staggering hardships to provide for our family. At first, they toiled in the fields of the San Luis Valley. Later, Papi struggled to scrape the money together to start the restaurant. Besides raising children, Mami worked two jobs to help get the restaurant off the ground.

Although we kids never lacked necessities like food, shelter, guidance, and loads of love, we weren't showered with toys and clothes. Neither were we tucked up in the comfortable surroundings that many young people in wealthy Boulder enjoy. Let alone the privileged children from the New England elite like Michael Kent. While our schoolmates jetted off on vacations to the Bahamas, Europe, or Asia, the Castillo clan trekked to the mountains and camped, rain or shine, snow or sleet. I'm not complaining; some of my fondest family memories are of those holidays. Life might not always be a bowlful of *dulce de leche*, but every time I switch on my TV in my own bedroom in my own condo, it tickles me pink.

I combed through my closet for something to wear. The News rumbled in the background along with dry thunder and lightning from the storm that, as weather systems along the Front Range sometimes do, was skipping over Boulder and racing toward Denver. Too bad! Our city can always use the moisture.

Here's another thing: clothes mean a lot to me. Not because I like pretty things, which I do. Or because I want to impress people, which I don't. But growing up, I didn't have much. As an adult, I believe I should always try to look my best to honor the noble profession I've chosen to follow. So, I selected black jeans, not designer-tagged, but a flattering, feminine cut and a red silk blouse I'd snagged for peanuts at Secondhand Rose. Then I hauled out a pair of blocky but simple and elegant Spanish-style heels so I could keep abreast, as it were, of my taller friends. Tall people don't intimidate me; I subscribed to the Latino maxim that "the size of a person is measured from the eyebrows up." But I love the shoes, and it's coincidental that high heels are slimming. I swear!

I sat in front of the mirror and attempted to add height to my hair by rolling it up in plump braids. I'd pinned the left side more or less the way I wanted when the anchorwoman's voice on the TV rose a couple of notches in breathless excitement.

"—news just in. We take you live to North Denver, where a hostage situation is underway."

The scene switched to a location I recognized as across the street from La Loquería Cantina, one of the sleazier watering holes in a Denver Hispanic barrio infamous for drug trafficking.

Reporter Rita Estrella, the token Latina at the station, clutched the microphone and squinted in the lights at the camera. The storm had made it to Denver. Her hooded, nylon rain slicker clung to her face as rain pummeled all around.

Above the downpour, her voice shrilled, "It began when an unidentified man allegedly threatened the life of a patron inside the bar you see behind me."

The camera panned to the cantina's neon sign, then refocused on Estrella. "The patron left and called police. He informed them that the suspect claimed to be toting a cache of fentanyl that he wanted to sell. When officers entered through the back door, the suspect fled through the front entrance."

The reporter's eyes grew wide. "A SWAT team was also closing in on the street. The suspect grabbed a female passerby and is now using her as a human shield."

The camera swooped in on the drama unfolding. I stared in horrified disbelief as I recognized Angela dangling like a marionette in the leather-gloved clutches of a bearded desperado, a hunting knife at her throat. As the camera zeroed in closer, I stood mesmerized. I didn't think about what my sister was doing in Denver. In *that* neighborhood. Pinned down by a madman. I was transfixed by the sight of the knife's sharp point making a dimple in her flesh.

The jangling phone freed me from the spell. As I sprang to answer, I screamed at the screen, "*Ay, hermana!* Don't move an inch. *Ni una pulgada!*"

"Have you seen the News?" My mother's voice choked with emotion.

"*Sí, Mami.* Just now. What can we do?"

"Papi and I are going there *ahora mismo.*"

"Wait for me!" I cried and slammed down the receiver.

I grabbed my purse and keys and fled the house, leaving the TV squawking in my wake.

✳ ✳ ✳

The next five hours seemed like five years. Papi's pride and joy Serrano-pepper red '59 Chevy (vanity plate HTMAL for The Hot Tamale Restaurant) flew like the Devil to Denver. Jaw set in dogged determination, Gustavo Castillo weaved in and out of traffic like a seasoned racecar driver. He drove so fast I swore I heard the car's fins flapping behind us in the breeze.

By the time we slid up to La Loquería, the crisis had resolved, and Angela was safe in the arms of the Men in Blue, *gracias a todos los santos!* They had just piled her into an ambulance and were heading off to Denver General Hospital. The Chevy cooled its jets and followed behind. I think it was the first time I've ever known my parents to go completely silent. We might have been riding in a hearse.

Angela checked out okay at the hospital. She was scared but physically alright, with no drug residue on her clothes or body. However, she had some road rash on her knees and hands, a pulled muscle in an arm, and a small band-aid on her throat where the knife had scratched her. Mami and I smothered her in tearful hugs and kisses, but Papi, strangely enough, held back.

The police took Angela's statement with us present. We learned that she'd snuck off to Denver after school to meet some of her militant friends whose current cause was justice for Lupita. I wondered whether my sister had gone there with Juventino Guerrero. If so, he'd have to answer to *me*, never mind Papi.

Angela told officers that she was crossing the street with an armful of FLA flyers when this smelly, wild-eyed *taco* grabbed her.

As SWAT closed in, the perp squeezed Angela tight around the neck and shoulders and dragged her toward his car. He began to sweat and tremble, then tripped on a manhole cover. The knife—*gracias a Dios,* it wasn't a gun, or it might have gone off—flew from his hand. But not before it left a scratch on my sister's throat. He toppled backwards, and Angela got pushed forward and fell. The worthless *frijol* was taken into custody.

Papi was *furioso* with Angela for associating with the Aztec Liberation Front. Not to mention the little matter of going AWOL to Denver. At fourteen, she's not allowed to leave town alone, much less travel to an unsafe barrio in the late afternoon with the intent of staying until after dark in the company of revolutionaries and malcontents. She's *supposed* to be at the restaurant working her after-school job, setting the tables for the dinner crowd. She's *supposed* to eat there, go home, do her homework, and go to bed. She's *not supposed* to talk the hostess into covering for her so she can fly the coop.

Though I realized a lot of Papi's show of anger masked his worry and sense of helplessness for not having better protected his daughter from danger, we all still suffered through his lecture all the way back to Boulder, where we arrived after midnight. The one time he got off Angela's case, he turned to me and complained that not only was he saddled with one delinquent daughter, but now The Jailbird was combing her hair like a punk rocker. My hands flew to my head, and I realized I'd run out the door so fast I'd forgotten to undo the half-finished braid. I'd traipsed all around Denver looking like that!

Mami insisted Angela stay home from school the following day to rest from her ordeal and also so she could fuss over her baby. By the time evening rolled around, it wasn't hard for me to persuade my sister to come along to Elsbeth's for some aromatherapeutic rescue. I figured if Angelita was going to keep getting into trouble, she'd need all the protection she could get. Besides, this would give our Bolder Women Detective Team a golden opportunity to find out what the teen knew about Juventino Guerrero.

I texted Elsbeth and Olivia from the hospital. I explained what had happened, and we rescheduled for the following evening. Then, I told Mami and Papi that Elsbeth wanted to perform a holistic examination on Angela and prepare an herbal concoction to settle her nerves and help her sleep. They let her go, provided I promised not to let her out of my sight. *¡No problema!*

Chapter Twenty-Two

"La mentira es un bicho de patas cortas."
"Lying is a short-legged creature." — Spanish Proverb

I drove to work the following morning because I wanted to use my wheels to get to Elsbeth's as soon as possible that evening. The plan was to bolt down some fast food at Taco Loco after work, swing by my parents' house to pick up Angela, then head over to Elsbeth's. Since I hadn't been granted one of the coveted reserved spaces in the front faculty lot, I parked in a back lot. I ended up hiking almost as far as I would if I'd walked from home. Maybe I should join the crowd and spring for an E-bike after all.

I caught up with the chairman, who was exiting his custom-painted, ice-blue Mercedes in the second row. We walked together along the tree-shaded walk to the department. Today, Vigil's perennially polyester attire was rumpled around the edges, and he wasn't bustling along at his usual officious pace. He also was in a suspiciously civil humor.

"I've been so busy with this fundraiser," he said, wiping perspiration from his brow with a monogrammed handkerchief he took from his breast pocket, "I'm afraid I haven't had a chance to ask how you're getting on."

He replaced the handkerchief in his pocket and gave me a smile so brittle it reinforced my impression that this was a face not accustomed to expressing solicitude. Which made me wary of why he was making nice now. I noticed a couple of other uncharacteristic details. For one, his little Hitler mustache twitched like he had a nervous tick. For another, his dominant eye, which so often flashed with arrogance, had an opaque curtain drawn over it today. Both eyes were smudged underneath with blue half-moons. I wondered whether the Chair had spent a sleepless night, and if so, why? I wished Ana would get back from her trip and call about him.

I smiled back. "I'm doing fine, Professor Vigil. Thank you for asking."

"*Bien, bien.* Please call me Baldomero. And your parents, I hope those fine, upstanding people are doing well and are happy you have joined our little faculty family?"

Faculty family, ha! "*Sí,* everything's fine with them, too." We paused at a crosswalk to let three skateboarders whiz by. *So that's it. Vigil learned that Papi is a respected member of the Latino business community and that he and the police chief are compadres.* Aloud, I said, "I hear Michael Kent's parents are flying in for the fundraiser."

We continued on our way, and Baldomero's face brightened. "Yes, they'll be here tomorrow for the kickoff reception at the College Club. They're staying through the weekend to watch their son perform in the play."

"I hope the event is very successful."

Vigil gave me a sidelong glance, and his mustache twitched twice. "I realize your first weeks here must have proved a bit more tedious than you expected, given the contretemps over Eduardo Calderón. Thankfully, that little scandal seems to have blown over."

I felt the blood rush to my cheeks. What nerve to dismiss Eddy's murder as a "contretemps" and "a little scandal!" I would have loved to challenge him but was not in a position to do so, at least not yet. I took a deep breath.

"Do you know who will replace Professor Calderón?" I asked in the plainest vanilla tone I could muster.

"A couple of candidates have applied, including a new Ph.D. from Bolivia, Oscar Fingir. However, we can't schedule interviews until more faculty return from summer break. We're working with a skeleton crew over the summer." He gave a short laugh.

So, Baldo's crony was already applying for the position. Imagine that! I'd have to let Olivia know her prediction had come true so soon.

We reached the department, and Vigil held open the door for me. "Mrs.

Webber tells me you're writing a paper to submit to the Celebrate Galicia Conference in the fall."

"I am, but I'm not done yet, and I don't know if it will be accepted."

He reached out and patted me on the shoulder with a well-padded hand. "It will. Given your past academic achievements, we're expecting great things from you, Isabel. Great things." He sniffed, and the way his nose pinched in his rotund face with the cobalt-smudged eyes and little twitching mustache, he reminded me of Mr. Pickwick on Thorazine. "I must leave you now, but you have a *wonderful* day." With that, he headed toward his office.

I trotted through the bowels of the almost-empty TA bullpen and into my office, rolling over in my mind the reason why Vigil looked so stressed. Was it solely the fact that, after the murder, the department appeared several times in the newspaper portrayed in an unflattering light? For a man so concerned with outward appearances, any whiff of scandal associated with the department probably filled him with anxiety because it reflected on his name. Was I reading too much into his behavior and he only was on edge about the fundraiser? Or was something more bothering him?

* * *

I wasn't surprised to see that Michael skipped class. After the way he behaved toward me, if I were he, I wouldn't show my face again this semester. Then I'd have to give him an "F." *Qué lástima!* As a bonus, Bibi was also absent. Bibi and Michael sat together in class and often left together. Perhaps she and Michael were cavorting on that nauseating waterbed of his. No matter. At least I wouldn't endure Uma Clone's unsettling stares today.

With his nemesis out of the way, Javier appeared relaxed and willing to participate in class discussion. He even made some insightful comments on medieval love poetry. This reinforced my impression that he had the makings of a successful academic.

Such an auspicious moment for questioning him wouldn't arise again any time soon. At the end of the hour, I stopped him before he could gather his books and run off.

"Excuse me, Javier. Do you have a minute?"

"I am on my way to the Recreation Center." Today, he wore a red bandana around his neck. The color complemented his brown skin and black curly hair, making him look like a jaunty character from the swashbuckler movie *Pirates of the Caribbean.*

"I'm headed in the same direction. Mind if I walk with you?"

"Por supuesto que no, profesora. I am happy to walk together."

We set off across campus on a footpath that diagonally traversed a grassy quad. Magpies, inured to the myriad human intrusions on their territory, strutted around the sunny patch of lawn, picking at who knows what delicate morsels, cawing to each other noisily.

After exchanging a few pleasantries about the play, I decided there was no subtle way to broach the subject, so I waded in. "Since you guys were first on the scene after me," I began, "you know I was the one who discovered Professor Calderón's body. The thing is, now I'm a suspect, and I'm trying to find out what happened so I can clear my name."

Javier's face flushed, but beneath his shaggy eyebrows, his eyes exuded pure sympathy. "If you do not mind me saying so, *Profesora,* it did look odd when we came upon you kneeling over the body. I apologize if I spoke anything out of turn, but we were all in shock. After I calmed down, I realized you could not have murdered *Profesor* Calderón because you and he were such good friends."

"I understand and appreciate your vote of confidence," I thanked him. "I'm still wondering, though, who might have a reason to kill him? You were at rehearsal on that night, weren't you?"

To his affirmative nod, I said, "Was the entire cast there?"

"No, *Profesora.* That night, it was *Profesor* Calderón and the principals, who would be me, Suzanne, and Miguel. *Profesora* Oakes and Dolores were there, as always, discussing the rose petal clouds with the set director. Oh! I remember that *Profesora* Rampage was backstage putting the cues into the musical score. But Bibi, who does the prompting, was away. I remember because Rampage had to fill in."

"Did you notice anything out of place, or did anything unusual happen?"

Javier stopped to shift his backpack to a more comfortable position. "Nothing out of the ordinary occurred that I can recall. Let me think." He looked out across the quad as if the scene at the rehearsal were unfolding again before his eyes.

He turned to me. "Suzanne wanted us all to go for pizza afterwards. *Profesor* Calderón said that he had already invited you, and we could all meet in his office and leave from there."

We began walking again, and he added, "One thing was different, but it was not anything I would call unusual, given the people involved."

I raised both eyebrows.

His gaze shifted away from me, then back again. "Oh, those *locos*, Miguel and Suzanne, were flirting around. In fact, they went off together after rehearsal."

"But I thought you all were going to meet Professor Calderón and me for pizza?"

We reached the student recreation center and stopped beside a bed of blushing tea roses. The musky, spicy odor of the roses, along with a familiar, underlying sweet scent I couldn't identify, enveloped us in a tantalizing fragrant cocoon as we stood face-to-face. How I wished Eddy were still alive to enjoy the flowers with me!

"We did plan to go for pizza," Javier explained. "Since *Profesor* Calderón still had to review some details with *Profesora* Oakes and the set director, we were going to meet in his office after three-quarters of an hour. Dolores and I went to her office to wait, and Suzanne stopped in a little while later."

Suddenly, butterflies started dancing in my stomach. I remembered how the group of three had burst in on me moments after I discovered the body. "What happened to Miguel?"

"I do not know. When Suzanne got to Dolores' office, she told us he would not be coming along. From the way she huffed in, nobody wanted to ask her why not."

I was having such a hard time keeping the butterflies from escaping my stomach and flying up into my mouth that I barely heard his last words. Perspiration beaded my forehead, and the sweet smell rising from the flowerbed became so cloying it made me feel sick. If I were to believe Javier, Michael didn't have an alibi. I willed myself to remain neutral.

"I know you and Miguel don't get along."

Javier's face reddened, and he shifted his weight. "I do not like the way he treats women, especially Dolores. Ever since Miguel was a boy—we went to the same high school, you know—he was not nice to some people. I think he is an unhappy person."

"Why is that?"

He shrugged. "Maybe his parents expect too much from him. They want him to be a master of all things and uphold the exalted reputation of the family. Stress kicks in, and he ends up mastering no trade, contributing nothing to the Kent name. At least, that is what *Profesor* Calderón told me."

"Did he?"

"Yes, *Profesor* Calderón was helping me overcome my own feelings of… certain inadequacies. I come from a family of prizefighters who started out on the wrong side of the tracks. He encouraged me in my academic work. I will miss him." He looked suddenly anguished, like a man lost at sea whose life preserver just floated away.

"I'll miss him too, as will many others. Thanks, Javier. You've been most helpful. I've got to run now."

Javier recovered his composure. "Me, too. Literally. I am glad to assist. I hope you find the killer soon." He turned and pushed through the glass doors of the campus sports facility.

I scurried off in the opposite direction back to my office as fast as my sandal heels could carry me. As I prepared a strong cup of not-very-good-but-useful-in-an-emergency instant coffee from bottled water with my electric heating element, I fixed on this new nugget of information. Why hadn't I thought of it before? The only people to enter the room after I discovered the body were Javier, Dolores, and Suzanne. Michael hadn't been with them. So where had he been? Murdering Eddy, then running away? Somehow, I'd have to worm my way into Suzanne's good graces so I could interview her about Michael's whereabouts.

Chapter Twenty-Three

"La voz del pueblo es la voz de Dios."
"The voice of the people is the voice of God." — Attributed to Hesiod, Greek Poet,
active 750-650 BCE

That evening, Angela and I sat in the parlor of Elsbeth's gingerbread house, waiting for her to put her children to bed and serve tea. Staring at each other, I imagined we looked as impassive as two Toltec warrior statues in a face-off.

Angela kicked her Crocs under the coffee table and folded her grasshopper legs yogi-style on the overstuffed couch. Then she looked away from me and became fascinated with a spider inching across the carpet.

Perched on a straight-back Victorian chair, I listened to the ticking grandfather clock and turned my attention to the tiny choo-choo puffs of steam that emitted from a tabletop aroma diffuser. The scent was citrusy refreshing, something I couldn't quite place. Maybe a blend?

What to do with my baby sister? Angela reminded me of that line from the old Joni Mitchell song about a "devil wearing wings." My heart cried out to the girl, but I knew if I even tried so much as to put my arm around her, Angelita would recoil. Would my sister ever grow up to be my friend and companion? *Hijo,* I'd settle for a human being who lived to see her twenty-first birthday.

The doorbell chiming "Bonnie Banks of Loch Lomond" broke the silence. Since Elsbeth was still busy in the kitchen, I rose and opened the door to Olivia. My friend breezed in, all smiles and good cheer, in black leggings, blocky sandals, and a crisp white blouse with a French collar and cuffs. She had a file folder tucked under her arm.

"I'm so pleased to meet you, Angela," Olivia said after introductions were made. "What a frightful experience you had. How are you doing now?" She took a seat in the companion to my chair and set the folder on the floor under her purse.

"Okay, I guess," Angela mouthed in a monotone I recognized as implying that she wouldn't get excited if the Earth suddenly spun out of orbit, much less fret over her recent so-called trauma. Angela went back to staring at the carpet. Olivia, still smiling, glanced at me with raised eyebrows.

Elsbeth sailed in from the kitchen, bearing a tray with four steaming mugs of tea, a honey pot, napkins, spoons, and plates with sliced, home-baked gingerbread, all of which she deposited on the coffee table. "Refreshments!" she announced.

"The tea smells wonderful," I chirped too exuberantly to cover Angela's bad temper.

Olivia sniffed the fragrant steam. "What kind of tea is it?"

Elsbeth arranged herself on the couch next to Angela, who made the concession of uncurling her legs, but edged to the far corner and hugged a throw pillow to her chest.

Looking as unperturbed as Mary Poppins in the nursery, Elsbeth said, "I prepared two different tisanes. One is for Angela to help calm her. The hops in it helps prevent nightmares about her ordeal." She took a mug from the tray and, with a radiant smile, set it before my sister.

Angela glared at the cup. "I don't have nightmares, and I don't feel like drinking tea right now," she mumbled.

Still hugging the throw pillow, she stared out the window at the rosy evening clouds tinged with gold, the kinds of clouds that prompt Boulderites to describe such evenings as "just another lousy sunset in Paradise." Apparently, an outing in Paradise with her older sister and friends was marginally more exciting than staying imprisoned at home.

As she distributed the other mugs to us, Elsbeth explained, "I call the second recipe, which includes some yarrow, 'Courage' to help put us in the proper frame of mind to solve our first case."

At Elsbeth's last words, Angela shook her head almost imperceptibly.

"How thoughtful of you to prepare something special for us," I said and directed a look at my sister that told her under no uncertain terms to mind her manners.

Olivia tested a forkful of gingerbread. "Yum! What a treat!"

"Ginger aids digestion and also sparks the intellect," said Elsbeth, "which I reckon we can all use if we're going to try to discover who killed Eddy."

At the mention of the murder, Angela's face took on a pout I knew well.

"But first," Elsbeth continued, "since you're a new guest in my home, Angela, I thought I'd share with you one of my aromatherapy concoctions for stress reduction and protection."

When Angela gave Elsbeth a laconic glance, I quickly put in, "It's good of you to think of my sister, Elsbeth."

Unruffled by Angela's disgraceful behavior, Elsbeth said, "My pleasure."

Striving to keep my seething annoyance at my little sister under control, I made an effort to turn my attention to our hostess.

Elsbeth produced a dram vial from her pocket, uncapped it, and presented it to Angela. The girl extricated one arm from around the pillow long enough to receive the vial and take a tentative sniff and then another.

"Doesn't it smell lovely?" Elsbeth enthused. "I use this 'Inner Balance' recipe whenever I feel I need a lift. Dab some on your pulse points at your wrists and ears. Lovely!"

We all watched as Angela dropped the pillow to the floor and rubbed a few drops of the essence into her skin.

"How does it feel?"

"Okay, I guess." Angela shrugged, but some of the peevishness had left her voice.

"This oil will also calm and protect you when you go on those special missions to Denver."

"Angela won't be going on any more special missions to Denver," I couldn't stop myself.

"Says who?" Angela snapped.

"Says Papi, Mami, and me."

Elsbeth intervened in a careful, modulated tone. "You've been doing some important work in Denver, haven't you, Angela?"

The teen's eyes sparkled with righteous pride. "Oh, yes. The marches and protests are important to the movement." She flashed me a malicious glance. "As we Latinos say, 'Ten who shout obtain more than ten who remain silent.'"

"I think it's admirable for a person your age to care so much about the plight of the less fortunate." Elsbeth's tone was as mellifluous as honey on a warm sopaipilla. "Why don't you sip the tea?"

Seemingly unaware, the girl reached for her mug and began sipping it.

"It's so brave of you and anybody who holds a strong belief to march in public," Olivia put in. "Why don't you try some gingerbread?" She moved Angela's untouched plate closer to her. With her free hand, Angela took a bite of cake, chewed slowly, and then gulped the tea.

I understood what my friends were doing, lulling Angela into a sense of security so she'd be open to answering questions. But given our volatile sibling relationship and my own sometimes impatient nature, I had to put an end to this admiration fest and move along with the investigation.

"Did you go into Denver alone?" I wanted to know.

Angela regarded me, and I saw that the look of spite in her eyes had softened. I wondered what Elsbeth had really put into that tea.

"No," said Angela. "I took the bus after school with Erica and Beto."

"You didn't go with your friend Juventino?" I insisted.

As Olivia discreetly stepped on my toe, Angela put down her fork, but still cradled the mug. She half-shut her eyes and some of the familiar look of disrespect crept back into her face, but less sharp now. "Juventino wasn't involved in the march. He had an even more important mission." To everyone's surprise, she yawned.

"It looks like you've finished your tea," Elsbeth said softly. "Let me take your mug."

She reached for the cup and took it to the kitchen. Angela yawned again and stretched her legs on the couch.

Prudence and Olivia's warning cautioned me not to interfere again with my friends' interrogation. I realized that I, too, could do with a cup of whatever Angela had been drinking to sweeten my own disposition.

Now Olivia took up the gauntlet. "More important missions? What could be more important than the march for Lupita?"

Angela blinked twice and said, "You should know 'cause your office is right above his. Juventino's saving undocumented workers from almost certain death."

On her way back from the kitchen, Elsbeth stopped stock-still in the doorway. I sensed the three of us holding our collective breaths lest we throw Angela off-topic.

"Is that so?" Olivia said. "And how is he doing that?"

For a long moment, silence reigned except for the steam puffing from the diffuser and the loud ticking from the grandfather clock that reverberated through the room.

Angela picked up the throw pillow, placed it along the arm of the couch, and leaned her head against it. A look of suspicion passed over her face. Then she sighed and seemed to come to a decision.

"I guess it doesn't matter if you know. It's an open secret among activists anyway. Juventino saves mules from the clutches of The Low Riders." After that declaration, she commenced staring at the opposite wall, seeming to have forgotten our presence.

From her position in the doorway, Elsbeth brought back Angela's attention. "You were telling us how he saves mules. I assume you mean people who carry drugs across the border."

Angela nodded. "They hook up with one of Big Carlos' coyotes in Mexico. He promises to bring them across the border and provide transportation to the interior of this country, a valid ID, and a job if they carry the drugs. Only once the coyote gets them away from the border, he makes them hand over the drugs."

"To Big Carlos himself? I asked.

"No, no," she said with a lackadaisical wave of her hand.

She settled deeper into the pillow, and her voice became sluggish. "The FLA's people in New Mexico take the undocumented ones off the coyote's hands and drive them to Walsenburg. There, they change vans. Kind of like an airport shuttle." The corners of her mouth turned up at the image brought to mind.

"They go to a safe house in Boulder and visit Juventino at night in his office, where he gives them prepared IDs. Then he drives them in his van to Greeley. From there, I think sometimes Juventino, but also others, transport them to towns around the Midwest where they can find jobs." This time she let out a mighty yawn.

The light dawned. Guerrero drove a big, nondescript, gray van to fly under the radar.

Elsbeth moved through the stunned silence to sit on the couch next to Angela's feet.

"Poppet, you know what Professor Guerrero does is illegal, don't you?"

"Yes," Angela responded in a small voice, "but he's helping so many people."

"That's good because you wouldn't want to get involved in anything against the law," said Olivia.

Elsbeth gave my sleepy sister an endearing smile. "We understand that you feel undocumented workers are getting a raw deal. Your legal protests and marches are admirable, but you must realize Juventino Guerrero has crossed the line."

Angela nodded in hazy agreement.

"I'm certain your family don't want to see you get into more trouble."

"And you've got to think of the larger Latino community you could harm if all this came to light," I added. "People might think all Latinos are lawbreakers, which isn't true."

"Hmm." Angela bobbed her head again and closed her eyes.

"You've never helped in this mule running, have you?" Olivia asked.

Angela's head lolled. "Nah. She makes sure I don't go along."

"Who's 'she'?" I interjected, raggedness creeping into my voice.

Angela's eyes were having a hard time focusing. "You know," The Numbers Girl...2...4...1...7...9...3..." With that, she closed her eyes and snored.

Elsbeth covered her gently with an Afghan and turned down the living room lights. Then, the three of us tiptoed into the kitchen.

Chapter Twenty-Four

"Incluso la mejor tela tiene un hilo desigual."
"Even the best cloth has an uneven thread." — *Spanish Proverb*

"*Válgame Dios!*" I exclaimed as we took seats around the kitchen table. "No wonder Juventino looks like he's on caffeine overdrive. He's been burning the candle; that is, rubber at both ends. Did you ever suspect him, Olivia?"

"I assumed he drove that big van because he loved camping. Eddy's journal showed me how wrong I was."

"What did the journal say?" "Where did you find it?" Elsbeth and I spoke at once.

Olivia pressed her index finger to her lips. "Shh! You'll wake Angela."

"I'll make us more tea, and we'll sort it," said Elsbeth. She got up and went to the stove. Olivia tiptoed to the living room, retrieved her folder, and returned.

"What did you put in my sister's tea, anyway?" I was curious.

"Exactly what I told you," Elsbeth said with a wicked grin. "But I filled the aroma diffuser with lime essential oil. While lime refreshes adults, it tends to relax children. I use it in my bairns' rooms when they're being contrary, and it does the trick."

"Something so simple! You should patent it."

"Its effect is common knowledge among herbalists, which tells you that your sister is a bundle of adolescent nerves. Relaxing her so profoundly undoubtedly helped pave the way for her to make revelations that, otherwise, she might not have done."

I felt my cheeks turn pink. "I guess I should remember to pay more attention to Angela's problems and try to help her during this difficult stage in her life."

Meanwhile, Olivia had opened her folder and was leafing through the papers inside. "Let's see," she said, getting us back on track, "I went to Eddy's office after the forensic investigators finished their job. Unfortunately, I didn't find anything interesting." She paused.

"But," she continued with a flourish, which showed me that Olivia, like Eddy, has a flair for the dramatic, "I unearthed this at the theater." She held up a memory stick. "Eddy squirreled it away in one of those hidden wall compartments that store small props."

I swallowed, remembering Eddy's backstage tour.

"I thought it might contain notes on the play," Olivia continued, "so I took it back to my office and popped it into my computer. To my surprise, it was Eddy's personal diary. I ran one hard copy of the entire journal. Then I took notes on the pertinent information and made copies for you." She distributed some papers around the table.

Elsbeth returned from the stove with a fresh pot of Dragonwell green tea. "Let it steep for three minutes before drinking." She covered the pot with a red and yellow flowered tea cozy.

"I take it the argument between Eddy and Juventino at that Saturday rehearsal was about transporting undocumented workers," I said.

Olivia nodded. "According to his journal, Eddy got wind of Juventino's illegal trafficking last winter when he worked on a Posadas Christmas play with a youth outreach program. Some of the kids in the holiday production came from drug rehab. They looked up to Juventino as something of a White Knight of the Underground."

"Evidently, Eddy didn't feel the same way," Elsbeth pointed out as she poured tea into our cups.

Olivia took a tentative sip of the steaming liquid before continuing. "Eddy never hid the fact he didn't approve of illegal workers crossing the border and taking jobs from legitimate immigrants and guest workers. But he also resented the degradations and risks these desperate people are forced to undergo to get into this country."

I blew on the hot liquid and sipped, letting its warmth trickle down my throat to revive my innards. "Sounds just like Eddy the Idealist. He came from a second generation of legal immigrants who hoped that one day all immigration would be legal and aboveboard."

Olivia said, "Eddy was in the process of homing in on Juventino's sideline. In fact, he thought he might discover something in the works on the night of the murder."

"Gosh!" Elsbeth exclaimed. "Juventino's galloped to the top of my suspect list. Now that we know he's up to something, even if it isn't murder, we can't sit back and let it go on."

"Somebody's got to inform the police," Olivia agreed.

I poured honey into my tea and stirred it, then fiddled with my spoon. "I suppose that person should be me. I can tell Papi, and he and I will go together to my *padrino*." I gazed disconsolately at the clear, golden-green liquid in my cup. If snitching on a colleague weren't bad enough, I could only imagine what Angela would think of me.

"Before I go on," said Olivia, "do you have something to tell us, Issy?"

I pulled myself together and recalled the last two days' events. "My big news is about Michael Kent. My brother told me Michael is a drug addict in debt to The Low Riders and that he blackmails people to support his habit. Then yesterday morning I found Georgina crying in the bathroom at work. She told me Michael learned something about her unsavory family background from Eddy and threatened to expose it unless she gave him an 'A.'"

Olivia frowned in disgust. "That doesn't surprise me. Michael got bent out of shape when I told him I was failing him in my Galdós seminar. He implied he'd dug up some dirt on my husband's suicide." She pursed her lips. "Since there's no dirt to dig, I assume he was faking. I wish there were a grade lower than an 'F' so I could stick him with it!" Her gray eyes flashed like a storm in a Turner painting.

"Looks like you could use some of Angela's aromatherapy recipes," Elsbeth observed.

Olivia exhaled through compressed lips and tapped her spoon on the table to emphasize her words. "What with the pressure of having to take on the director's role and not getting time to grieve over Eddy, all I need is for somebody to needle me about Roger's death."

She put her spoon back on the table. The sea swell within had calmed. "Sorry if I sounded sharp, but Michael didn't show up for rehearsal *again*. I had to call his understudy."

She gulped her tea and reached for the pot to replenish her cup. "Michael annoys me because he's talented but fritters it away. I suppose that as long as he makes it to tomorrow's dress rehearsal, he'll pull it off."

Just then, my cell rang. I pulled it from a pocket and saw on Caller ID that Mami had called. She probably was worried about Angela being away, although we hadn't been out very long. I'd talk to her when I took my sister home.

"You're right to be concerned about Michael," I said as I put away the phone. "After his behavior with me at his apartment, I can say without a doubt that he's more of a *ratoncito* than we thought. I talked to Javier today and realized Michael wasn't with the group when they discovered me with the body. Olivia, do you remember if Michael left with them at the end of rehearsal?"

She shook her head. "Sorry. I was wrangling with the stagehands over the rose petals. Eddy was aware of Michael's drug habit, though. In his journal, he mentions that he found out from the kids at the outreach program."

While we talked, Elsbeth got up and went to the refrigerator, brought out a bowlful of cherries, and sat it in the middle of the table. The warm color contrasted appealingly with the golden-hued wood. She invited us to dig in, and we chomped away, leaving the pits on a small dish she provided.

"Eddy was a reformer at heart," Olivia reminisced as she bit into a juicy piece of fruit. "He saw Michael as coming from a home with an absent father and a pushy mother. They want him to follow family tradition and become a Wall Street Wiz, a chip off the old Doric column."

Elsbeth snickered. "Sounds like Michael is into something financial, only not what his parents intend."

I reached for a plump cherry. "Javier said something similar today."

"From what I know about Michael," Olivia mused, "he's more into the artsy, creative side of life. So, he's rebelling in a self-destructive way. Eddy was trying to get him into rehab and turn his life around before it's too late."

"How terribly sad!" Elsbeth commented.

"Now it probably is too late," I concurred. As yet, I hadn't mentioned Germán's suspicions about Eddy blackmailing Michael because they didn't ring true. Especially since we now had proof that Eddy was genuinely concerned for Michael's welfare.

Olivia sipped her tea. "When Eddy mentioned the rehab program, Michael came at him with…. Here, I'll read the precise words." She shuffled through her journal copy.

"According to Eddy, Michael threatened him with, 'You've had a relation-ship with Dolores, who's a student, and you know that's a no-no. You've also hit on Suzanne, Issy, and even that dried-up prune, Georgina. If you don't help me graduate with honors, I'll tell everyone what a letch you are. You'll never get tenure. Not here, not anywhere!'"

Olivia put down the paper and said, "Eddy knew it was mere gossip, but in these things, truth doesn't much matter. Once the word was out, he wouldn't be able to stem the tide. His play was yet unpublished, and he had few academic papers under his belt. He was pinning his hopes on taking this play on the road to make up for his lack of publications. Even that wasn't certain."

She took a big cherry and twirled its stem. "A scandal like that would tip the balance against Eddy's chances for getting tenure, and Michael knew it."

I leaned back in my chair, popped a cherry into my mouth, and stared at the ceiling. "Ah, gossip!" A vision of my ancestor's proverb about slanderers and assassins flitted through my mind.

We sat in silence for a few minutes, each of us lost in her own thoughts. My cell rang again, Mami calling. I chose to ignore it. I drained my teacup and said, "It's possible that when Michael balked about going into rehab, Eddy threatened to tell the boy's parents about his habit."

To my friends' astonished looks, I clarified, "I don't mean I think Eddy was blackmailing Michael back. He might have thought he was doing something for the boy's own good. That could have pushed Michael over the edge."

"Suddenly, Michael has catapulted to the head of my suspect list," Olivia said with relish.

"Before we rush to judgment," said Elsbeth as she refreshed everyone's tea, "let's look at some other angles. Assuming Eddy didn't gossip about Georgina's past to Michael, how did Michael find out?"

"That's easy," Olivia volunteered. "Eddy mentions that Bibi once visited him in his office when he was writing background information for his play."

"I knew it," I interjected. "That girl's a snoop."

"You're right," said Olivia. "Eddy had the screen saver on and got a call to run down to the main office to pick up some papers. When he got back, Bibi was gone, and the file was showing a different page from the one he'd been editing. Eddy figured that given Bibi's and Michael's friendship, she'd tell him about the notes. Knowing Michael's penchant for blackmail, Eddy worried the notes would be misinterpreted."

I clicked my tongue. "Bibi sure gets around. Do you know anything about her, Olivia?"

After sipping her tea, she said, "Not much. I see her a lot in the student union with Michael, but I don't think they're dating. They seem friendly, but not intimate."

Elsbeth chewed on a cherry then said, " It is possible Bibi was hitting on both Eddy and Juventino. Maybe because Eddy was putting the moves on you, she killed him out of jealousy."

I shrugged. "I don't think she's the type to let her emotions run away with her."

"Getting back to the play Eddy was writing," said Olivia, "he wrote in his diary that he worried about Georgie's sensitivity concerning her background. He regretted having based his play, in part, on her life story and was sorry Bibi and Michael found out about her family."

I said, "When we tell Georgina, it will comfort her to know Eddy cared for her so much."

"And it probably lets her off the hook as a suspect," Olivia commented.

Again, we fell silent, sipping tea and munching cherries.

"You know what it means when the conversation dies?" said Elsbeth.

"What?" Olivia and I chimed in unison.

"That an angel is passing overhead."

A vision of my ancestor filled my mind. Was my spirit granny watching us? If so, why wouldn't she help us figure this thing out?

"Did you glean any more information from the diary?" Elsbeth wanted to know.

Olivia shuffled through the pages again. "No, but I found this photo of an antique clock like Mark's."

She took a small picture from the folder that looked like it had been cut from an auction catalog and passed it around.

"Too frou-frou for my taste," I commented.

"Clocks like these are prized in Europe," said Elsbeth as she ate the last cherry. "I'm sure some collector would pay a pretty penny for it. We'll learn more about the clock when we pay a visit to the repairman in Nederland."

I reached for the journal, but Olivia was already tucking it back into the file folder. "I wonder, did Eddy mention anything about others involved in the play who weren't actors?"

"He was concerned about Dolores becoming morose after Michael dropped her," said Olivia. Suddenly, she smiled. "Also, he wondered if Suzanne was getting the wrong idea about her relationship with him."

I chuckled, remembering Suzanne's bizarre declaration about running off with Eddy. "No kidding!"

"It seems," said Elsbeth with a wiggle of one eyebrow, a gesture I found reminiscent of Eddy, "that even a worldly-wise fellow like Eddy Calderón could sometimes be blindsided. Typical male behavior! And I speak from experience."

We all laughed.

She went on, "If I understand from your description of her, Suzanne is unhappy with both her body image and menial job. She envies anyone whom she thinks looks better than her or has something she wants."

"If that were the case," I said, "she'd try to kill one of us, not Eddy." I shifted in my chair. "There's something I've been meaning to mention. Somebody left two dead scorpions tacked to my office door and, later, a Voodoo doll."

"Ugh!" Both my friends grimaced.

"So," I continued, "I think Suzanne is capable of doing at least that. Not that I have any proof."

Elsbeth said, "We know she was jealous of the attention Eddy was paying you. She could have decided it was time to declare herself to Eddy, and when he told her he wasn't hot for her bod, she flew into a rage and strangled him."

"She's capable physically, and we all know she runs on a short fuse," Olivia noted.

"If she left the rehearsal with Michael as Javier told me," I said, "and for some reason, Michael walked off, she would've had time to do the deed before joining Javier and Dolores."

"Now we have four more suspects." Elsbeth counted. "Juventino, Michael, Suzanne, and Clive."

"Don't forget the redoubtable Bibi," I said, "whom I saw on the staircase and perhaps also the chairman."

"So far, we don't have anything to link Vigil to the murder except he didn't want Eddy to get tenure," said Olivia. "That would give Eddy reason to kill him, not the other way around."

Elsbeth sighed. "It's such a muddle."

Olivia rubbed her forehead. "I just remembered something Eddy once told me."

Elsbeth and I looked at her in anticipation.

"He said Javier made several appointments to see him in his office. The student would indicate it was urgent to meet, but when he arrived, he didn't seem to want to talk about anything in particular."

I said, "I remember seeing him lurking around Eddy's office on the day I broke my heel."

"That is curious," commented Elsbeth.

"Eddy thought so," said Olivia. "He also told me he tried to press

Javier about his longstanding antipathy toward Michael to see if that was causing the problem, but Javier clammed up. After the dustup outside the department, Eddy advised Javier to bury the hatchet and get on with his life."

"Javier mentioned that Eddy encouraged him to pursue a career in Academia," I volunteered, "so maybe that was the reason for the visits."

"But it was the student's own decision to give up a potential boxing career for research and teaching despite the fact his family thought university employment wasn't manly enough," said Olivia. "Eddy certainly honored the boy's commitment." She glanced at the file folder, and a shadow passed over her face.

"Okay, Olivia. Spill the beans." I said, wiping cherry juice from my fingers with my napkin.

"It's nothing. I mean, I don't think it has anything to do with why Eddy was murdered, but it gives some insight into his character." She sighed. "Better I read it." She opened the journal again and searched for the entry. "Eddy says that throughout these recent troubles, and I quote,

"'Two of my most recent successes have been first, Olivia the Oak, whom I rescued from her doldrums. I consider her one of my prime success stories. The other is Issy. I like her sense of humor and spunk, but she's too naïve to move in this jaded environment without guidance. I'd like to make something of her, too.'"

Olivia gave us a wry look. "You see, Eddy seems to have taken to this directing stuff perhaps too well. He fancied himself something of a puppeteer."

"A veritable Svengali." Elsbeth's voice was laced with sarcasm.

Eddy in the role of puppet master! I preferred to remember his warm smile and engaging sense of humor and not that, despite his good intentions, he manipulated people's lives.

I said, "On the positive side, we must remember that Eddy set alight a spark in all of us."

"In one," Elsbeth reminded us, "he set a conflagration."

* * *

It was getting late, and we were getting nowhere, so we packed it in for the night. We agreed on Michael Kent as our prime suspect only because he was the sentimental favorite. Before leaving, Elsbeth and I made a date to go to Nederland the following afternoon "to see a man about a clock," follow through on Eddy's intentions and eliminate Clive Strange as a suspect. I offered to bring Lady Spymistress to record the interview so Olivia wouldn't miss out.

After rousing Angela from the sofa, I thanked Elsbeth, and we left. On the drive back to our parents', I ruminated on the disappointing revelation that Eddy had been into manipulating people's lives. Elsbeth was right. Maybe he'd disillusioned someone enough to want to kill him.

Now I had to face Papi and tell him about Juventino. And Mami about keeping Angela out late. I glanced at my sister's serene expression as she dozed in the passenger seat, a Botticelli angel framed in a mass of golden curls. I regretted having to upset her.

When I pulled into my parents' driveway, I was startled to see the lights inside the house ablaze. Surely, they couldn't be that mad about my keeping Angela out. As we stepped up the walk, Mami held open the screen door.

"*Ven, ven!*" She motioned us inside. "We have been waiting up for you."

"Oh?"

"Lucio Mondragón stopped by the house tonight."

"I hope he doesn't want to question me again." My voice sounded as dispirited as air seeping from a deflating cushion. "I told him everything I know."

Mami waited until Angela drifted past us and closed her bedroom door. "No, *hija,* it is not that. The place where you work at the college, you know, it is not a nice place to be. I think you should quit your job and come to work at the restaurant with us. We could use the help."

"Mami, you know I can't do that," I began, but sudden apprehension overcame me. "Why do you say the department is not a nice place?"

Mami put her hands on her hips and looked me straight in the eye.

"Because that colleague of yours, that Professor Guerrero, was arrested tonight in a sting operation for moving *indocumentados* across Colorado."

Chapter Twenty-Five

"Piensa mal y acertarás"
"Think the worst and you'll be right." — *Attributed to Niccolò Machiavelli*
(1469-1527), Italian Author, Diplomat

I love watching old movies. In some of these films, an inmate unjustly convicted of murder escapes the electric chair courtesy of an eleventh-hour call from the governor. That night, I came to fully understand the relief and elation those prisoners must feel, even if the scenarios only take place on a Hollywood movie set. I was so glad I didn't have to rat out a colleague and ecstatic about not needing to ruffle Angela's feathers that the warm and fuzzy feeling stayed with me until the letdown the following morning at work.

According to what Chief Mondragón told my parents, Juventino had been under police surveillance for some time. On the night of the murder, they managed to videotape him moving undocumented workers to Greeley. That he could now be eliminated as a murder suspect didn't disillusion me; in fact, I was heartened: one less dubious character to worry about.

This, however, was not the opinion of the department. One would think that with the gala about to kick off the long-anticipated fundraiser, everyone would be in a party mood, bustling around, frenetic but ebullient. I was only right about the frenetic part. Tension radiated from the chairman's office in waves like the old RKO Picture Studio logo and threatened to engulf the entire building. The reason for the agitation was splattered across the front page of *The Boulder News*: "GMU Spanish Prof Arrested in

Illegal Immigrant Sting." With Michael's parents arriving that afternoon, the headline undoubtedly was the chairman's worst nightmare.

I was curious about Michael's parents. It would be interesting to see what kind of people had raised such a crazy, mixed-up kid. The chances of me meeting them, I knew, were unlikely. As a low woman on the department totem pole, I wasn't expected to attend prestigious, invitation-only events. But I'd have an opportunity to catch a glimpse of university royalty at the play. Baldomero had convinced the dean to have the lone theater box repainted and replace its faded dusty curtains. The Kent parental unit would watch in style as their child trod the boards.

On leaving my air-conditioned classroom at noon to get lunch, I hit a wall of heat so intense I would have fled back to the dark, cool interior if I hadn't promised Elsbeth we'd go to Nederland today.

I drooped over to The Mound to grab a sandwich before heading to Elsbeth's. Shuffling out of Merkowicz' Deli, I caught sight of two figures as incongruous as Laurel and Hardy, and not only because of their sizes, disappearing around a corner by the gelato store. The one poured into a red tank top and boyfriend shorts was Bibi Pomodoro. The other, as wide as he was tall, turned out to be none other than Big Carlos Machado, AKA The Drug King of The Front Range. I never would have conceived that those two had met, much less played footsie together.

However, one of Boulder's many attractions is known as "Compatible Lifestyles." This means that people can choose from many like-minded groups to associate with. Today, it seemed, I was dipping into "the criminal lifestyle."

I was dying to know what they were up to. I checked my phone to make sure I wouldn't be late for Elsbeth and have its camera ready in case I needed to take pictures. Then I stuffed my bagged sandwich into the empty space in my purse. Energized for the hunt as if I'd just quaffed a Red Bull, I scooted into the gelato store's doorway. From there, I peeked around the corner and watched the duo hotfoot it into an alley.

Was Bibi involved with pushing drugs? If she was, perhaps Eddy had found out. Feeling responsible for his student, he may have confronted her in an effort to save her from a life of crime. And for his efforts, she sneaked up on him and strangled him to keep her nefarious activities secret.

The picture I painted made my blood boil, and, in my mind, I ran with the scenario. If I found evidence, however slight, of Bibi selling drugs, I could take it to Chief Mondragón. I'd help bring down a dealer and unmask a killer in the bargain. And I'd be off the hook for the murder. The Chief might even praise me to Papi, and I'd be back in my father's good graces. I trembled with anticipation.

Creeping from dumpster to dumpster, I followed Bibi and Carlos three blocks up the alley in an off-campus neighborhood mostly comprised of old houses converted to student rentals with a few modern apartment buildings thrown in. They walked as swiftly and silently as a couple of Dementors. I huffed and puffed and sweated to keep up. Then, they shimmered through the back door of a rundown Victorian. Panting, I hustled along a narrow walkway between two houses and emerged at the front sidewalk.

For a short while, before he mostly straightened up and married Juana, Germán was into drugs. I'd answered his rescue calls many times from places like this, where pushers shopped their wares and kept Papi from finding out. Such dives weren't particularly dangerous places because many residents were strung out and oblivious to what was going on around them. Even if I encountered Big Carlos face-to-face, he always remembered the childhood punch-out incident and would treat me with grudging respect. So I wasn't afraid. I simply wanted to find evidence. Still, I approached the building with caution.

Badly in need of a coat of paint, the house featured four oversized dormers, one with a broken window. The other windows had moldy-looking air conditioners hanging from the sills that chirped like giant crickets. The dwelling, which in its heyday probably boasted a manicured lawn and a vibrant flower bed, was now landscaped in gravel with wild lettuce, dandelions, and bindweed poking through.

Half a dozen bikes littered the sagging-covered veranda. A line of white mailboxes tacked to the molding like so much forgotten underwear on a clothesline overflowed with junk mail. Stepping over some loose newspapers and a couple of empty beer cans, I passed through the unscreened main open door to the hall.

I stood still for a moment to reconnoiter and let my eyes adjust to the gloom. The hallway smelled like a combination of unwashed bodies and someone smoking weed. Overhead, the floorboards creaked with the sound of pacing, maybe the marijuana smoker or a crackhead. Behind the nearest closed door, the base boom of *Sweet Dreams*, a popular song by the 80s band the *Eurhythmics*, pounded relentlessly. In front of me loomed a steep staircase with a couple of spindles missing on the grimy banister.

I had placed one foot on the lowest step when—uh-oh—Bibi materialized from behind the staircase. She came up close and towered over me.

"Why, if it isn't my Spanish teacher! Are you following me?"

Remembering the adage about intelligence being measured from the head up, I stood my ground. "What are *you* doing palling around with my childhood classmate?"

"None of your business unless, of course, you're here to score a lid." Bibi's eyes seemed to shoot through me like two laser beams. "Or maybe you're into something with more kick?"

I needed to set her straight right now. "No way am I into drugs. I followed you because I want to know why you took information about Professor Rampage from Eddy Calderón's computer and gave it to Michael Kent." I saw the beginning of a blush tint the girl's flawless cheeks and knew I'd scored.

"Who told you I did?" she challenged.

"In a way, Eddy himself. He wrote about it in his journal, which is now in the possession of my friend and colleague, Olivia Oakes. She told me about it."

"Look, I know you're trying to find out who offed your boyfriend. If you think I had anything to do with it, you're barking up the wrong tree." Her eyes became slits, only the pupils showing. "But I'll give you a free piece of advice. If I were you, I wouldn't put too much stock in your friendship with Olivia Oakes. She and Eddy were going at it hot and heavy, and I think she's jealous of you muscling in on her turf. Maybe *she* killed him."

My chin jutted out, and my tongue burned in my mouth as if I'd eaten a kilo of serrano peppers, seeds and all. I took a deep breath and let out the air slowly. Lest I say or do something I'd regret, I turned and, without a word, stalked out the door.

Chapter Twenty-Six

"Amor y celos, hermanos gemelos."
"It's rare to find love without jealousy." — Spanish Proverb

Fuming and no longer hungry, I dropped my uneaten sandwich in a trash can and hopped on a bus that would take me near Elsbeth's. Since she had a bigger and moderately faster car that would accommodate the children, she'd offered to drive.

On the bus, I reviewed the most recent incident. Was Bibi telling the truth, or trying to get to me out of pure maliciousness? Yet I remembered how Olivia had folded away the copy of Eddy's journal as I reached for it. Had she hidden something Eddy had written about their relationship? Had he thrown over Olivia, and she followed him back to his office to have it out with him and then murdered him in a fit of rage? Last night, I'd seen how angry she could get.

Stop that! Now you're being silly. I scolded myself as I climbed Elsbeth's steep stairs. I have to let this go for the moment. Better to concentrate on the antique clock issue. I'll ask Olivia about Eddy after I calm down and can think more clearly.

* * *

Because of the more than mile-high altitude, Boulder's weather is usually mild in the day and cool at night. But it does suffer from some hot weeks. At least it's a dry heat, not like back East, *gracias a Dios!*

Nobody was in a good mood because of the weather. Elsbeth, the children, and I drooped into Elsbeth's car, which unfortunately was not equipped with air conditioning. With windows yawning open, we sped up the canyon past stands of fir and pine so brittle in the summer heat it was a wonder they didn't candle into flames on the spot.

We tried to talk about Juventino's arrest, but between the wind whistling through the car and the kids, who fussed all the way, it was impossible to sustain a conversation. By the time we arrived at the little town perched at the top of the canyon, everyone was thirsty and cross, and I felt a hunger headache coming on. Perhaps, I thought while rubbing my neck, I was better off not having children. At least for now.

We unpacked ourselves from the car and stretched our arms and legs in the clear, cool, high-altitude air. Then we walked to a local café for Auntie Issy's ice cream soda treat, which also treated Auntie Issy. Afterwards, we unwound by visiting the local rock shop, where the children crawled around to their hearts' content among the kids' bins, brimming with fossils, quartz points, geodes, and polished stones.

When we'd rocked out, so to speak, we stepped outside onto the sidewalk inlaid with fossils and semi-precious stones. Then we strolled to where Eddy had gone through the gap between two buildings into the unpaved alley. There sat a tidy row of wooden artisan shops, each dedicated to a specific trade. Nestled between a tannery and a woodworking studio was the clock repair store, with a sign hanging over the door showing the face of a grinning moon.

Inside, clocks of all sizes and shapes ticked away the minutes on every available inch of wall space. And not a cellphone or Apple watch in sight. A white-haired man with a snowy beard and a big, cherry-colored work apron girded to his ample frame sat on a high stool bending over a worktable. He lifted his head, peered at us over wire-rimmed glasses, and boomed a hearty greeting. "What can I do for you folks today?"

At that moment, the hands on the clocks hit three o'clock, and they all began chiming at once. The little doors on the cuckoo clocks flew open, and wooden birds strutted forward on perches to chirp the hour. Ginger and

Jamie were dumbstruck. Elsbeth and I pressed our hands to our ears until the racket died down. The proprietor was unfazed.

"Sorry about the noise," the jovial clock man apologized. "When you work here all day, you get used to it."

"Wow!" "That was so cool!" the kids cried. They ran to inspect the clocks, hoping for a repeat performance.

Elsbeth and I approached the workbench. I slipped my hand into my purse and switched on the record function for Lady Spymistress.

Elsbeth said to the proprietor, "I rang you up the other day to inquire about an eighteenth-century clock my friend and I are trying to locate."

"Yes, I remember. You're the lady from Scotland."

She took Eddy's picture from the outside pocket of her purse. "The clock looks something like this."

He took the photo and studied it. "Ah, an exquisite specimen!" he exclaimed as if referring to a rare animal species. "I repaired a mantle clock recently that looked much like this."

"Was your customer a tall, red-headed gentleman with blue eyes?" I asked.

The repairman bobbed his head. "Yes indeedy. I remember his eyes. They were so blue I thought he might be wearing tinted contact lenses."

Elsbeth and I exchanged glances.

"The clock was authentic, but perhaps not quite as grand as the one pictured," the proprietor volunteered. "Why do you want to know?"

"What a relief," I said and crossed my fingers behind my back as I do when about to tell a white lie. "You see, the clock is a retirement gift for a colleague, but we knew it needed repair. Another of our colleagues, the red-headed man whom you met, is a great admirer of timepieces of all kinds. He offered to take it to the best repairman in the region, who we assume is you."

The artisan beamed.

"Since that fellow is something of an absent-minded professor," Elsbeth put in, "we wanted to make certain he had the clock fixed because we're the ones who have to wrap it."

The clock man bobbed his head again and said, "I can assure you; I did repair it. The customer picked it up yesterday." He added, "You must value your colleague a lot to give him such a fine mantlepiece."

"We value all of our colleagues," I said. "Thank you, sir, for the information."

"You've been most helpful," Elsbeth thanked him. "Come, children. Time to go."

As we emerged from the dark shop blinking in the sunlight, little Ginger piped up. "Mummy! Now I know where Santa hangs in summer. I can't wait to tell Lizzie and Cora!"

On the ride down into town, Elsbeth and I agreed that the time had come to pay Clive a visit. He had the clock and, therefore, motive for murder. I took out my cellphone and called Olivia in her office. I put the phone on speaker and played Lady Spymistress's recording for her. She offered to look up Clive's office hours on her computer.

After a couple of minutes, she came back on the line. "He's in tomorrow morning between ten and twelve."

"Elsbeth's telling me she can't go tomorrow because she has to take her kids to the d-e-n-t-i-s-t. I'll feel more comfortable if I don't have to go on my own," I shouted into the phone because of the bad reception in the mountains. Besides, I wanted to get Olivia alone so she could straighten out details about her and Eddy's relationship.

Olivia's voice came faintly through the phone, mixed with static. "Gotta run...deliver programs...tent...gala at...College Club. See...tomorrow. Bye."

Chapter Twenty-Seven

"La mentira tiene patas cortas"
"The truth will out." — Spanish Proverb

Since it was getting on toward five o'clock, I asked Elsbeth to drop me off at Taco Loco. Exams had sneaked up on me, and I needed sustenance to inspire me to write tests. As a graduate student, I'd been accustomed to sitting on the other side of the podium. Now I realized that devising exams and grading them fairly, as well as considering factors like class participation, creativity, and improvement wasn't a slice of *tres leches* either.

I entered the bright yellow-walled fast-food joint with the red-tiled floor. Harried-looking students crammed into the lime-green vinyl booths, slurping sodas and stuffing burritos into their mouths while they team-studied.

I recognized Suzanne sitting alone, hunched over her computer, alternating between sucking an electric-pink-colored smoothie through a straw and chewing her nails. The queen of the TA bullpen was concentrating so hard she didn't notice me. Recognizing that the Fates had dealt me a golden opportunity, I wasn't going to waste it. I made a hasty order at the window, picked up my bag of goodies, and sauntered over to Suzanne's table.

"Hey," I said in a cheerful, surprised tone as if I'd just noticed her. "I didn't know you came here."

It took Suzanne a beat to focus. When she registered that I was the one talking to her, she curled the edge of her upper lip in a scowl. "Yeah, I hang here when I'm trying to get something done. So?"

"So, nothing," I said and dug deep to muster an ingratiating smile. "I drop in here for a quick meal from time to time, too." Feigning curiosity, I said, "Is that a spreadsheet of the exam rooms, times, and proctors?"

"Yeah, and as you can tell, I'm busy with it," Suzanne said with the air of someone brushing off an insect.

"I see, but do you mind if I sit for a minute?"

The woman shrugged her shoulders, embarrassingly exposed in a tank top the shade of a Florida orange. "It's a free country." She focused on her computer and proceeded to ignore me.

Slipping into the seat opposite, I set down my bag of food and purse. "Listen, Suzanne, I'm sorry we got off on the wrong foot because of Eddy."

Suzanne harrumphed but didn't look up.

"Believe me, I never would've accepted a date with him if I'd known he was already taken. I assumed that since you're married, you weren't interested."

Suzanne shot me a viperous glance. "Never assume anything around here. You're better off that way."

I kept my lips firmly pasted into a smile. "Now that Eddy's passed on, I'd like us to bury the hatchet."

"Whatever."

"Excellent!"

I paused, uncertain how to proceed. The smell of old grease burning on the tortilla griddle wafted toward us, causing me to briefly reconsider my recent dinner selection. *Do not let yourself get distracted. Concentrate!*

"Since the cops haven't given up on me as a suspect," I said, "I'm still trying to reconstruct the events of the night Eddy was killed. Maybe you can help me remember."

Suzanne pressed the exit button and clamped her computer shut. "Alright. I've lost my train of thought anyway. What d'ya wanna know?"

"I was wondering if the four of you left rehearsal that night together or separately. And did everyone go straight to Dolores' office to wait?"

"You mean Dolores, Miguel, Javier, and me? Sure, we left together."

"But Miguel wasn't with you when you arrived at Eddy's office."

Suzanne's eyes darted to the left, and she pushed her pointy-rimmed glasses higher on the bridge of her nose. She took a swig of her smoothie before answering.

"Yeah, I forgot. Miguel left us at the crosswalk to the department. He went off toward the parking lot."

"You think he went home?"

"How should I know? I'm not the boss of him."

I said, "You didn't see him again that evening?"

"Nope," said Suzanne with a bitter laugh. "I only saw Dolores, Javier, *you*, and Eddy *dead* on the floor."

I thanked her, picked up my dinner bag, and left. Somebody was lying about how they spent the time after leaving the theater on the night Eddy died, Suzanne or Javier. But, which one? Or both? And why?

* * *

As I headed in the direction of my condo, I realized I'd left a memory stick that held my exam information in my office. With a sigh, I went back to retrieve it. Tired from my long day, I chose to walk home a faster route that would take me past the College Club. I checked the time on my phone and noted that the gala must be in full swing by now. Maybe I'd catch a glimpse of Michael's parents.

Padding along in the comfortable running shoes I'd changed into to go to Nederland instead of my usual toe-pinching sandals, I was struck again, as I had been on the night of Eddy's murder, by how quiet campus was. The light evening breeze, which always cools things off in high-altitude Colorado no matter how hot the day, poured balm over my troubled thoughts of jealousy, blackmail, and suspicions toward friends. On this tranquil summer evening, the colors of the grounds and buildings became muted, and everything stretched out in peaceful repose. The perfect environment for research and study. I sniffed the piney mountain air and savored academic life.

I was so engrossed in these ruminations I didn't realize I'd reached the College Club until I was almost upon it. A large, white tent had been erected on the green lawn, and blue folding chairs were set in neat rows in front. Colorful balloons gently bobbing in the breeze festooned the club's walkway railings, and people were milling around.

On closer inspection, I realized something was amiss. The people weren't guests, but workmen, busy taking down the balloons and folding up the chairs. Puzzled, I walked to the tent. The only person inside was Olivia, who was gathering what looked like programs for the event and storing them in a box. Her eyes held a glazed look, and her face was paper-white as she set about her task.

"What happened?" I asked. "Where did all the people go?"

Olivia gave me a gray stare. "They went home," she said. "The gala has been cancelled. Michael Kent is dead."

Chapter Twenty-Eight

"La muerte es la segadora que no toma una siesta del mediodía."
"Death is the reaper who doesn't take a midday nap." — Spanish Proverb

Stunned into silence, I gaped at Olivia. When I found my voice, I croaked, *"Dios mío!* A drug overdose?"

Olivia's gaze slid away toward the summer-green quad. "No." She spoke so softly I had to lean forward to catch her words. "It wasn't a drug overdose, although it may have been an accident—or not. The police are at Michael's apartment now."

"An accident *or not?*" I echoed. *"The police aren't sure?* Why not?" Perspiration broke out on my forehead, and a dizzy wave of nausea passed over me.

Still staring blankly at the placid landscape where birds were flying home to roost, Olivia said, "A neighbor saw a flashy car speed away from Michael's apartment last night. He noticed because it's not the kind of neighborhood where anyone, but Michael would drive a high-end vehicle. After the body was discovered, the neighbor came forward."

"If it wasn't an overdose, then how did Michael die?"

"The hot water heater," Olivia said as if it were obvious. "Either it was faulty, or somehow tampered with." She turned back to the programs, smoothing each one, and placing it tenderly in the box.

"Faulty or tampered with?" My voice darkened with sinister patience. "What do you mean by 'faulty' or 'tampered with?'"

Olivia turned her reflective eyes on me and spoke as if to a child.

"Somehow, it filled the entire apartment with carbon monoxide. Michael died in his sleep. He never knew what hit him."

"*Ay, no!* Carbon monoxide like your husband!"

I clapped my hand to my mouth, but too late. The words had escaped before I could prevent them. Now, they hung in the early evening stillness like a dirty layer of smog.

Olivia picked up the box. As she brushed past, she said, "Excuse me, I have to get these back to the department."

* * *

Dios me perdone! I didn't mean to upset her with my big mouth. I know very well that "wounds from the knife are healed, but not those from the tongue." Now I'd spoken out of turn and couldn't take it back. Worse, on the slow walk home, niggling doubts about Olivia crept into the dark corners of my mind like spiders finding refuge from the falling autumn temperatures.

Could she be a double murderess who killed her husband for reasons unknown? Then, panicked at Michael's insinuation that Roger's death hadn't been suicide, she did away with him, too? I remembered how Olivia had ranted about wanting to give Michael a grade lower than an 'F.' If she *had* killed her husband, perhaps she found carbon monoxide a convenient weapon and decided to use it twice.

Why stop there? The devilish voice in my head fueled my imagination. *Remember how Olivia closed up Eddy's journal when you tried to take a look at it? Maybe she once had, and still was engaged in an affair with Eddy, and he wrote about it. When he started to take up with you, she killed him in a jealous fury. That would make her a triple murderess.*

"Pipe down!" I demanded aloud, then glanced around to make sure nobody had seen me talking to myself. Whew! Only a couple of errant magpies were strutting about, and they sidled away from me cautiously.

It was a ridiculous assumption. Olivia couldn't have killed Eddy, or her husband, or Michael. Olivia was one of the good people. She was a friend until I stuck my foot in my mouth.

* * *

By the time I arrived home, my dinner from Taco Loco was beyond rescue by microwave; in fact, it had collapsed in on itself. The crisp, fried tortillas had gone soggy as sponge cake, and the guacamole was turning black around the edges like it had been stricken with blight. *Fuchi!* Obviously, I wasn't going to get anything substantial to eat tonight. I didn't feel like eating anyway because my stomachache. So, I threw the whole mess into the bin and made myself a double espresso.

Shaking so much that I could barely hold the tiny cup and saucer, I took my coffee into the living room. Not bothering to turn on a table lamp in the gathering dusk, I collapsed on the sofa. Enough backlighting streamed in from the kitchen for me to see what I was doing, which, at the moment, wasn't much. I stared out the picture window, mesmerized by the line of car headlights crawling along the road up to Flagstaff, our city's signature mountain. They resembled a shimmering strand of pearls as they snaked up the 2,000-foot climb.

What a revolting development! The recent deaths had unhinged me so much that I'd entertained the notion that one of my friends could be a serial killer. How could I even consider such a thought?

Speaking of thoughts, how could I assume I was a good enough detective to solve these murders? Even with help from my friends. I was a Spanish teacher, not Mis Marple of Agatha Christie fame.

What must my family be thinking of my new role? Probably that they wasted time and effort encouraging me to follow my dream and get an education. Maybe I should heed Mami's advice, quit teaching, and go to work at the restaurant. It would be easier, and I wouldn't be interfering in so many lives. Everybody would be happy. Everybody but me.

A loud rap at the door made me jump. I clattered my cup and saucer onto the coffee table and went to peer through the peephole. Chief Mondragón, as gloomy as a bloodhound with a bad case of pinkeye, slouched on the doorstep. *Ay!*

"Just a minute," I called and rushed to turn on more lights and straighten the magazines and books that littered the coffee table.

"May I come in?" the Chief asked in the sepulchral voice of a pallbearer coming to collect the body. "I want to ask you a few questions."

I showed him to the sofa, where he lit without taking off his signature black raincoat he wore no matter the weather. He perched on the edge like a melancholy crow on a wire. Then he slipped a notebook and pen from his pocket and balanced them on his knee. Refusing my offer of coffee, he regarded me, unsmiling. "Michael Kent was found dead of carbon monoxide poisoning in his apartment this afternoon."

"I know. Olivia Oakes told me. *Qué lástima!*" As I spoke, I wondered why in the world the Chief wanted to question me about Michael's death.

His tone was flat and cheerless as a cold winter day. "There were some suspicious circumstances. In fact, we know it was homicide."

"Oh?" I tried to sound innocent. *Caramba! I am innocent!* Nevertheless, my mouth went dry, and I felt my espresso rebel in my stomach.

"He died in his bedroom on Monday night. Your fingerprints were found on the bedroom door molding." With an expression as solemn as The Grim Reaper's, he asked, "Can you explain how your prints got there?"

"Dios mío! How can that be?"

"Indeed, how *can* that be?"

Then I remembered leaning my hand on the door jamb when Michael was showing me around. My face went hot as if I were standing in front of the fires of Hell, and my fingers tingled. This interrogation felt worse than my oral comps, and there, I had to confront a committee of five.

I licked my lips and swallowed. "I-I was there, but only once. On Sunday."

Mondragón chewed his mustache and waited for me to continue. "Michael Kent is—was a graduate student of mine. He gave me a lift home from Regal Foods after my car broke down, and we stopped so he could show me his apartment."

"Isn't his place a bit out of the way from yours?"

I felt my face redden even more. I began speaking quickly. Too quickly, I knew. But once I opened the faucet, there was no plugging it. "He wanted to show me his collection of rock concert posters. I was only there for a few minutes. *De veras.* No more than ten minutes max. My friend Elsbeth MacLeod picked me up, and when we left, Michael was very much alive. In fact, he was so happy he was laughing." *True.* "At least he was on Sunday. Alive, that is. I mean, I wouldn't know about Monday. He was alive and kicking on Sunday. You can check with Elsbeth." Out of breath, I stopped.

The Chief bent over his pad and meticulously made a note. "I'll speak to Mrs. MacLeod." He turned his sad-eyed gaze on me again. "Where were you on Monday night between nine and eleven?"

A cool feeling of relief washed over me like an afternoon shower on a hot day. The flames in my cheeks were being quenched. I answered with as much confidence as I could muster under the circumstances. "I was with Mami, Papi, and Angela from six o'clock on. That was the night my sister was taken hostage in Denver. I didn't get home until after midnight. Papi will verify that."

After informing me that the police were following up several leads and that if I remembered anything important relating to the murders, I should tell him directly, the Chief left. Through the window, I watched him walk to his car, the corners of his unbuttoned raincoat flapping in the breeze, chewing on his mustache all the way. He eased his scarecrow-thin frame into the driver's seat of his cruiser and pulled away. I fell back on the sofa.

* * *

Muy bien! Now, I was a possible suspect in two murders. Having an alibi for the second one didn't bring me much comfort. I wiped the perspiration from my neck with a tissue and blew my nose hard. What was that proverb Germán had spouted when talking about Dolores? "A woman's reputation depends on the good opinion of others." I didn't think that Chief Mondragón's or Olivia's opinions of me were very good right now, let alone Papi's, if he found out I'd visited one of my male students in his apartment. My self-image wasn't earning high marks either, especially when I remembered I'd just been suspecting a friend.

Suddenly, I saw everything in a different, crystal-clear light. My padrino's visit, strangely enough, had come in the nick of time. The accusation he implied was so wrong that it bordered on the ridiculous. And I really, really needed to do something about that misconception and many other things. I had been moaning about quitting teaching and moving back in with my family. But it was now obvious that this would be the wrong decision. There was still a lot that I, with the help of friends and family who had faith in me, could do.

Isabel Castillo, I addressed myself. *You are not a quitter. Quitting would only bring more shame to rain on you, your family, your department, and even your community. The Castillo clan may have suffered many setbacks in their time, but one thing they don't do is quit. So you can jettison all those weenie thoughts right now and figure this thing out."*

More than ever, it was vital to find a solution to these crimes. And I wasn't thinking only of my own reputation and career. Someone in the department was a killer, and that person might not stop at two victims. Everyone was a suspect, and everyone was in danger. Time to stop feeling sorry for myself and get going!

Chapter Twenty-Nine

Shuffling through the papers I'd hurriedly tidied, I unearthed a pen and the suspect list that The Bolder Women Detective Team had made. I needed to add what new information had been gleaned since the Team's last meeting and consolidate the list. Maybe if I wrote everything down in a concise and logical order, a new idea about the identity of the murderer would surface.

First, I copied each person's name in alphabetical order and left a few spaces to register new information and my thoughts. I crossed out Michael's name, even though he could have killed Eddy because Elsbeth, Olivia, and I had already hashed out enough about him. I reminded myself that I could be dealing with two killers because the methods had been quite different. At least, this is what Conventional Police Wisdom claims. But this case was not conventional.

Baldomero Vigil

I remembered his and Eddy's grim faces the day they left the chairman's office. Had they been talking about Eddy's tenure bid? Baldo may have killed Eddy because he wanted or needed to bring in the relative of a friend. I'd also observed him at the door to the department that evening, so he had opportunity.

As to a reason for murdering Michael, perhaps the chairman harbored some dark secret that Michael uncovered and threatened to tell his parents about unless Baldomero coughed up a lot of lana and/or graduated him with honors. A fancy car was seen leaving the scene of the second murder. The only person I knew with such a vehicle other than Michael was the Chair. But would Vigil know how to make a hot water heater malfunction? If he were like some male academics I've known, he could be mechanically challenged.

Bibi Pomodoro

Uma Clone could have set her cap for Eddy. Not accustomed to rejection, she cracked. The long-limbed Amazon looked strong enough to strangle him. I'd seen her sneak up the back staircase on the night of Eddy's murder, so she was in the right place at the right time.

Why kill Michael? Maybe he found out something about her that he could use as blackmail. But I couldn't even guess what that could be.

Clive Strange

If he'd stolen the clock, and Eddy and Michael knew about it, he could have killed them both out of fear of losing his job if word got out. Eddy already harbored suspicions, and Michael, with his Nederland connections, could have found out. The repairman could be wrong in his appraisal; the clock could be worth enough to put Clive on Easy Street for a long time. Anyway, Carrot Top might not have needed a logical motive. As a true believer in astrology, it seemed he let the stars guide his life. He didn't like Eddy because their signs clashed. Maybe his and Michael's signs were also incompatible. I'd seen him at the door to the department on the night of the first murder, so he had opportunity.

Dolores Lopes

When she thought Eddy was going to throw her over for

Suzanne, she might have confronted him, flown into a green-eyed passion, and lashed out. However, if she and Javier had been together the entire time after the rehearsal, she had an ironclad alibi. Did she possess enough muscle to strangle Eddy? Maybe. Never underestimate the strength that adrenalin-fueled wrath can pump into a person's system. Eddy was probably taken by surprise, which made him a relatively easy target.

Dolores could have killed Michael for the same reason. Michael had rejected her and blabbed about it. If Suzanne had gone off with him on the night of the first murder, Dolores could have killed Michael out of revenge. She did her own sewing and decorating and had plenty of experience taking care of a home for her brother, so she probably was handy enough to fiddle with a hot water heater. I sucked on my pen. When I thought back on it, Dolores, with her unassuming demeanor, lurked everywhere.

Olivia Oakes

As much as it pained me, I had to list my friend's name, too, if for no other reason than to exonerate her. Maybe her relationship with Eddy blossomed into more than friendship when he comforted her after her husband's death, and their affair had continued into the present. She could've been envious of the attention he paid others. And she was on campus the night of the murder.

Olivia made no bones about being angry with Michael and his accusations, but had she been irate enough to kill him? What linked her in my mind to Michael's murder was the carbon monoxide, which could be a coincidence. Taking another tack, someone who knew about her husband might have been trying to implicate her. Who would want to do such a nasty thing to a nice woman like Olivia?

<u>Georgina Rampage</u>

She had both the opportunity and strength to strangle Eddy. Having grown up on a farm, she also probably understood how hot water heaters work. Only after Eddy's death did she indicate that Michael had claimed Eddy was going to ruin her reputation with the play he was writing. She could have killed Michael for the same reason: he knew about her family background and threatened to expose it.

<u>Javier Malecón</u>

I remembered a proverb Doña Isabella had spouted earlier that "two sparrows on one ear of corn cannot agree." Did he kill Eddy because he resented the professor's interest in Dolores?

Ditto as a reason for murdering Michael, with the addition of what in his mind might be justifiable homicide over Michael ruining Dolores' reputation. My mind drifted back to the scene in front of the department when the two grad students had come to blows. It appeared that Javier and Michael hadn't gotten along well since childhood. He, or any of the suspects could have sneaked to Michael's apartment and tinkered with the hot water heater. However, if Javier and Dolores had gone back to her office together, then he, too, had an alibi for that evening.

<u>Suzanne Selos</u>

I wished Suzanne were the killer because the woman was so annoying. But I knew I had to analyze this suspect's motives as impartially as the others. Suzanne could have killed both victims because they rejected her. According to Javier, on the night of Eddy's murder, she and Michael had gone off together. If they had, they didn't stay together long because later, Suzanne turned up at Dolores' office alone. The question was, how much later? I wouldn't put it past La Celosa to sneak to Michael's place and do something heinous to make him pay for rejecting her.

I was chewing my pen and contemplating my list when a noise in the kitchen startled me.

190

Chapter Thirty

"Choices are the hinges of destiny." –Pythagoras (c 570 BCE-c 490 BCE), Greek Philosopher

I dropped the pen and wracked my brain to remember where I'd parked my cell. *Caray!* In my purse in the bathroom where, it wouldn't do me any good. I eased myself off the couch and crept toward the kitchen, pausing on the way to heft a Mexican onyx paperweight from a table. If such a weapon was good enough for Lupita González, it was good enough for Issy Castillo. Raising my arm with the paperweight, I tiptoed to the doorway.

My ancestor stood hunched over the kitchen stove, clad in her familiar tattered, plum-colored skirt and rough cotton blouse. Over this ragged ensemble, she'd donned an incongruous-looking, white, ruffled 50s housewife apron. With a wooden spoon, she stirred a big black pot steaming with something so yummy it made my mouth water despite my recent scare.

Then Doña Isabella sang out in a high, reedy voice something about senses reeling in a wind-swept field. She called over her shoulder,

"Quit skulking around in the doorway like a mangy dog that ain't 'et in three days and get your buns in here! You can lose the paperweight, too, *Chica.* I ain't gonna attack ya." She kept stirring and humming. "Dum-deedle-dee-dum. How d'ya like my new duds? They make me feel all domestic." She turned toward me, with a spoon in one hand, the other on her hip, and struck a model's pose.

"Impressive," I said with a lift of my eyebrows. I entered the room, plunked the paperweight in the center of the kitchen table, and took a seat. "I thought you were an intruder."

"If you'd trust your sniffer," my ancestor huffed, "you'd know better. What intruder rustles you up a pot of scrumptious Make the Right Choice Soup?"

I slumped in my chair, and my spirit granny clicked her tongue in disapproval.

"Tsk! Tsk! You even look like a mangy dog and no wonder. You don't eat real food."

"I do eat," I protested and stifled a yawn. "I eat food every day."

"Not today, you haven't," my ancestor grumbled. "You call that dog's dinner you dumped food?" She wrinkled her nose. "How can you expect to solve this mystery on such a puny diet?" She wheeled back to the pot and stirred furiously.

I was too done in to argue. "*Bien*, so my eating habits haven't been all that great." I wrinkled my nose, too, but with hungry anticipation. "What's in the soup?"

Doña Isabella ladled some liquid into a bowl and brought it to the table for me to inhale the rich aroma. "A lot of stuff that's good for you," she replied, "and which, not incidentally, will also help you finger the right suspect in your little murder investigation."

"It looks like bean soup," I said, ignoring the last half of my ancestor's comment. I picked up the spoon and dug in.

"No kidding, Sherlock. It's a *fifteen*-bean soup, which I gotta say is a lot easier to assemble now that it comes packaged at the supermarket. In my day, we had to plant and harvest each crop. Sometimes, we foraged far and wide to gather fifteen different kinds of beans."

The spirit shuffled over to the sink, leaned against it, and folded her arms. "Beans, *m'hija,* are one of the best divination vegetables that exist, especially if the results of your prestidigitation"—she drew out each syllable long for emphasis—"require swift action. I sprinkled a little ranchero cheese on top to give your brain an added boost of protein."

I stopped with my spoon half-raised to my lips. "Where did you find the ingredients?"

"I told you, at the supermarket."

"But how did you *pay* for everything? I mean, nobody but I can see you, *verdad?*"

"Oh, I took care of that," the old lady said loftily as she opened the refrigerator door and began poking around. She brought out a frothy glass of a dark, purplish-colored liquid, set it before me, and dropped down in a chair.

"When you're done with the soup, I've whipped up this juice potion to open your paths to Spirit so you can discover the truth about who's knocking off all of your friends in the good ole Spanish Department. It's got good stuff in it to buck up your body, mind, and spirit."

I looked up, spoon poised in the air, and jutted out my chin. "Michael Kent was no friend of mine."

"Maybe not when he was alive, but now that he's Up There—" she glanced piously toward the ceiling — "he's one of your biggest fans."

"He went Up There?" I gestured vigorously with my free thumb. "Not Down There?"

"Simmer down, Sweetie Pie. It's not for you to judge another's life."

I put down my spoon, folded my arms across my chest, and glared at my ancestor.

The old lady's smile was beatific. "He's rooting for you to discover who did it."

"That sounds more like him," I said in a sour tone, but unfolded my arms. "I imagine he wants vengeance."

"No," my ancestor said in an uncharacteristically low and serious tone, "he doesn't want you to become Victim Number Three. And neither do I. So there!"

She took her shawl from her shoulders, draped it across the back of a chair, and gave me a broad grin. "I don't want to be reduced to communicating my teachings to Angela. You're a hard enough nut to crack. Are you going to polish off that fortifying soup I slaved over, or do I have to spoon-feed it to you?"

Too confounded to react, I did as I was told.

Doña Isabella began humming, breaking into song again, warbling something about earth-bound misfits.

"Isn't that an old Pink Floyd tune?" I remarked between mouthfuls. I hadn't realized how hungry I was, and the soup was delicious.

"Good for you, *Chica*! You should go on *Jeopardy*."

I rolled my eyes. "Except I can't even remember the name of the song you're hamburgering, let alone the album."

Doña Isabella answered quickly, "What is 'Learning to Fly' from the album *A Momentary Lapse of Reason*, 1987?" She leaned across the table and winked like Beulah the Witch. "I'll clue you in on something: I ain't singin' it for no good reason. Nor am I winkin' at ya 'cuz I got sand in my eye. And here's another song for you to put into your pipe and smoke, that is, if you smoked a pipe. These lyrics are from the tune 'One Slip' on the same album."

She got up, arranged her shawl around her shoulders, and swayed as she crooned about being in love and fate intervening to keep a lover from fulfilling a desire.

By now, she'd hiked up her skirt to reveal thick, gray woolen socks and moccasins. She swirled around the room, screeching about a person with a sudden lapse of reason falling down a hole. With that, she fell into a chair.

"*Ay!*" she panted. "All that twisting and turning takes it out of you when you're a little old lady of a hundred and fifty." She wiggled her Groucho-like eyebrows. "And if that Pink Floyd lullaby didn't reveal the murderer to you, I've mixed up some Concentration Bath Salts for you to use tonight to help you ponder things. Now, where did I put them?"

While she groped in her capacious skirt pocket, I finished the soup and started on the fruit juice potion.

"I appreciate the hints you're giving me with all the proverbs and songs," I said, "even if I don't have the foggiest notion what they all mean."

"That's because you don't eat enough protein. Ah, here it is! No, that's my pipe and tobacco."

She took out the old cherry wood pipe and worn pouch, along with some matches, and laid them on the table. Then she fumbled inside her pocket again, and her eyes lit up.

"There you are, you rascal. I knew you were hiding somewhere." She produced another pouch and tossed it on the table.

I picked it up, opened it, and breathed in the refreshing, slightly sweet scent of perfumed, orange-colored salts. "Aah! They smell wonderful."

"The ingredients will help you clear all that library book dust from your noggin and give your undivided attention to the matter at hand."

How I wished I could reach over and hug my granny. But I suspected the little Native woman only existed in my mind, as ephemeral as a white contrail left by an airplane on the blue horizon. I bit back a tear that was threatening to well in my eye.

"*Ay, abuelita,* you're so good to me. I want you to know how much I appreciate your assistance and encouragement, even though you can't interfere in the course of events on Earth. But…but…." I felt my lip tremble and could no longer hold back the tears. One by one, they dribbled down my cheek and landed in my empty soup bowl.

"It's all been too much. I can't seem to get a handle on things. I even suspected my friend Olivia. And then, for a moment, I wanted to give it all up, including teaching. Am I losing my mind?" I implored.

"No, *Chica.* You just suffered a momentary lapse of reason, as the song says. You wouldn't be human if sometimes you didn't question your motives and the path you're on. What you briefly lost were your self-confidence and trust in your intuition. Yet you've trusted Eddy, Olivia, and Elsbeth. Ask yourself, what is the one characteristic they share?"

I dabbed my eyes with my napkin and sniffed. "I don't know. Unless maybe it's because I see in each of them an independent streak, which I admire."

Doña Isabella clapped her hands in delight. "Right on, *Chica!* You're a chip off the old totem pole, that is, if we had totem poles in our pueblo, which our tribe did not. But there's more to it than that."

"Oh?"

"As you said, you've trusted them 'cuz, like you, they're independent-minded. They also possess another quality which you esteem but haven't yet fully developed in yourself."

I wasn't sure I liked where this was going. "What do you mean?"

"Take Eddy, for example. He never hesitated to tell people what he thought as long as he believed it would do them some good. Even if it meant the person wouldn't like him as much. He didn't curry favor with The Powers That Be to help him get ahead, either."

"I guess you're right. His attitudes probably would never have gotten him tenure."

"Same thing with your other friends, only different. Olivia's been known to stand up to your Chair when he starts spluttering nonsense like all that about the department letterhead. She speaks her mind if she believes she's right despite the fact it doesn't show her to be a player."

"That's true, but I don't understand where you're going with this."

Doña Isabella ignored my comment and went on. "Your new friend Elsbeth is a woman from another culture whose husband left her flat. Somehow, she's managed to overcome the double stigma of being abandoned and a single mom. She's built a career teaching about alternative healing techniques, a field often pooh-poohed by many of the more uptight elements of your society. You admire these three because they're not bothered by what others think of them. They're concerned with doing the right thing and helping others."

"And I am not?"

She shrugged. "To put it bluntly, you're too self-conscious of body image and the face you portray to the world."

"Not me!" I protested but knew in my heart my spirit granny was right.

"It's okay, *Chica.* I like your caramel-colored, moisturizing lip-plumper and little sandal heels. I really do. Even if those shoes are going to end up giving you corns. By the way, I have a recipe to cure corns, if you're interested. And I know you're still trolling around for Prince Charming, so you're fanatic about watching your weight."

"It's better for my health to be thinner."

"It's better for your health to eat better."

I stared at the dregs of my juice and fell silent. Was I a shallow person? If I weren't so concerned with body image, would Dolores and Suzanne not dislike me so much? Would I not have sent the wrong message to Michael? Would Eddy not have considered me to be naïve? And the way I treat my sister, is that more about how Angela affects *my* life rather than how I can help her?

I sighed and regarded my ancestor, whose bright, burning eyes had softened into pools of compassion.

Doña Isabella said, "You know I can read your thoughts, and you're not such a terrible person. After all, nobody's perfect except maybe me. And I'm dead, so I don't count." She cackled. "I'm trying to point you in the right direction. My advice to you in this case is to look toward the principals. And, oh yes, I almost forgot. Follow the scent trail like…well, like a bloodhound."

As I continued to gaze into my ancestor's eyes, I thought I noticed them grow larger. I didn't understand how this could happen, but the spirit's eyes now encompassed the entire room. I blinked to clear my vision, and my ancestor disappeared.

I sat at the table alone for a few minutes, contemplating her last words, then finished my juice. I rose, covered the remains of the bean soup, and placed the pot in the refrigerator. After putting the dinnerware in the dishwasher, I turned out the kitchen light.

In the bathroom, I drew a warm bath and poured in the Concentration Bath Salts. While I soaked in the tub, Doña Isabella's words kept echoing in my head like a raspy old 78 rpm record played at 33-1/3 speed.

By the time I emerged from the tub, my thoughts had crystallized. As Bibi told me, I'd been barking up the wrong tree. I may not have figured out everything yet, but I'd discovered one of the key pieces that would fit the entire puzzle together. Time to verify my discovery and put a plan into action before everyone dispersed in clouds of dust at the end of this term.

Chapter Thirty-One

"Cada mochuelo a su olivo."
"To every owl its own olive tree." — *Spanish Proverb*

"Are you busy?" I tapped on Olivia's office door, opened it, and craned my neck around the corner.

It was early enough that Olivia was still drinking her morning coffee and reading the campus paper. She looked up and smiled. "I was browsing the news. Come on in."

I ventured inside and perched on the edge of a chair, as nervous as a student coming to dispute a grade. From Olivia's second-floor double-hung windows, she had a panoramic view of the quad. Dappled sunlight filtered through the trees and illuminated the empty broad walks, deserted of students and professors while classes were in session. At the moment, we might be the only two people on campus.

"I'm sorry if—"

"Listen, I'm sorry—"

We both began at the same time and then laughed.

"You first."

"No, you."

"I'm sorry," I began again, "if I offended you by blurting out that business about your husband. I guess the news of Michael's death overwhelmed me."

"No worries. I was just shocked to hear he died the same way as Roger. I'm sorry if you mistook my numbness for feeling affronted. And, Issy, I've a confession to make."

"Oh?" My tone was nonchalant, but I squeezed my knees together. What would I do if Olivia confessed to the murders? Insist on calling the police? I wished I were suddenly struck deaf so I could claim I hadn't heard a word of it. But Olivia was swiveling in her chair and asking me something.

"Hello? Issy? Do you want some coffee?" She held up her electric coffee pot and a mug.

"Please."

"Four sugars, right?"

"Just three." I patted my waistline. "I'm trying to cut back."

Olivia prepared my drink, handed it over, and refilled her own cup. "I admit I wasn't straight with you and Elsbeth the other night."

I sipped the sugary brew. "Oh? What about?"

"About Eddy's journal. I didn't tell you everything he wrote."

At that moment, the carillon bells rang to announce the end of a class period. Olivia set her mug on her desk, and we both looked out the window at the throng of students and professors streaming to and from a myriad of destinations.

Olivia turned her silvery gray eyes back to me. "I don't want you to misinterpret something that might compromise our friendship."

"I doubt there's anything you can do that would interfere with that," I said, and meant it.

Olivia sipped her coffee and began. "When Eddy wrote that he lifted me from the doldrums I'd fallen into after my husband's death, it was true. The way it happened, though, was that we had an affair. It only lasted a few months, and we remained good friends afterwards, but without sex. The point is Eddy mentions in his journal that both Michael and Bibi were trying to blackmail him over it. I understand about Michael, but not Bibi. Eddy doesn't say why, either." She pursed her lips. "I'd hate for the whole thing to go public. But I don't want to hold back information about Bibi from the police."

I looked from Olivia to the neat stack of exam papers already graded on her desk, to the bookshelves groaning with heavy tomes and periodicals having to do with Spanish literature, to the little bust of the nineteenth-century Spanish novelist Galdós, then back to Olivia. So that was all, an affair that ended long ago.

"I don't want to hide anything either," I said. "I was going to tell you and Elsbeth anyway that yesterday I saw Bibi with Big Carlos Machado, my former elementary school classmate and Drug King of the Front Range. Bibi insinuated that she could get drugs for me if I wanted them. So, she's into something more than blackmail. How this links up with Eddy's and Michael's deaths, I don't know. For now, all we have is this journal entry."

I watched a bicyclist race down the walk and narrowly miss knocking into three female students. "Let's hold on to what we know for a short while. Once we get a few other details cleared up, like Clive and the clock, we'll tackle this problem."

It was as if a heavy fog had dissipated from the room, and our friendship had strengthened.

I turned the conversation to another topic. "Anything in there about Michael?" I asked, indicating the open newspaper on Olivia's desk.

"It's Page One news. The police are calling it homicide. According to the reporter, Michael's hot water heater vents outside behind his place. Someone clogged the exhaust vent so that carbon monoxide escaped into the bathroom. From there, it spread throughout the entire apartment."

I scrunched my nose. "Wouldn't Michael have smelled it?"

Olivia scanned the article. "Remember, carbon monoxide is odorless. The autopsy results aren't in yet, but from what we know about Michael's habits, I suspect he drugged himself into a stupor and never woke up."

"Or he had help," I noted. "Either way, it's terrible!" I recalled my previous night's encounter with the police chief. "Did they find fingerprints on the exhaust pipe?"

"They don't say, but the article mentions they found the driver of the classy car, whom they're interviewing. I wonder who he or she is?"

"One person I can think of besides Michael himself is our chairman," I said, and made a silent vow to call Boston ASAP to see if Ana was back yet.

"Mrs. Webber will know if the police have interviewed him."

"I need to stop by the department office today anyway. I'll ask her. Any other news?"

Olivia folded the paper and tucked it into a magazine rack on the floor beside her desk. "Only some weird story about a pig found at Regal Foods."

"What?"

"Yesterday, they found a live pig roaming around the stockroom. Weird, huh?"

"I'll say," I concurred, but my intuition ignited.

"Even stranger," Olivia continued, "an Indian blanket was tied around the porker's middle, like on a horse. The manager thought the blanket looked very old and had an unusual design on it, so he took it to the Anthropology Department. They're examining it to see whether it's an artifact. If so, it could be worth a small fortune. Can you believe it?"

I closed my eyes, then opened them and glanced toward the ceiling. "Oh, I can believe a lot of things." *Like Doña Isabella's notion of currency exchange.*

Olivia eyed her wall clock. "*Cielos!* It's almost ten. Do we want to talk to Clive now?"

I patted the outer pocket of my purse. "Lady Spymistress and I are ready when you are."

* * *

If someone held a nationwide contest for professors' office decor, Clive Strange's would be a contender in the "vous já-dè" "I've-never-seen-anything-like-this-before" category. The room looked like Captain Kangaroo's playhouse gone berserk. Every wall overflowed with collages of objects relating either to clocks or astrology. Bookcases transformed into shadow boxes displayed in three-dimensional detail scenes from novels, all centered on the themes of time and clocks. On one shelf, Alice conversed with the White Rabbit, who, in turn, consulted his watch. In another tableau, Tristram Shandy's father stood suspended in the act of winding the grandfather clock. In yet another, Julio Cortázar's cronopio was inventing the wild-artichoke clock and plucking its leaves to know the time.

As to astrology, colorful framed reprints of paintings of natal, lunar, and even sidereal charts of both the famous and unknown, along with Medieval and Renaissance renditions of the zodiac, crowded the remaining wall spaces. The effect was so dizzying I imagined that if I stared at the walls long enough, they'd spring to life and sweep me up into the vortex of the cosmos. Over the floor was stretched a multi-colored wool rug with a natal chart woven into its pattern.

"Nice rug," I commented as Clive offered us chairs.

"It's my very own chart." He beamed. "All my planets are above the horizon." He gave me a knowing nod.

"Yes, I see," I said, hoping I sounded impressed.

"According to astrology, it means I've chosen this to be one of my final incarnations." He paused for dramatic effect. "I may be about to nova onward to The Inner Planes."

Not, I hoped, before he answered a few questions.

Clive sat behind his desk and sipped from a glass full of a thick, cream-colored liquid. He announced, "But ladies, where are my manners? May I offer you some buttermilk?"

After we politely refused, he said, "Are you certain? It contains fewer calories than regular milk and does wonders for the complexion."

When we turned down the offer again, he shrugged and took another sip. "Isn't it simply awful about these murders? Awful, but thrilling!"

"That, in a way," said Olivia, "is what we came to ask you about."

"Really?" His eyes widened more than usual, and he rubbed his hands together in apparent glee. "I knew that with a Scorpio," he waggled his head at me, "and a Libra in the department," he joggled toward Olivia, "it wouldn't take you two long to get involved in the investigation. Scorpios are the detectives of the world, and Libras possess a keen sense of justice. How can I help?"

Olivia looked thunderstruck by Clive's speech, so I waded in. "Olivia and I are trying to clear up a few minor points, none of which probably relate to the murders, but which…"

"Which, in one way or another, have us puzzled." Olivia, by now recovered, finished my sentence. "We want to sort out some extraneous details so we can view the real mystery with more clarity."

Clive settled back in his chair and clasped his long hands behind his head. I noticed that around his neck today, instead of the Dalí watch, hung a dog tag chain with a medallion of a tiny Ouija board set inside a bottle cap. I wondered if he consulted the bottle cap on a regular basis.

"Yes," he agreed. "Clear visioning is important in such serious matters. I should know; I'm a Sag—Sagittarius. We're called 'the far-seeing ones' after the archer god of myth."

"I guess we've come to the right place then," said Olivia with a faint smile. "Seeing all your clever shadowboxes representing time in literature, I'm reminded of the beautiful clock Mark used to keep on top of his filing cabinet."

A satisfied smile spread over Clive's face. "Indeed."

Olivia cleared her throat. "Mark mentioned in an e-mail that the clock seems to have gotten lost in his move to Montana. Do you, by chance, know what happened to it?"

Clive's smile erupted into a grin. "I do, I do!" He reached inside a bottom desk drawer and produced a large gift box decorated with a swirl of pink ribbon. "In fact, I took it." He raised the lid. "Isn't it a gem?"

I held my breath as we leaned forward and peeped into the box. Nuzzled in a nest of protective wrapping sat a mantle clock encrusted with angels, porcelain birds, and flowers.

"What's it doing in your desk drawer?" I blurted.

"Well," he began in a voice that showed he had a sweet tale to tell, "during the move when I carried it from dear Mark's office to his truck, I noticed that the mechanism wasn't working properly. I couldn't let such a gorgeous example of a Louis XVI timepiece go west in such a deplorable state." As he spoke, he shook his head vigorously from side to side.

"So, I spirited the poor ailing child away and had it fixed by the best repairman in the region. I'll have you know the repair cost me a pretty penny. But it's worth every dollar to give dear Mark a fitting going-away present: a well-oiled timepiece in perfect running order."

He gently lifted the clock from the box as if he were taking a baby from a crib and held it up for inspection. Olivia and I nodded in admiring approval, even though I, for one, wouldn't know whether the clock was broken in the first place, repaired, or even that it was an antique.

Clive carefully replaced the precious cargo in its box, set the lid on top, and slid it back into the drawer. "I'm sending it off today by overnight FedEx. It will be my little surprise. I love surprises, and I'm sure Mark will, too." He grinned again, showing two rows of gleaming white teeth. "But I digress. It's a failing, I know, and another reason I insist that the clocks around here keep proper time. How can I help you ladies with your investigation?"

"Ah…."

"Well…."

Olivia and I looked at each other. With our thunder having been stolen, we were at a loss for words.

"Um," I began, "we wanted to know if you've noticed anything unusual going on in the department these days. Besides the murders, I mean."

"Unusual?" he echoed. "In this establishment, my dears, you'll find that the usual would be considered unusual." He leaned forward and said in a conspiratorial whisper, "I suspect this building is constructed over a confluence of ley lines. It's the only explanation for the kind of energy it attracts."

I hadn't the foggiest notion what a ley line was nor what kind of energy it might attract, but I straightened on my chair and bobbed my head in agreement.

Clive straightened in his chair, too. "Of course, if you consider changes in relationships among our comrades as something unusual, there's been plenty of that going on."

Now Olivia straightened on her chair. "What do you mean?"

With a wave of his hand, he indicated, "Dolores, Suzanne, Javier. All is not as it once was with that gay and carefree trio."

"It wouldn't be," I said. "Not after Michael's and Eddy's deaths."

"Of course not," said Clive, "but…" He paused and his eyes widened so much they looked like two bright blue marbles dancing in their sockets. "Consider this astute Argentine aphorism: 'A quarrel is like buttermilk; the more you stir it, the sourer it grows.'" He gave a sage nod and gulped his drink.

The odd saying confounded me. It must have confused Olivia, too, for she stood and prepared to leave. I followed suit.

"We'll consider your advice, Clive," Olivia said, "but we've already taken too much of your time."

"Yes, thanks for your time," I chimed in.

But Clive wasn't finished spouting proverbs. His blue eyes grew misty, and he sat back in his chair, contemplating the constellations gracing his ceiling. "It must be the ley lines," he mused. "The convergence has served to illustrate the fact that 'power has no friends, envy has no rest, and crime has no satisfaction.'" He sighed and shook his head.

As we passed through the door, I heard him say, "As a night owl myself, although not a bird of a feather with the miscreant in question, I can say with confidence, 'Every owl to its own olive tree.'"

When we rounded the corner of the corridor, I called softly to Olivia, "Hoot, hoot!"

Chapter Thirty-Two

"Donde la trama espese con cada vuelta y vuelta de tuerca."
"The plot thickens." — Spanish Proverb

Back in my office, I searched my desk drawer for a protein bar snack. I tried calling Ana but got no answer. She was probably teaching; I'd try again later.

I also transferred the interview with Clive from Lady Spymistress to a computer file, something I'd also done with the clock repairman's interview. This way, I'd have plenty of memory in case I needed it. Not that the discussion with Clive had led to anything more productive than to eliminate him as a suspect. He'd said some interesting things, though, about relationships, quarrels, and one who remains aloof. His words, coupled with Doña Isabella's singing about earth-bound misfits, untenable attractions, and lapses of reason, her advice to adhere to the principals in this case and to pay attention to fragrances were making sense. Maybe the protein was kicking in.

As I was leaving my office, Dolores was entering hers. After greeting her, I asked, "Mind if I have a word?"

"If it's short," Dolores said in her characteristically toneless voice. "I've got a stack of Portuguese grammar tests to correct, and I'm not looking forward to the chore."

Entering the office behind her, I was struck by how thin and stooped the young woman's shoulders were and how little she weighed. Seeing her, I couldn't imagine Dolores, even in a rage, mustering the strength to strangle anyone.

I sat in the same chair as before with the charming violet-colored slipcover, and Dolores sank into her desk chair.

"First of all," I began, "I owe you an apology."

A surprised look came over Dolores' face. I assumed the Portuguese teacher was the one accustomed to making apologies, not the other way around.

"I had no idea you also applied for the position in Medieval," I said. "No wonder you're vexed with me."

Dolores' eyes widened, making her look a little like Olive Oyl in *Popeye*, only sadder and more subdued than the cartoon character. "No need to apologize. I'm not vexed with you, Isabel. If anything, I'm at odds with the world in general. I knew I hadn't a chance of getting the position. But Eddy made me feel so hopeful about my work and future that I applied anyway."

I smiled, remembering how Eddy had made everybody feel special. "You miss Eddy, don't you?"

"Things won't be the same around here without him."

"You'd never have done anything to hurt him?"

Dolores focused on me more intently, and a hint of color tinged her complexion. "Of course not! I loved Eddy. Even though he was into other women. He was my inspiration."

"Did you know that Olivia found his journal, and in it, he said that your translation of the Gil Vicente play was brilliant?"

It was the first time I'd seen Dolores crack a smile. She said, "He did? How sweet!"

I wanted to ask her about the night of Eddy's murder. I took the deep purple-colored throw pillow in my hands that I'd been leaning against and began twirling it slowly, trying to think of a way to broach the delicate subject. Suddenly, I stopped twirling: I'd seen that material before. It was the same as the Voodoo doll still lurking in my bottom filing cabinet drawer.

I tried to sound casual. "This violet material is so pretty. Do you have any leftover?"

Dolores shook her head. "I had some scraps but gave them away."

"To whom?"

"Suzanne asked me for them. God only knows why. I've never seen her sew a stitch in her life."

Except to hand-stitch together a Voodoo poppet and leave it in front of my office door for me to step on. I said, "I've noticed you and Suzanne aren't hanging around together as much as before. Has anything happened?"

Dolores shrugged. "Nothing new. I guess I got fed up with Suzanne muscling in on all my men. Not that there have been many of them."

I nodded in sympathy. "Besides, she's married."

"Suzanne should be content with Joe. He's a nice guy and provides for her well. But she's never satisfied. She feels compelled to go out and make one more conquest."

"I assume you're talking about Eddy."

"Yes."

"And who else?"

Dolores shifted in her chair, and the ghost of animation that had enlivened her face folded in on itself. "You must know about Miguel and me. Everyone else does. He saw to that."

"I had heard something. Did Suzanne set her cap for him, too?"

"During rehearsal on the night Eddy was killed, Miguel was putting the moves on Suzanne. I think he was trying to flaunt in my face the fact that our affair was over. Even Javier agreed with me."

Even Javier? I wondered why, with her words and tone, Dolores had dismissed her good buddy.

Dolores shifted her gaze to her desk, then back to me, and it seemed like she drew a veil down over her face. But she said, "Suzanne and Miguel must have had some sort of a blow-up because she stalked into my office hopping mad. It may have been over the drug issue. I saw Bibi hanging around the stage door at one point, and I think Miguel went to talk to her."

I was confused. "So, you think Miguel and Bibi were hooking up?"

"Not in the way you're implying. Bibi supplied him with cocaine and who knows what else? Suzanne doesn't approve of drugs, you know, since her mother's something of a suburban cokehead, and there always have been family problems over addiction. She and Miguel could have had an argument over that."

"Whoa! You're telling me Bibi is a drug pusher?"

"Everyone knows she deals."

Everyone except me, who only recently suspected it. But we were getting off-topic. "Do you remember exactly when Suzanne got to your office?"

Dolores pushed back a strand of black hair that had fallen over an eye. "Not the exact minute, but it was right before we left to go to Eddy's office."

"Was it a long time between you seeing Suzanne at the end of rehearsal and her turning up at your office?"

She considered. "I'd say almost forty-five minutes. We all left together, but Suzanne and Miguel took off to the parking lot, probably to hook up in his car." She rolled her Olive Oyl eyes. "For whatever reason, things didn't work out to either party's satisfaction."

Suddenly, she gave me what could only be interpreted as an impish look. "Maybe the quarrel wasn't over drugs. Maybe Suzanne broke a spring on the Porsche."

Chapter Thirty-Three

"El árbol frondoso no siempre da fruta dulce."
"The leafy tree does not always give sweet fruit." — Panamanian Proverb

"Is the chairman in? I need to ask him about a student who expects to graduate, but still wants to take an incomplete."

After talking with Dolores, I went upstairs to the department office to attend to business before giving my first final exam. As I collected my mail, I glanced out the window. The fully leafed trees swayed in a stiff, hot breeze, but inside, air conditioning kept everything cool and dust-free. I couldn't even hear the wind, let alone smell the leaves as they thrashed around.

It struck me that the last afternoon of the first summer session had arrived. It was hard to believe that only a few weeks before, I'd entered the main office for the first time and met the head administrative assistant.

Mrs. Webber, as efficient as always, was entering data into her computer from a mountain of papers stacked to her left. She paused, fingers poised over the keyboard, and regarded me over her tortoise-shell rimmed glasses.

"Sorry, Isabel. Chairman Vigil is at the police station, as the British say, 'helping the police with their inquiries.'"

She took her hands with their short-filed, clear-polished nails from the keyboard and said in a low voice, "I've never seen Vigil so frazzled. On his way out of here, he told me that not only was his car seen at Michael Kent's on the night the boy died, but the police also found his prints on the door knocker. He swore he only stopped by to invite Michael to coffee and ask him to join his parents at the gala, but no one answered the door."

Ha! I'd been right about the car. "I wonder why the Chair didn't just call Michael?"

The secretary gave me a knowing look. "I asked him that, too, and he claimed he happened to be passing through the neighborhood. Smells fishy to me. Unless he was coming in from Lyons or Estes Park, there was no reason for him to be on the far north end of town since he lives in a southeast neighborhood."

"Oh, I don't know," I said. "I hear a dynamite yoga studio opened out there. Maybe Vigil wanted to clear his chakras for the big event."

"That would be the day!"

* * *

On the way back to my office, I pondered the possible reasons for Baldomero visiting Michael. I didn't have time to mull this over, for when I got to my door, my phone was ringing.

"How was London?" I responded to Ana Torres' lively greeting.

"Ooh, dahling, it was fab!" my friend gushed in a pseudo-British accent that overlaid her natural Cuban one. "I met the most chahrming man at the conference, a professor of Latin American Politics at London College. Frahncis fflaumer, with two little fs."

"Do the f's go before Francis?"

"No, *tonta*, before his last name. He took me absolutely everywhere— Harrods, the Royal Academy, the Tower. We rowed on the Serpentine, and even went up in a pod on that big Ferris wheel they call The Eye to view the city. So-o romantic!"

"Did you find time to attend the conference?"

"I did more than that, *mi amor*." She lowered her voice a few decibels. "I uncovered a veritable gold nugget of gossip about Chairman Vigil."

I clawed in my desk drawer for a clean sheet of paper and pen and tried to keep my voice from squeaking with excitement. "You found out something about Vigil in London?"

211

Ana's voice took on a worldly-wise tone. "You know, ours really is a relatively small field. Dahling Frahncis told me he's met your Chair on several occasions at conferences. The scuttlebutt is that Baldomero Vigil never earned a real doctorate."

I poised with pen in hand and mouth wide open. "How can that be?"

"This sort of thing occasionally happened some years back," Ana explained. "People didn't check records and transcripts as rigorously as they do now. The story goes that Vigil arrived from Bolivia with a degree from a storefront education mill. He had a connection at Brownell who—"

"Let me guess," I cut in. "Was the connection's name Fingir?"

"Appropriate name, don't you think, since *fingir* means 'to pretend' in Spanish."

I nodded my assent even though I knew Ana couldn't see me.

She went on with her story. "Rodolfo Fingir got Vigil a tenure-track appointment at Brownell as if he had a Ph.D. Since Fingir vouched for Vigil, no one was ever the wiser. By the way, how do you know the name?"

"I'm assuming Fingir has a nephew, son, or grandson whose name is Óscar. It looks like our Chair is complying with the old payback routine by getting Little O a job here."

"Your poor department!" lamented Ana. "Cross your fingers that the new hire is competent."

"We can always hope." I set my pen on the desktop without having written down a word of our conversation. "Thanks so much for sleuthing. I owe you one. By the way, since you always keep your ear to the ground, have you heard of any positions in Medieval coming available in this region?"

"Why? Do you want to fly the coop so soon?"

"No, no," I demurred. "It's for one of my, ah, students. She's about to graduate and wants to remain in the area. She's bright and quiet, but a deep thinker."

Ana laughed. "Not a motor-mouth like us, *eh*? You may be in luck. My friend Miranda Vásquez, who teaches Peninsular History at Fort William, was at the conference, and she told me something is about to open up there in Medieval Lit. The position's so new it hasn't even been announced yet in the Modern Language Association job listing."

"*Perfecto!* Fort William is just up the road from here."

"*Oye*, I'll give you Miranda's number. You can call her for the details before you talk to your student."

"Thanks, Ana, I will. And thank you again for the skinny on Vigil."

* * *

All the time I proctored my exam and, on the way back to my office, various murder scenarios starring Baldomero Vigil ran through the editing room of my mind. I envisioned him preparing to strangle Eddy because the tenure track professor knew too much about his personal history. Then there was the vignette where Vigil, clad in a Clive-clone black turtleneck and ill-fitting tights, skulked behind Michael Kent's apartment building, his hands encased in black leather gloves, preparing to sabotage the hot water heater because Michael had threatened to expose his charade.

Yet whenever my inner editor reached the crisis scene, it made a brutal cut, and the celluloid tumbled away across the editing room floor. Somehow, I couldn't see Baldomero getting his fingers on my scarf and twisting it around Eddy's neck. Nor could I conceive of him pussyfooting around on the wrong side of the tracks in the dark. For the moment, I had to set aside my suspicions about the Chair. More pressing matters required my attention.

* * *

"We need to talk," I told Suzanne in no uncertain terms. I caught La Celosa leaving her office as I returned from giving my exam at the end of the afternoon.

Suzanne tried to fob me off with, "Later, alligator," but with blood coursing red-hot through my veins, I stood my ground square in the middle of the narrow hall.

"Excuse me," Suzanne complained haughtily but nevertheless backed into her office. "I've a dress rehearsal to get to, and since I'm the star, the show can't go on without me."

"Relax. You're not J Lo. Besides," I lied, "your director said it would be all right if you're a few minutes late."

The big woman slumped in her office chair with all the ill will of a hippopotamus cut off from its favorite watering hole. "If you're going to ask me more questions about Eddy's murder, I already told you—"

I cut in. "Why did you leave a Voodoo poppet and dead scorpions at my door?"

For a moment Suzanne looked taken aback, then managed to pull a wide-eyed face. "I'm sure I don't know what you mean."

Exhausted, I flopped onto a hard, open folding chair. "It's no use denying it. I know you took the scraps of material left over from Dolores' pillow to make the doll. You knew Eddy, and I were Scorpios because, on the day I arrived, I heard you lurking in the hall when Clive blurted it out. So, you left that donation as well. I simply want to know why. What did I ever do to you?"

La Celosa clicked her tongue in disgust and narrowed her eyes. "Chicks like you get everything handed to them on a silver platter. You even snag scholarships and the best jobs because you're a minority. With your surgically enhanced bee sting lips and fluttering fake eyelashes, you con men into falling all over themselves to get into your panties. All they see is what's on the outside; they never bother to look for a woman's inner beauty."

It was my turn to be taken aback. I'd never expected to be viewed as a *femme fatale* who only got ahead because of my physical attributes and ethnic background. And my lips and eyelashes were my own, thank you very much! As to the "inner beauty" comment, I had yet to see it in Suzanne. Then again, I, like the men Suzanne accused, have never looked beyond her physical appearance, and that's my own shortcoming.

"*Bien*," I said, satisfied that, at least obliquely, I'd gotten the TA maven to admit her guilt. "Let's put the dolly and insects aside for the moment. I want to know how long you were with Michael on the night Eddy died."

"You're one suspicious broad. I'm glad I'm not like you."

"Look, I'm trying to get all the details straight so I can figure out what really happened."

"You want to know what *really* happened? I'll tell you, and you'll find out how Mr. Preppy, who fawned all over you, wasn't all he was cracked up to be. That night, Miguel and I went off to his car for some hanky-panky, only he didn't want to play. Typical, self-centered jerk!" She gave an acidic "harrumph," and suddenly, tears welled in her eyes.

"He was only playing up to me during rehearsal to put a bug in Dolores' ear. It took me a while to catch on. Guess I'm a slow study."

Her arrogant demeanor had vanished, replaced by a painful expression of vulnerability. "I was so stupid. All I thought about during rehearsal that night was how I might lose my chance with Miguel because I was afraid he'd run off."

"What? Where to?"

"That bimbo Bibi stopped by, and I heard them talking. She wanted him to start going with her on drug runs to nearby states. She figured his good looks and charm would help with sales. She tried to get him to go with her to Nebraska, Wyoming, Kansas, and as far away as Iowa. Would you believe?"

She reached for a tissue and honked her nose. "So, when we got to his car, I asked him about it, and that's when he started dissing me. And I mean, real bad. He told me he was only using me to get back at Dolores, and I was as useless a hanger-on as she. With that, I finally got the picture and walked off. It was the last time I ever saw him. I didn't tell you when you asked before because it was too damned humiliating."

I said gently, "His behavior had nothing to do with you. We all know now that Michael was a troubled young man who projected his unhappiness on others."

Suzanne gave me a lopsided smile and blinked rapidly. "Sorry about the blinking," she said. "It happens whenever I cry."

I waited for her to remove her glasses and dab at her raccoon eyes, smudged from running mascara. After she composed herself, I asked, "Do you think you can remember how long you spent in Michael's car? It may be important."

"More than a half hour for sure. I checked my watch under the department foyer light because I thought I might be too late to go for pizza. Didn't want to miss two parties. I had to hustle down to Dolores' office to make it there on time. So no, I didn't have time to kill Eddy even if I'd wanted to."

She put her glasses back on and with them, her composure. "As to the night Miguel died, Joe and I spent the entire evening at home." She gave a scornful laugh. "Playing Strip Scrabble."

* * *

Later that night as I pored over exam papers with my Smart Phone TV humming in the background to keep me company, bizarre scenarios spawned by the latest information I'd gleaned kept replaying in my mind.

Bibi and Michael, zooming around the region in his Porsche, dispensing drugs like ministering fallen angels. Suzanne and Joe, engrossed in a Las Vegas-style Strip Scrabble game. A black-clad Baldomero searching for Michael. Dolores and Javier, waiting patiently in her blue-and-violet office. Poor rejected Suzanne fleeing Michael's car.

A puff of air from the open window raised some dust, and a mote landed in my eye. I should pay more attention to housekeeping, I thought as I eased out of my chair and felt my way to the sink to rinse my eye with water. I stood for a few moments, blinking hard to dislodge the particle, and tried to focus on the newscast. The evening's big story was a rash of tornadoes descending over the Eastern Plains and into Nebraska and Kansas. Twisters had touched down over the Colorado border near Route 243 in Kansas and Route 769 in Nebraska.

Then it hit me. The tornado report, along with Doña Isabella winking at me, Suzanne blinking back tears, and me blinking to dislodge the dust particle, made everything gel. I jumped up, ran to my purse in the bathroom, and trolled for a scrap of discarded paper. Yes, there it was! I retrieved the paper and smoothed it out on the sink. It was the fragment Bibi had dropped in the stairwell. On it was written the word WINK followed by a series of numbers.The same numbers that Angela had spouted at Elsbeth's before she fell asleep. I'd catch my sister tomorrow.

Before I drifted off to sleep, I turned my face toward the ceiling in case my ancestor was floating around in the vicinity and winked.

* * *

"Do you remember at Elsbeth's you mentioned something about 'WINK,' 'a numbers girl,' and a series of numerals?"

My sister finished painting her nails the color of Concord grapes and was waving her fingers in the air to dry. Evidently, Angela was in Goth mode this morning. Her nail color matched the deep purple eye shadow smeared on her lids. Unfortunately, they clashed with her honey-blond hair, but I wasn't about to point that out.

"Uh, I guess. I was pretty wasted that night. That herb lady friend of yours must've doctored the tea."

"Not with anything that would do you any harm. Do you remember what "WINK" and the numbers refer to and who the numbers girl is?"

"Bibi is the numbers girl. She's always hanging around Juventino." Now Angela was applying black lipstick, a brand-new item for me at the cosmetics counter. "The numbers 2-4-3-7-6-9 are the routes that Juventino took to get immigrants to other towns, but I don't know what 'wink' means. All I know is they both said it a lot."

"I think I know," I said. "WINK stands for four nearby states: Wyoming, Iowa, Nebraska, and Kansas. The numbers, as you say, are county roads where Juventino traveled with the *indocumentados*." I looked in Angela's mirror and caught sight of my own black eyes dancing. "Listen, *'mana*, I've gotta dash. You've been more help than you know. Thank you so much!" I gave my astonished sister a quick squeeze and was out the door.

* * *

I caught up with Olivia as she was leaving her office to take her grades to

Mrs. Webber.

"This is how I see it," I told her after I persuaded my friend to retreat to my office for a minute. "Bibi is a dealer. She probably supplied Michael, which is neither here nor there, except that it bound them together in a kind of alliance. She was putting the moves on Juventino because she wanted him to let her go along on his immigrant runs to push drugs."

"Juventino wouldn't condone something like that," Olivia objected.

"So, he turned her down. That's when she started working on Eddy. She went to him thinking he'd let her travel with his troupe when it went on the road, and she would sell drugs on the side. This may be why she participated in the play at all. Eddy would have found this out through those drug rehab kids and rejected her. So, she had Michael dig up dirt on Eddy so she could blackmail him and force him to acquiesce."

"Makes sense, but would this provide enough motive for Bibi to kill Eddy?"

"As devious as Bibi is, I don't think she murdered him."

"She seems a perfect candidate."

"For one thing, not that she's necessarily trustworthy, she told me she didn't kill him. Other pieces of this puzzle don't fit the Bibi scenario either." I was thinking of scents, other motives, and some of Doña Isabella's proverbs, but didn't want to get into a complicated explanation.

"Whatever your reservations are, I think the time has come to tell the authorities what we know about Ms. Pomodoro," said Olivia.

With the ghost of the image of Chief Mondragón still haunting my brain, I said, "I couldn't agree more."

Chapter Thirty-Four

"A pillo, pillo y medio."
"Deal with the wicked on their own terms." — Spanish Proverb

What with the free publicity generated about the department, the play's opening night drew a standing-room-only crowd. Since I had an in with the director, I reserved places for my entire clan in the fourth-row center which, according to Olivia, were the best seats in the house.

Despite Doña Isabella's scolding about my obsession with appearances, I was determined to dress to the nines. I wanted to show respect for Eddy's memory and encouragement to Olivia and everyone involved in this star-crossed production by donning my best summer attire. Besides, on the day I was traipsing around The Mound after Bibi, I'd spied this to-die-for lavender silk, knock-off Armani suit in the display window of a chic boutique. I convinced myself I had to have it because I already possessed a sweet pair of violet-colored sandal heels that matched the outfit perfectly.

I unearthed a tiny beaded purse from the back of my closet into which I stuffed my lipstick, a couple of tissues, ID, and money for intermission refreshments. My cell had died, and I had no time to recharge it, but didn't anticipate needing it. I did, however, think Lady Spymistress might come in handy, as I had unfinished business at the theater. Since she wouldn't fit into my skinny purse, I attached her with her "clip thingy" to the inside of my skirt waistband.

So we wouldn't have to take two cars, I offered to pick up Elsbeth and her brood. My friend looked and smelled as cool as a frosty margarita in a lime-green floral sundress bolero-style jacket, and a touch of neroli perfume. The kids were so excited to see their very first play they burst out the screen door the minute I pulled into the driveway. Elsbeth had dolled them up. Jamie was *monísimo* in short pants, white shirt, and red faux bow tie. Ginger, her hair wound into two bejeweled pigtails and wearing a hand-sewn blue granny dress with pink appliqué flowers and white trim, was the spitting image of Elsbeth in miniature.

My family beat us to the theater. Mami radiated warmth and simple elegance in her chiffon dress, tinged the delicate blush shade of a cactus blossom. A valentine-pink rose from the garden graced her hair. As I drew closer, I noticed that my mother had applied rouge, lip gloss, and—wonder of wonders—eye shadow and mascara. With Papi sitting tall beside her in his best beige summer suit, they looked, at least to my eyes, like a distinguished Thirties film star couple attending a premiere.

Germán appeared casual but neat in a fresh guayabera shirt and gray slacks. Juana had found time to paint her nails fiesta-fire coral, a shade I recognized as this season's hottest color. She'd swept her luxuriant hair into an artistic knot on top of her head and fastened it with an elegant sequined comb. I always thought my sister-in-law would thrive as a beauty salon operator, and her appearance confirmed my theory. She'd wrapped Sarita in a summery cotton blanket adorned with a pretty cornflower design and attached a pink bow to the top of the baby's head with double-sided tape. The little one slept in her basket on her mother's lap, oblivious to the surrounding chatter.

I was thankful to see my sister had forsaken her Goth uniform for a pair of not-too-skin-tight designer jeans and a flowing, deep turquoise poet's blouse with puff sleeves. A delicate gold chain adorned her neck and there wasn't a henna tattoo in sight. As I made my way down the aisle toward our seats, my first thought was that the Castillo clan cleaned up pretty well.

My second thought, when I recognized Chief Mondragón seated next to my parents, was that I hoped he hadn't told Papi about my escapade at Michael's apartment. Although no one could accuse the Chief of being the life of the party, when he caught sight of me, the wrinkles around his mouth and eyes curled up slightly instead of sloping toward the floor. Maybe he scratched me off the suspect list for good after what Olivia and I told him about Bibi.

While helping Elsbeth settle her children in their row, I glanced around the audience. Michael's parents, in mourning and still waiting for the coroner to release the body, were not in attendance. Instead, the spiffed-up theater box was occupied by Dean Tilson and a red-headed babe from Contracts and Grants. The dean, who I'd only seen once before in passing, looked a little like Leonardo di Caprio in his role as Howard Hughes. The tall, solidly built fellow in a stylish white summer suit and bronzed-to-perfection golf course tan wore his light brown hair smartly slicked back. The gold stud in his left ear caused me to speculate whether he had it because he was cool or because he thought it made him look cool.

Settling into the box next to the dean were the Vigils. Baldomero, gussied up in a fussy summer suit that gave off an unfortunate bluish-green sheen, surveyed the audience with the eye of a monarch inspecting his vassals. I hadn't realized at the barbecue, but Penelope towered over her husband by at least four inches. As she took her seat, the shoulder strap on her powder-blue gown slipped. She hastened to lift it back into place, but not before her husband noticed and glowered at her with his right eye.

Olivia, Georgina, Suzanne, Javier, and Dolores were busy backstage, and Juventino still languished in jail. Bibi was answering questions at the police station, or so I'd learned from my *padrino*. The only other people whom I recognized from the department besides some students were Clive Strange and Mrs. Webber, who sat together. Clive stood out against the summer-clad crowd in his signature black turtleneck and pants, accessorized with a jaunty red cravat and the Dalí necklace watch. Maybe he thought his attire made him seem more part of the theater scene. Mrs. Webber looked up from studying her program and motioned to me. I made my way over to her seat to have a word.

"What do you make of the police arresting Barbara Pomodoro today?" Mrs. Webber asked, fanning herself with her program.

"Ah," I nodded. "I suspected something like that might happen."

"Do you think Our Girl Amazon committed both murders?" Clive's eyes vibrated with anticipation.

Mrs. Webber stopped fanning. "Hush, Clive, we don't know that. We wondered if, since you have a relationship with the police chief, Isabel, you might know."

"All I can tell you is that Bibi is being questioned about drug trafficking, not about the deaths. I suppose the police went ahead and arrested her."

Of that, I was certain, since Olivia and I had gone to Mondragón with the journal and WINK paper. I'd also signed a statement saying that Bibi offered to supply me with drugs. But neither Olivia nor I had hinted that we suspected her of the murders.

Mrs. Webber patted her freshly clipped and dipped hair. "I was thinking that Barbara may have had a motive to kill Eddy if he found out about her activities from that youth group and threatened to turn her in."

"But why would she do away with Michael?" I asked. Nobody had yet answered that question to my satisfaction.

Clive fiddled with his watch. "Perhaps it was a drug deal gone south. Alas, poor Michael was known to overindulge." He flicked a veiled glance in the direction of what would have been the Kent's box.

"I'm sure the truth will soon be revealed," I said.

"How right you are, dear lady." Clive cast his blue orbs toward the ceiling. "This evening, the stars are well aligned toward revelations."

I glanced at my more terrestrial timekeeper and excused myself. The curtain would rise soon, but Elsbeth and I had a few minutes to pop backstage to give Olivia a good luck bouquet.

Doña Isabella's proverbs, songs, and advice had been marinating in my head since the night my ancestor appeared in my kitchen, and I felt I needed to salt my inquiry into the murders with a few more questions. I might not get a better opportunity to see all the principals in one place at the same time until the fall semester began. By then, the trail might have gone cold.

Dolores would squirrel herself away in a carrel to finish her thesis; Georgina was traveling to a conference in Puerto Rico; Baldomero meant to take a short trip to Bolivia to visit relatives and probably Little O, leaving

Olivia in charge of department matters. Javier had finished his course work and indicated that he wanted to return to Boston to visit a few libraries to begin thesis research. And Dolores was preparing her thesis defense.

Only Suzanne would still be plodding along, lording it over her captive audience in the TA bullpen. The professors who weren't teaching during the summer term would be back, a new semester would have begun, and memories of the summer terms would all but be erased.

The mood on the other side of the curtain roiled with nervous excitement. Extras, half-dressed in their costumes, orchestra members toting unwieldy instruments, and stagehands laden with props, steamed around, appearing and disappearing between sheaths of black velvet curtain, and bursting from hidey-hole wall panels with the suddenness of ships rising from a fog. A mist of rose fragrance permeated the air. Peering up at the cavernous reaches of the stage, I discovered that the source was masses of fresh rose petals packed tight into muslin sacks, ready to cascade down at the finale.

Elsbeth and I delivered the bouquet to Olivia, who was dictating last-minute reminders to Suzanne, Javier, and Joe Binks, Michael's replacement. We wished everybody to break a leg.

I was exiting the stage behind Elsbeth looking around for Dolores, when Georgina emerged from behind the wall panel that provided a shortcut from the Green Room. We almost collided like the iceberg and the Titanic. Elsbeth didn't see Georgina, so she proceeded through a side exit door into the auditorium. I stayed behind.

"Georgie, you look *fabulosa!*" I enthused.

The feminist literature professor had exchanged her mannish-looking pantsuit for a below-the-knee, wisteria-colored, spun silk dress. A touch of Lycra gave her bony body an elegant sleekness. In place of her customary sensible shoes, her feet were encased in a pair of low, navy pumps. She'd created a new look for herself with her makeup, too, using a muted rose tone more flattering to her complexion. I glanced at the musical score she held in her hand and noticed that she'd invested in rose-colored acrylic nails etched with sparkling silver stars.

"Thanks," Georgina mumbled, but looked pleased that her makeover had been noticed. "Thought I'd make myself presentable for the occasion. Looks like you went all out." She indicated my attire.

"Oh, this? It's a knockoff. Listen, I know you're busy, but something has been bothering me, and I wonder if you could cast your mind back to the night of Eddy's murder."

A frown creased the professor's forehead, and she pursed her lips like the Georgina Rampage I first met. "Do I have to right now?"

"Please, just for a moment. Do you recall, on the night Eddy died, who left the rehearsal with whom and in what order?"

Georgina folded her musical score and rubbed her chin thoughtfully with an acrylic nail. "Let's see. I don't know about Olivia because she stayed behind with the technicians." She counted, "Eddy took off first and alone after talking with the lighting crew. Then Michael and Suzanne went together, and Javier and Dolores left at the same time, too."

I took a sharp intake of breath. "Javier and Dolores left *at the same time*? Not together?"

"At first, yes, but as I was gathering my things, I walked past the open stage door and overheard them arguing. Dolores said, 'You're not the person I thought you were!' She raced off toward the department. Javier stood still for a minute, then went in the same direction. I presumed he went after her."

A knot of excitement twisted inside my stomach. "Thanks, Georgie, you've been immensely helpful."

As we spoke, with a swish, the orchestra conductor materialized from between two curtains. I recognized the long-limbed man with salt-and-pepper hair, Jumbo ears, and dimples that made him look perpetually amused as musicologist and Latin American percussionist Franco Martinelli. To my surprise, Georgina's color rose, and she gave him a shy smile.

"Hullo, Frankie," Georgina said in a husky voice.

Martinelli's dimples deepened into small craters. His smile revealed a gap between his front teeth.

"Georgie, I've been searching all over this maze for you. You know the music so well. Would you mind being my page-turner tonight?"

CHAPTER THIRTY-FOUR

Her eyes brightened into sunny disks. "I would be honored!"

I wished them both success and watched them disappear down the short staircase into the orchestra pit. Georgina Rampage and Franco Martinelli an item! The fragrance of roses, the romantic queen of scents, was wafting down from the rafters and working its subtle enchantment on at least one couple.

I didn't ponder the budding romance for long, as I knew the play would start at any moment. I needed to get one more thing straight before I took my seat in the audience.

I caught up with Dolores in the prompter's box, checking that her flashlight was working properly. She'd taken over Bibi's job.

"*Hola,* Dolores."

"Issy, what are you doing backstage? The curtain's about to go up."

"I know. I wanted to wish you and everybody the best of success tonight."

"*Gracias.* We're dedicating the performance to Eddy's memory."

"I'm sure he'll be watching over you all tonight; in fact, I can feel his presence here."

"I hope so." Dolores glanced down at her script.

"Before you go back to your work," I said, "could you answer a quick question?"

Dolores raised her Olive Oyl eyes to stare at me. "What?"

"Something you said about the night Eddy died wasn't clear. You mentioned that you and Javier left together, but you didn't go into the department together, did you?"

"No. We got into…well…kind of a misunderstanding, and I took off. Javier joined me in my office a few minutes before Suzanne rolled in. Is it important?"

"I'll say! And I think I know what you had words about."

Dolores blushed. Just then, the bell rang for the audience to take their seats. I thanked her and hurried out of an exit and back into the auditorium.

Chapter Thirty-Five

"La ira de la mente es veneno para el alma."
"Anger of the mind is poison to the soul." —Spanish Proverb

When the curtain rose, the audience gasped in delight. The stage was transformed into a tri-level fairyland representation of Heaven, Earth, and Hell. Tiny white lights twinkled in a deep blue sky, portrayed as if at dusk. Papier-mâché figures of angels rendered in a European medieval style floated gracefully above the scene. Upstage, trees that could have rivaled Sherwood Forest grounded the main action on Earth. A blue-painted moat with a turreted castle adorned with several colorful flags stood mid-right stage. Downstage left and at a lower level, the fires of Hell crackled hot and menacing. Whenever a blast of steam shot from the faux embers, Jamie and Ginger squealed with delight.

From a window in the turret, Suzanne, in a long yoked green taffeta dress, tall pointed hat, and veil, waved a sad farewell to Javier, The White Knight. Sheathed in chain mail, he trudged away from the castle toward the forbidding forest on his way to the Crusade.

Although the play captivated the audience, I was too distracted by the information I'd gleaned backstage to pay proper attention. Words from my previous interviews with suspects I'd almost forgotten suddenly took on significance. I realized that Eddy, who once directed this play and the lives of many associated with it, overstepped his boundaries with the wrong person. That mistake was his undoing. And Michael transgressed by attempting to blackmail the one individual with whom he should never have tangled.

At intermission, my group made our way through the crowd to the lobby to stretch our legs and take refreshments. Once everyone had icy glasses of ginger ale punch in hand, I announced, "Hey, guys, I need to check on something. I'll see you back in the auditorium."

Elsbeth gave me a quick glance, but I pressed my forefinger to my lips and mouthed, "Later."

* * *

Backstage, I swiftly made my way down a staircase into the basement, which housed the dressing rooms. I was met by a cool draft that bore on its wings a dry but musty odor of sweat and old costumes. Here, the dead silence swallowed the lively clattering of shoes and scenery moving overhead. It was as if I'd entered a burial chamber where the spirits of actors from former eras and the characters they portrayed lay entombed within the walls for all time, like flies caught in amber. Even the lights cast an eerie ochre glow over the walls. I stood for a moment, waiting for my eyes to adjust to the gloom.

I figured Olivia and the cast were upstairs in the Green Room, reviewing last-minute details about the final act, so the dressing rooms would be vacant. I peered at the closed doors and smiled. Thank heavens for Dolores' academic attention to detail. I recognized the Portuguese instructor's precise handwriting inked on cardboard nametags and tacked to the doors that noted each actor's name and role.

I moved along the row of doors until I found the one I wanted. As I eased it open, the door creaked mournfully like a soul in Purgatory. The occupant was not in residence, so I closed it lightly behind me.

The small dressing room was crammed with a dresser shoved against the left wall and three or four chairs packed with costumes and other accouterments of the acting profession. To the right, a coat rack leaned half-buried with more costumes. I stepped to the dressing table against the back wall, laden with the usual assortment of makeup. Taking a seat on the vanity chair in front of the mirror, I placed my little purse on the floor.

Pots of makeup were arranged on the narrow glass shelf in two neat rows.

There were a couple of tubes of dark-colored pancake, eye pencils, eye shadow, and rouge to make cheeks appear rosy under the bright lights that washed out faces onstage.

Like a bloodhound on the trail of a scent, I spied, wedged between a brush and a jar of cold cream, a small glass bottle. I picked it up, opened it, and sniffed. My head swam as I inhaled the cloying scent with the tart finish that I'd smelled three times before: once in Elsbeth's classroom, again hovering around Eddy's body, and yet again, at the flowerbed in front of the student recreation center. A wave of nausea overpowered my senses, and I almost dropped the bottle as I remembered the words, *"Eddy was helping me get over my feelings of inadequacy."*

A rustling caused me to glance toward the back of the door on which a pair of gray sweats and a muscle shirt that read "Boston Boxers' Gym" faintly swung from the peg where they hung. The door creaked open.

* * *

"Like my aftershave?" Javier indicated the bottle I clutched. He entered, prop sword in hand, and shut the door firmly behind him. Suited up in his breast armor costume, he looked even bulkier than he appeared in his street clothes.

I slammed the bottle on the vanity so hard I almost knocked off the cold cream jar. I jumped to my feet. "Hyacinth, isn't it? *Muy fragante.*"

"How would you know?"

He moved to the dresser and leaned the sword against it. I told myself it was only a prop sword, and he couldn't harm me with it. Anyway, why would he want to? But my stomach churned and the ginger ale punch inside it fizzed like Mount St. Helens about to erupt. The fact that Javier had positioned himself between me and the door didn't escape my notice either.

"I learned about that fragrance in an aromatherapy class I took," I said. "Our instructor told us that in Ancient Rome, homosexuals and hermaphrodites wore it to enhance their sex appeal. Some still use it today as a sexual attractant."

Javier's upper lip curled back in a smile, revealing big, straight, bleach-strip-white teeth that bore an uncanny resemblance to wolf fangs. I wondered whether his incisors had been knocked out in a boxing match and replaced with implants. But this was not the time to venture into a conversation about the pros and cons of cosmetic enhancements, as my adversary, at the moment, was growling softly and ominously.

"*Bien, bien, profesora,*" he grumbled. "You have managed to uncover my little secret. And it was not because I proposed to you to write my thesis on homosexuality in Cavalier poetry, no. It was all because of a lowly bottle of aftershave."

I was amazed I'd never noticed before how much Javier's voice resembled Peter Lorre's in his role as the murderer in the classic Fritz Lang horror film *M.* If he broke out in an eerie whistle of "In the Hall of the Mountain King" now, I'd collapse in a dead faint on the spot.

Somehow, I found my voice. "I made the connection between the odor I smelled clinging to the air when I discovered Eddy's body and, again, on you when we talked outside the Rec Center. It wasn't the roses that smelled so sweet; it was you. But this is only part of the story. I think I understand why you killed Michael. He's been a craw in your throat for a long time. I'm guessing he discovered your secret and was holding it like a heavy sword over your head. And then, he told you he was going to reveal it to the world so you could never have a relationship with Dolores or any woman."

My brain scrambled to find a way to maneuver past Javier to the door and freedom, but he cocked his head toward me, and I couldn't risk the move. He lifted his shaggy eyebrows to reveal eyes that sparked dangerously in the vanity mirror's bright lights.

"Right again, *profesora.* If this were your final exam, I would award you an A+." He chuckled. "Come to think of it, this is turning out to *be* your final exam."

At his words, the hairs on my arms stood straight up, and I felt prickly all over. What had ever possessed me to come to Javier's dressing room alone to look for a clue to link him to the murders?

The pen! The pen! Where did I put the pen? I had to record this before he realized what I was doing. That's right, on my waistband. But I was afraid that any movement might galvanize the youth to pounce on me and strangle me like he had Eddy.

Javier was speaking now, almost as if to himself. As he did, he picked up small objects from the dresser, one by one, and toyed with them. A tissue box, a bud vase, a tin of mints.

"It is no secret that Miguel and I have engaged in a rivalry that extends back to our childhood days," he admitted with a shrug that flapped his shoulder armor and made me start. "After all, we are two different types from opposite sides of the tracks. Miguel had the pedigree, but I gained renown with my fists. And my success…" he waved a hand dismissively, "let us say that my success troubled him."

His thoughts veered in another direction, as he favored me with an earnest look. "You have been so supportive of me, unlike some others, by encouraging me in my academic endeavors. So, I don't mind telling you all this. Please understand, *Profesora*, I think Miguel was more perceptive and talented than many gave him credit for. I truly believe that once he made it through this bad patch and got his act together, he would go far. But things being as they are…"

He was so intent on stroking the makeup brush he now held that for a moment, I hoped he'd forgotten my presence. I shifted my weight to prepare to sidle past him, but the slight movement snapped back his attention. He pivoted to face me head-on. I coughed, pretending it was the reason I'd moved, slipped my hand inside my waistband, and activated Lady Spymistress.

Now if he would only make a full confession. My family, friends, the department, even the community at large would be so relieved. And why not? Javier was an actor and as Eddy once commented, he was fond of upstaging.

His sad eyes, the tortured eyes of Lon Chaney Junior in the horror flick *Wolfman,* riveted my attention. "One time, long before either of us found our way to the same graduate school, Miguel caught sight of me leaving a gay bar in Boston in a more than comradely embrace with my partner at the time. So, I knew that he knew."

He held up his hand. "I don't want you to think he ever threatened me with anything specific. Miguel was too adroit for that. He simply kept the knowledge tucked away where it festered like a wound that never heals."

I had to keep him talking. I needed that confession even if it killed me. Which it probably would. "At what point did things change?"

"It all started with *La Dulce Dolores*." He smiled, presumably at her memory. "She and I were close friends, two outcasts, birds of a feather. At least, up to a point." He gave a mirthless snigger. "That day in front of the department, the day when you arrived on campus, I confronted Miguel about the malicious gossip he was spreading about her. Dolores needed a champion, and I stepped into that role as her knight in shining armor."

For a moment, he dropped his gaze to regard his costume gleaming in the makeup lights. The thespian was in full soliloquy mode. He continued. "My decision to defend and protect Dolores is something that, no matter how this ends, I will never regret."

He went back to rearranging objects but didn't step far enough away for me to get around him in the small room. Perhaps the action helped order his thoughts. I wished he'd quit making those distracting, repetitive movements but dared not comment lest I interrupt the flow.

"Later," he continued, "I told Miguel that if he did not stop maligning Dolores and apologize to her, I would let his family know about his drug use. That was, as they say, the trigger. He threatened to tell the dudes at the gym in Longmont about me. You know, all the bruisers and gay bashers who hang with Big Carlos."

So, Javier, not Eddy, was the one to think of turning in Michael.

He sighed, chose a small framed photo of Dolores, and fondled it. "I might have married Dolores to keep up appearances. But it would not have been fair to her. The night Eddy...died...I told her my secret. She rejected me soundly, even as a friend. *Fíjate!*"

He shot me a look full of reproach and carefully replaced the photo on the dresser.

"I took her reaction as a harbinger of things to come. If Dolores shunned me, so would everyone else once they found out."

Suddenly, he looked at me as puzzled as if I'd asked him to derive a differential equation. "It could not have been only because of my aftershave. Tell me, how else did you know?"

I took a deep breath. I was going to have to measure every word as if my life depended on it, which indeed it might. "Someone mentioned that you didn't get on with the crowd at the gym. He sensed that you and they were poles apart in some indefinable way. Then you and Dolores became estranged for no obvious reason. Also, Clive Strange hinted there was something…different about you."

He guffawed. "Strange should know. That *tipo* is a rare bird, but not of my species."

I recalled Clive's proverb about owls keeping to their own olive trees. "He said something like that about you once. What I don't understand," I said, because my bird brain still hadn't come up with an escape plan, "is why you didn't come out of the closet when Michael threatened to expose you. Tons of people around the university and in the community are gay and make no bones about it. There's no stigma anymore."

Again, he laughed his curiously vacant laugh as if he were laughing down a long, empty hall. "*Sin verguenza!* As a Latina, *Profesora* Castillo, you should know better. What you say may be true for some, but not for those who move in a macho society. Especially not for me with my pugilistic background." He mouthed the word "pugilistic" with a curl of his upper lip.

"I am the youngest of four brothers, all professional boxers, and my father and grandfather before me were boxers. What shame such a confession would rain down on my family, I cannot think! I could never bear the dishonor I would visit upon them. Miguel understood this, and he played it for all it was worth."

With this last string of words, Javier had managed to work himself into an agitated state. He paused, red-faced and panting, then pulled himself together. The visible signs of anger were beaten under control, but not spent.

"You do agree that it was vital I rid myself of Miguel and his devilish influence? It was practically a case of self-defense. Any jury would see it that way."

The shaggy brows drooped over his eyes, leaving only the gleaming pupils exposed. "For two nights, I kept watch outside the scurrilous bastard's apartment. Finally, he came home drunk or high, as I knew he would. I waited until he stumbled into bed. I stole around the back and plugged the exhaust on the hot water heater so carbon monoxide would leak into the bathroom and spread through the apartment. Then I went away. Problem solved."

Again, I tried to inch around him, but he stepped even closer to the vanity. Now he loomed over me, caressing in his right hand one of the objects he'd taken from the dresser.

"I understand your anger and frustration over Michael," I said, "but it doesn't explain Eddy Calderón."

I almost didn't want to know the answer to my next question but was compelled to ask. "Were you two having a relationship?"

He gave a bitter chuckle. "I shall have to mark you down on that one, *Profesora*, because there, you are dead wrong." He stood so close to me I smelled his body odor mixed with the sickly-sweet scent of the hyacinth aftershave escaping from under the hot armor.

He frowned. "I thought there was a chance for me with Eddy because he was such an open, friendly person. So *simpático*. I kept devising opportunities to get the ball rolling when I visited him in his office. But he never grabbed the ball and ran with it."

Sports metaphors, even under the best of circumstances, annoy me. I needed to get to home base fast before my tape clicked off, alerting my adversary. "So, what happened that night, the night Dolores rejected you?"

He considered. "I was feeling exactly that way: rejected. After Dolores walked off to her office, I thought, 'I shall consult *Profesor* Calderón about this. He is the only one who understands, the only one to lend a sympathetic ear.'"

"When I arrived at his office, he was writing notes, something about Juventino Guerrero and donkeys, something ridiculous like that. He was so absorbed he did not want to talk to me. I must have looked *deprimido*…let down…for he reconsidered and invited me to go ahead and tell him my troubles. I confessed everything. I let loose with all the passion I felt for him, which, until then, I had bottled up inside."

I had a sickening feeling about what was coming, but I persisted. "How did Eddy react?"

Javier's face was turning red again. "I shall never forget his look of horror and revulsion. I had made a big mistake in judgment, but there was no taking it back.

"He became cold toward me in a way that made me feel I was lower than a cockroach. He told me that he definitively did not shave on both sides of the razor, our euphemism for being bi-sexual. He said that he was busy and had something important to finish. He got up to go to his other computer and turned his back on me. On *me*, the one who practically worshiped him. I was *furioso!* Two rejections within twenty minutes were more than I could bear."

He gesticulated, acting out the scene from memory. "I turned to stomp out, and my eye caught a scarf hanging on the door. Before I knew it, the scarf was in my hands. I wheeled around and surprised him from behind. With his back to me, he did not stand a chance. I had squeezed his last breath out of him before I realized what I had done. I ran out and got myself into Dolores' office without delay."

Footsteps clattered overhead, and the sound of the orchestra warming up filled the air. I glanced toward the ceiling. The intermission meeting in the Green Room must have let out, and actors and crew were taking their places. And here was Isabel Castillo, professor of medieval Spanish literature, trapped in this benighted basement with a double murderer. No one would hear my screams over the noise; not a soul would fly to my aid. I felt my breath come in ragged, shallow gasps. If only I could keep Javier talking, maybe someone would come looking for him.

Clutching at straws, I asked, "Did killing Eddy make the second murder… killing Michael Kent…easier to do?"

I couldn't see the object he was now stroking because he cupped his hand around it as if it were a captured bird. At that moment, I couldn't have cared less about the prop he held.

"It did make a difference. Although nobody lost his life by my hand until Eddy and Miguel, I grew up in the mean streets of Boston. I was a fighter in the 'hood before I channeled the aggressive side of my nature into boxing. After all, I come from a family of fighters." His boyish smile reminded me of Anthony Perkins in the Hitchcock classic horror film *Psycho*. "I sure whaled on a few bozos in the old days."

The fleeting smile disappeared. "After a while, I developed an interest in becoming adept with weapons other than my fists. In fact, I became something of an authority on knives."

With that, he uncurled his fingers to reveal that the object he'd been holding was a switchblade. He flicked it open, and in an instant, I found myself staring at its menacing point.

"To answer your question, yes, it does get easier," he said. "I must say that as intelligent as you are, and as much as I respect the knowledge you have communicated in the classroom and the sympathy with which you have listened to my story, I am going to have to put you away, too. You know too much."

Slowly, he closed the short gap between us. I backed against the opposite wall, grimacing as the blade moved inexorably closer.

At that moment, the buzzer rang to announce the final act. The two of us stood stock still like those actors who make a living in malls pretending to be statues. The play might be about to resume upstairs, but down in the basement, time and space had suspended.

Javier spoke. "I guess there is not enough time to finish this business now. I shall have to put you where you will be out of harm's way until I can return."

With the suddenness of a pouncing tiger, he sprang to the wall next to me and pushed a decorative piece of molding. A panel slid open, and before I knew what was happening, he shoved me inside. The panel slid shut, plunging me into total darkness.

Chapter Thirty-Six

"No hay peor consejero que el miedo"
"There is no worse counselor than fear." — Spanish Proverb

It took me a couple of seconds to realize I was trapped inside one of the theater's hidden wall compartments. Unlike the ones Eddy and Georgina used as passageways, this one had no exit. Because it was so small, I took it to be a storage bin.

The space was so narrow I couldn't move more than a few inches from side to side. Worse, I was tucked into it lopsided because a heel had ripped from one of my shoes when Javier slammed me in. The ghastly part, that which frightened me almost out of my wits, was that I'd been left completely in the dark. The kind of darkness Shakespeare describes as "sable night."

When I was five or six years old, Germán decided it would be hilarious to lock me in the attic closet. Everyone thought I was down the street playing at my cousin Manuela's, so nobody heard my frantic cries. Only when Tony happened to open the door to search for white-soled basketball shoes did I escape. Now, the memory of that unpleasant experience came flooding back. This time, no brother Tony would appear to rescue me.

In fact, nobody would ever look for me inside this coffin. My friends and family would think that since I was so buddy-buddy with the director, I'd been invited to view the rest of the performance from backstage. Neither Olivia, Georgina, nor Dolores would suspect anything because everyone would be whooping it up at the cast party when Javier delivered my final bow.

I'd left my phone at home because it wouldn't fit into my chic little purse. Even if I'd brought it along, I wouldn't have been able to reach it because my purse was sitting on the dressing room floor. That is unless Javier had already disposed of it.

I couldn't hear clattering above anymore. Either the last act had begun, or my tomb was soundproof. With the sides of my arms and backs of my hands, I felt the compartment walls and judged it was constructed from some sort of metal. I hoped it wasn't lead. I visualized my body being discovered decades hence during some remodeling project, fully intact, like a mummy in an ancient Egyptian sarcophagus. Only this mummy would be dolled up in a knock-off Armani suit, rebellious hair sticking out in all directions like a madwoman. Despite being wedged in as tight as a size twelve body in a size six bodysuit, I strained from side to side with all my might.

"Help!" I screamed. "Somebody, please help me!" Useless!

The more I thrashed around, the more breathless I became. The air was so fusty and close I feared I would suffocate. A dusty substance smelling of roses sifted over my head from above, choking me. Tears streamed down my face, and I wept.

Exhausted and by now losing sensation in my feet and legs from being pinned in, I gave up the struggle. What did it matter? Now, I understood the full meaning of the medieval concept of the "dark night of the soul." I let out a strangled sob. I was embarked on my final journey and would never get out of there alive, never see my family and friends again. Never see Doña Isabella unless we reunited on The Other Side.

Doña Isabella.

From somewhere in the depths of my psyche, a place as black as the primordial sea from which all life originates, I remembered how, during my first encounter with my spirit ancestor, Doña Isabella had advised, "If you can't modify a situation, you can change your physical and emotional response to it."

Either my ancestor was teleporting advice to me, or my survival instinct was finally kicking in. I must not let fear take the upper hand. If I remained calm and thought things through, I'd find a way out. I had to. I tried to slow my fast, shallow breathing so the panic would fade away, replaced by clear, down-to-earth reasoning. I straightened my body as much as I could. When Javier returned to put me out of my misery, I would get one slim chance to escape, and I had to concentrate on that moment.

A click sounded, and in the dead silence, it crackled like a thunderbolt. I would've jumped out of my skin if there had been anywhere to jump to. Trying to extricate myself from the tight space, I must have rubbed against the side of the container hard enough to inadvertently turn off the record function on the pen. At least I could console myself with the thought that when my body was exhumed, the coroner would discover the recording device and learn who had murdered Eddy, Miguel, and me. It wasn't much comfort, but I'd take what I could get.

In my mind, I played back the recording of what was probably going to be Javier's and my penultimate encounter. Maybe the apparent lack of oxygen was affecting my brain, but I began to think of my killer with a feeling that approached compassion.

Poor Javier! He wasn't such a bad person, at least not in the beginning. With proper counseling with someone to talk out his problems, he wouldn't have ranged so far out of control.

He did it all for *pundonor*, the traditional Spanish concept of honor and reputation. But he let rage take over and, consequently, ended up losing precisely what he hoped to preserve. As the saying goes, "Anger of the mind is poison to the soul." *Might I journey to my final destination without harboring a vestige of anger within my heart toward anyone?* I couldn't bear a grudge against Javier; indeed, I would not.

Suddenly, I felt my sarcophagus vibrate, and with a groan, it began to levitate.

* * *

Out of the depths of Hell, inch by inch, I was being transported upward. Even though I couldn't crane my neck to see above me, flashes of light illuminated the inside of my burial chamber. The lights flared so bright I figured they must be spotlights. They blinked on and off probably in accordance with the lighting changes needed onstage.

From the intermittent light, I deduced that my prison was a near-empty ballast box, positioned on a platform. The crate was one of those stage mechanisms that could be filled with material to make it heavier or left empty to act as a counterbalance for a weight on another platform. The other weight might be a piece of scenery, a large prop, an actor, or, in this case, my corpse.

The strobe-like flickering revealed something else. Hooks were attached to the wall in front of my face. Although I couldn't lift my arms to grab onto them, they were positioned close together and extended low enough on the inner wall that I might be able to gain a foothold on one. With difficulty, because of the numbness in my feet, I groped for a foothold. Since I was lodged somewhat diagonally, with my feet pressed into something that felt like a bale of hay, one foot and leg had a bit more swing room, as did one arm and hand.

I felt around for a hook that was about twelve inches off the ground and slipped my right foot into it. Next, I snaked my left arm up the front wall and grabbed another hook. This enabled me to hoist myself onto the wall. I inched my way up the wall, trying not to slip back down.

With another groan and a jerk, the crate ground to a halt. I almost fell but managed to keep my grip. I realized that the top from where the lights and the smell of roses emitted was open. First, my head emerged, then my shoulders, arms, and torso. I reached the top hook, tried to stand, and "Ow!" smacked my head on overhanging scaffolding.

My hands flew to my head. I swayed, almost toppled over, and went into a crouch. Steadying myself, I took a deep breath and crawled outside the crate. My hands and elbows hit something soft and yielding. It felt like tightly packed goose feathers inside an enormous down pillow. A stunning sweetness emanated from the material.

In the dim light, I discerned that I'd landed inside the opening on top of one of the muslin sacks packed with rose petals and that—*Cielos*—Heavens, indeed—I was in the remote upper reaches of the stage.

The sacks, gaping open on top and held in place by stiff netting, ropes, cords on the wall, and metal pulleys, extended in a row from one side of the stage to the other. I was not alone in this inky eyrie. On a catwalk, at the other side of the stage, knelt a stagehand. With his back to me, he appeared to be working on a piece of machinery.

"Hey!" I called, but he didn't turn around. *"Hey!"* Perhaps his ear was too close to the purring motor to hear.

The technician was probably up here getting ready to release the rose petals at the finale. I had to make it over to the catwalk before he tipped the bags and collapsed, my only means of escape. Gingerly, I pushed down on the mass of petals to see how firmly they were packed. A cloying cloud of scent fogged into my face and made my eyes water. I coughed, and the sack I was clinging to swayed dangerously. I held my breath, fearful that my sudden movement might cause it to rotate and empty it and me onto the stage forty feet below.

In a sickening wave of remembrance, I recalled what Elsbeth had mentioned in class about the Roman emperor who, at his coronation, had unfurled thousands of rose petals on his guests, suffocating them. Getting across to the other side of the stage wasn't going to be my only problem. I had to do it before I succumbed to the billowing waves of scent that threatened to inundate me.

I took as deep a breath as I could manage without drowning in fragrance. Instead of crawling, I extended my body flat over the sack to distribute my weight as evenly as possible. Then, I started worming my way across the top layer of petals toward the next sack.

With each breath, I choked on concentrated rose perfume. It took all my willpower to keep from sneezing and coughing and overturning the bales with me on them. Tears streamed from my eyes, blurring my vision, frustrating my efforts to move forward.

Because I had to stretch out completely to keep from sinking into the mass of petals and suffocating, I made excruciatingly slow progress. I reached the next sack and blindly grasped for the netting. Then, I eased my body over and onto its top layer of petals.

I slithered and slipped along like a lizard native to the tropics caught in its first snow blizzard. It dawned on me that not only was I probably claustrophobic, but I'd also managed to add yet another phobia to my list: fear of heights. I dared not glance down lest I panic and lose my balance. I had to keep what part of my dimmed vision could still focus on my goal, the catwalk on the opposite side of the stage where the technician still knelt.

The intoxicating odor was beginning to disorient me. Olivia must have added rose perfume oil to the petals to make them smell so strong. Gallons of it! Now and again, tiny ripping sounds like sailcloth tearing in the wind at sea did nothing to assuage my fears. I prayed that the ominous noises came from my clothes rather than from the netting but suspected the worst.

From somewhere far below I was aware of the actors carrying on a conversation. Suzanne, Javier, and someone, probably Michael's replacement, onstage. I realized that the play must be nearing the end.

I had no idea how far I'd traveled, only that I hadn't made it across the entire stage yet. I could only hope the technician would turn and see me before it was too late.

Then, my right hand touched something solid. Another platform! This one was shrouded in a sparkling white cottony material of the kind that conceals the bases of Christmas trees. I heaved my body onto it and clung on like to a lifeboat in a storm-whipped sea.

With the appalling moan of a soul in torment that I recognized only too well from attending rehearsals, the platform lurched downward. I barely had time to clutch at one of the chains to keep from falling off and going splat onto the stage floor.

The platform migrated down through the black night of the upper reaches and past cloud scenery, with me hanging half-on, half-off. Belly-down, my legs executing the flutter kick of a demented frog, I registered papier-mâché angels and glistening Moravian stars as I glided by.

Now, I was tossed amidst a world of deep blue light, churning ever downward into the brighter white lights of the stage. I was descending on the platform meant to retrieve Suzanne and Javier and carry them to Heaven. I pulled myself to my knees. Clinging to the chain, I straightened myself into an upright position just as the platform halted two feet above the stage floor with a teeth-rattling jolt.

Suzanne and Javier stood gaping at me. Javier dropped his sword. Joe Binks, the Black Knight, who had been lying face-down on the stage floor slain by the White Knight, forgot he was dead and propped himself up on an elbow to get a better view. The audience gasped.

Stumbling off the platform, I pulled at my skirt, which had gotten hiked up around my waist. Then, I extracted Lady Spymistress. *Gracias a todos los santos;* her "clip thingy" had kept her intact inside my waistband throughout my ordeal.

I fumbled for the pen's playback function and, in a shaky but loud voice, announced, "Though the White Knight has slain The Black Knight on this stage for pretend, in reality, he has killed twice. Here is the proof."

I held the recorder close to a microphone near the front center footlights. Javier's confession rang out loud and clear.

The last thing I saw before I slumped to the floor in a dead faint was the scarecrow figure of Chief Mondragón rising up from his seat in the audience, descending on the stage like an avenging angel.

Epilogue

"What you leave behind is not what is engraved in stone monuments, but what is woven into the lives of others." — Pericles (d. 429 BCE), Greek Statesman

The August full moon, which some Native Americans call the Red Moon because it often rises russet-colored through the sultry atmosphere, hung low in the sky. To my eye, it resembled a single gigantic halved blood orange. From Elsbeth's bluff-top front porch, we three friends sat admiring the panoramic view of Boulder. Olivia and Elsbeth shared the old-fashioned swing, and I folded myself into a Maplewood rocker. The children were tucked up in bed.

The Bolder Women Detective Team basked in the cool evening breeze, welcome after the ninety-degree day, and sipped frothy glasses full of Elsbeth's Friendship Smoothie. Elsbeth told us that besides cementing friendships, frozen raspberries, and currant juice provide loads of fiber and vitamins C and K, increase stamina, and promote weight loss. Always a good thing. The fresh scones topped with the whipped cream she served may have canceled the smoothie's slimming benefits, but at least the fruit added a healthy touch.

Elsbeth smothered a giggle.

"What's so funny?" I snaked my hand over to the round rattan table between us and plucked a scone from the earthenware serving platter.

Elsbeth looked sheepish. "I shouldn't laugh, but onstage that night you looked so daft. Your hair with the rose petals stuck in it made you seem like one enormous flower in full bloom."

"You were lurching around barefoot with a look of wild surmise in your eyes," Olivia put in. "And your poor dusty clothes were ruined with that revealing rip from knee to waist." She chuckled. "It's a wonder the audience didn't think they'd wandered into the wrong play and were watching Ophelia in *Hamlet*."

The corners of my mouth turned down. *"Muy gracioso.* I'll remember that the next time you find yourselves in a situation that makes you look ridiculous."

"You looked cute, really." Olivia clucked and slurped her smoothie through her straw. "As we say in Spanish, '*muy mona.*'"

"Which also means 'like a monkey,'" I huffed, but not too vigorously. If truth be told, I couldn't help but feel proud I'd managed to make a harrowing escape and bag Javier for good measure. My unorthodox stage debut served to speedily land the killer behind bars. With the confession taped on Lady Spymistress, no way could Javier weasel out of the murder rap.

To my immense surprise, Papi had been the most effusive with his congratulations. He crushed me in a bear hug, declaring over and over, *"Enhorabuena, m'hija! Enhorabuena!* Well done, my daughter!" Mami covered me in kisses of relief that I'd been delivered safe and unharmed. Even Angela's eyes glistened with tears of admiration, or so I presumed.

Elsbeth leaned across the table and squeezed my hand. "We're teasing you, Issy. We were petrified when we saw you careening down on that platform. It twitched around so much I thought it was going to throw you off onto the stage floor like from a bucking bronco."

I took a refreshing swig. "That wasn't the worst part. Climbing out of the crate and slithering across the top of the stage on those bales of stinky rose petals was more terrifying than anything I've ever experienced."

"Tell us again about how you escaped," said Olivia, her eyes shining.

"I already told you."

"We know," Elsbeth put in, "but we want to savor the details again."

I sipped my smoothie and sat it on the table. Now that I'd put the horror behind me, I didn't mind reliving the scene. "The hooks inside the crate where I was imprisoned were there so that ropes and netting could be attached to keep the ballast from falling out of the open side where Javier had pushed me in."

"But you didn't know that at the time," Olivia said, putting her thoughts in order aloud, "because the crate was in a chute."

"Like inside a laundry chute. Anyway, only a couple of bales of hay were at the bottom, so the hooks were available for me to climb; that is, once enough light shone from the spotlights for me to realize hooks were there."

Elsbeth wrinkled her forehead. "One thing I don't understand is why the stagehand didn't see you and try to rescue you."

"Because," I explained, taking another scone and nibbling it, "he was trying to adjust the motor that lifts and lowers the platforms. And it made a lot of noise."

"That motor plagued us throughout rehearsals," Olivia commented.

With a scone in hand, I waved my arms to demonstrate. "You see, it was harder to raise the crate I was in because of my one-hundred-plus pounds. And I won't say how many pounds over one hundred I weigh. It put more strain on the motor than it should have. The technician thought it needed to be fixed."

I swallowed, took another bite, chewed, and swallowed again before continuing. "I got to the platform that was being lowered, which set the weight off-balance again. When the stagehand began to lower the platform on cue, he realized somebody was on it. I guess he tried frantically to keep it from descending too fast by starting and stopping the motor. That's why the descent was so erratic."

"Gosh!" Elsbeth exclaimed. "As Clive would say, your lucky star was surely burning bright."

"While Javier's was being extinguished," Olivia added with a sad nod.

Her words brought to mind Javier's terror-stricken face, winter white despite the hot armor and makeup he wore. "I hope they don't treat him roughly in jail," I commented.

"Even with extenuating circumstances," Olivia differed, "he did snuff out two lives. He deserves to be put away for a long time."

I shook my head. "But he's been disgraced, which to him is far worse.

He's living a nightmare without support from family or friends, much less from the university that has disavowed him. We Latinos have a proverb to describe it: 'A man without honor is worse than dead.' I feel Javier deserves our compassion."

"You're right, of course," Olivia admitted as she polished off a scone. "Mrs. Webber told me he's undergoing extensive psychological testing. He may be sent to an institution for the mentally ill rather than to a hardcore prison to get the help he needs." She sucked on her drink. "Speaking of Mrs. Webber reminds me that she told me a juicy tidbit about Baldo."

"She did?" "What was it?" Elsbeth and I chorused.

Olivia wiped her hands on her napkin. "It wasn't about the real reason, at least the reason they believe Baldo went to see Michael on the night he died," she said, obviously enjoying dragging out her story.

"You mean he went there to pay Michael money to keep mum," Elsbeth confirmed what we all thought.

"Yes, but Baldo's history has been unmasked publicly anyway." Olivia clapped her hands in delight. As she spoke, she started the swing moving. "During the course of the investigation, the university conducted a thorough background check on him. The fact was brought to light that Baldomero Vigil doesn't have a genuine Ph.D. from Brownell, or from anywhere. It's what your friend Ana told you, Issy."

"What's going to happen to him?" I wondered.

Olivia shrugged. "You know how it is at the university. Vigil was hired with tenure and has cemented enough connections with The Powers That Be to ensure his position here. This scandal will soon blow over, and all will be forgiven and forgotten."

"But how can that be?" I jutted out my chin. "It's not fair."

"Oh, Issy!" said Elsbeth, shaking her head. "You still have a thing or two to learn about university politics."

I sighed and sucked on my recyclable straw. "At least *El Señor FLA Juventino* got what he deserved."

"I guess that man was fated to be a rebel," said Olivia.

Elsbeth leaned back against the slowly moving swing and gazed at the stars. "I read in the paper that Bibi is still in jail awaiting trial on charges for selling drugs across state lines."

"My brother tells me her rich parents hired a top-notch defense team," I said. "She'll get off with a slap on the wrist."

"Maybe with nothing better to do in jail, she and Juventino will fall in love," Olivia speculated. "That could be punishment enough for both of them."

As the moon rose higher in the sky, it lost its new penny color and transformed into a dazzling white disk. It shone on the tree-lined streets, houses, and gardens below like a spotlight illuminating a stage set cast against the black mountain backdrop.

"How's Georgina Rampage doing these days?" Elsbeth wanted to know.

Olivia replied, "Now that she's dating Franco, she's no longer on the rampage."

"She has another reason to be content," Elsbeth said. "The secrets of her past need never be revealed now."

"I'll never tell," I vowed.

"Nor I." "Nor I," my friends affirmed.

"The best part," said Olivia, "is that since Georgie's fallen in love, ten years seem to have dropped from her face."

"That's love for you," Elsbeth said with a sigh. "It's better than any beauty treatment aromatherapy can offer."

"Ah, love!" I said and tipped back my head to regard the moon.

Breathing the delightful fragrance of spicy, sweet, night-scented phlox that flourished in the beds around the porch, I listened to the sounds of the city. They receded into the distance, taken over now by the night rustlings of mountain meadow creatures and chirping crickets. My rocker and the swing creaked back and forth in rhythmic harmony.

"Remember how we all thought Clive Strange was…well, a bit hinky?" I mused. "Truth is, he turned out to know a lot more about what was going on than anybody else because he observed everything and everybody. It's a skill that, if we continue with The Bolder Women Detective Team, we should try to cultivate."

"We weren't wrong about Suzanne," Olivia reminded us. "At least you weren't, Issy. You knew she was up to something, even if it wasn't murder."

"Only because I was the target of her jealousy. You'd have suspected her, too, if she'd gone after you with those scorpions and that Voodoo doll."

"What's happened to her and Dolores?" Elsbeth asked.

"As far as I know," said Olivia, "Suzanne and Joe are still married and playing Strip Scrabble at night, and she's still reigning over the TA room. She seems as disgruntled as ever, especially now that she's lost Dolores as her foil."

Elsbeth straightened in the swing. "What do you mean?"

"You tell her, Issy. You had a hand in it."

I sucked up the last of my drink and placed the glass on the table. "After Eddy died, I was the logical one to take over as Dolores' thesis advisor. As I got to know her, I realized how brilliant she is, like Eddy said. Anyway, I found out about a position opening at Fort William teaching Medieval Spanish Literature and urged Dolores to apply. She did, and the day after she defended her thesis, the department at Fort William called her in for an interview and followed with a job offer.

"Dolores and her brother will go there at the end of the month. I've even talked my brother into helping her move with a truck borrowed from Al."

Elsbeth regarded me for a moment, then said, "It seems that not only did you make a friend of Dolores and help her lead a happier life, but the lion's share of the credit for solving this case should go to you."

I blushed. "That's not true."

"Come on," she insisted. "How did you know Javier was guilty? Olivia and I never guessed."

"I had tons of help from you guys and my family." I counted on my fingers. "Germán told me about Miguel's extracurricular activities and how Javier's peers outside the university viewed him. Javier himself even hinted he was gay by wanting to write his thesis on homosexuality in medieval poetry and telling me how Eddy was helping him overcome his feelings of inadequacy.

"My sister helped eliminate Juventino, who at one time, as you recall, had been our prime suspect. And although I put two-and-two together about Bibi, what Angela knew and Eddy's journal gave me some key information there. Then, both of you assisted with eliminating Clive. My friend Ana Torres let me know what was going on with Vigil. Georgina and Dolores clarified the timing issues for the night Eddy was killed."

I regarded my companions. "Olivia, your discovery of Eddy's journal added valuable details and confirmations. And Elsbeth, if you hadn't introduced me to hyacinth perfume and explained its history, I would never have discovered Javier's secret. So, you see, it was a joint effort with everybody pitching in."

Elsbeth smiled. "It's good to know that my workshops, though perhaps not on a par with university lectures, do some good and that my students listen."

"Don't go all self-effacing British on me," I protested. "You know your classes are fabulous. However," I said with arched eyebrows, "I've got to tell you something: I'll never wear rose perfume again."

Everyone laughed.

"I truly mean it," I said with conviction. "I think from now on I'll stick to jasmine, the 'king of scents.'"

We fell into a companionable silence, each pondering the moon and the infinite cosmos. After a while, the squeaking swing stopped, but I kept creaking back and forth in the rocker.

Family and friends. I had come home, among other things, to cement the bond with my family and make new friends. This had come to pass. I had also returned determined to forge a career at the university. After a rough beginning, this, too, was shaping up. Prince Charming was still being elusive, but I couldn't expect to fulfill all my cherished dreams in one short summer.

I'd taken a step toward discovering my roots through my relationship with my spirit ancestor. Doña Isabella's cryptic proverbs, off-key singing, and wacky advice had played an important role in helping me solve the murders by challenging me to think for myself. Doña Isabella. Fact or fantasy? My imagination or a vision from the world beyond The Veil?

As I gazed at the starry sky, the object of my reflections suddenly appeared. With a plum-colored skirt and scraggly shawl flapping in the breeze, looking like Beulah the Witch in silhouette, Doña Isabella sailed serenely across the face of the moon on a broomstick. And what a crooked, ratty-looking broomstick it was! As she reached the midpoint of the circle of the moon, she turned her face toward me and winked.

"If you remember nothing else, my six-times-great-granddaughter," she called, "keep in mind this ancient proverb: 'Until death, all is life!'"

With that, like a rocket accelerating after burning off most of its fuel, she vanished into space.

"Did you see that? Did you hear that?" I called excitedly to my friends on the swing. But they had fallen fast asleep.

Doña Isabella's Famous Recipes to Help Get the Most Out of Life

Sea Salt Detox Bath

- Large jar
- 1 pound sea salt
- 10 drops each of essential oils of eucalyptus, lavender, Siberian fir, and neroli fragrance oil
- 5 drops bergamot essential oil
- Honey

Fill jar with sea salt, add essential oils, and shake to mix thoroughly. Add 2 or 3 tablespoonfuls to each bath. If desired, add a tablespoonful of honey to the bath water.

Sleep Tight Herbal Tea

- 1-quart, wide-mouthed jar
- 1 cup chamomile flowers, dried
- 1 cup lemon balm, dried
- 1 handful rose petals, dried
- Rosehips to taste, crushed
- ½ cup orange peels, dried and finely chopped

Mix all the ingredients and store in the jar. For each cup of tea, use 1 teaspoonful in a tea strainer and boiling water. Brew to taste.

Calm the Troubled Spirit Oil

- 24 drops rose fragrance oil
- 12 drops vanilla essential oil
- 6 drops cinnamon leaf essential oil
- 3 drops angelica essential oil (or substitute clary sage)

Blend together and wear as perfume, or place in a room diffuser.

Balancing Act Oil

- 15 drops amber essential oil
- 15 drops neroli fragrancel oil

Blend together with a few drops of any combination of allspice, bitter almond, lavender, or spruce needle essential oils.

Protection from Another's Anger Massage Oil

- 24 drops red rose fragrance
- 6 drops cinnamon leaf essential oil
- 6 drops marjoram essential oil
- 6 drops basil essential oil
- 6 drops juniper berry essential oil

Add mixture to a four-ounce bottle of aloe vera carrier oil. Use as a massage oil.

Open Your Paths Juice

To 1 cup water, add:

- 1 cup blackberries
- ½ cu[cantaloupe, cubed

- ¼ cup apple, peeled, cored, and cubed
- ½ teaspoon ginseng

Blend and serve.

Concentration Bath Salts

- 16 drops sweet orange essential oil
- 8 drops frankincense fragrance oil
- 6 drops heather blossom essential oil
- 4 drops fir essential oil
- 2 drops clary sage essential oil

Combine in a 1-dram vial and top off with grapeseed oil. Shake well before using.

Elsbeth MacLeod's Aromatherapy Recipes

Inner Balance Perfume

For spiritual alignment

- 12 drops frankincense essential oil
- 12 drops rose perfume oil
- 6 drops Mysore sandalwood essential oil
- 3 drops mignonette essential oil
- 2 drops lavender essential oil

Safety and Protection Oil

- 15 drops red rose fragrance oil
- 6 drops myrrh fragrance oil
- 6 drops gardenia essential oil
- 2 drops lemon verbena essential oil

Elsbeth MacLeod's Culinary Recipes

Restorative Iced Tea

In a bowl, combine:

- 1 tablespoon fresh lavender flowers
- 2 teaspoons rosehips
- 1 teaspoon hibiscus flowers, dried
- ½ teaspoon hops, dried
- Handful of fresh pink rose petals

Pour a pot of boiling water over the mixture. After steeping the brew for five minutes, drain away the herbs; pour the tea into a pitcher, and chill.

Lullaby Tea

All the ingredients for this tea are dried.

- 1 tablespoon chamomile flowers
- 1 teaspoon dandelion leaves
- 1 teaspoon hops flowers
- 1 teaspoon St. John's wort
- ½ teaspoon catmint tops
- ½ teaspoon dried primrose flowers
- A few aniseeds to taste

Courage Tea

- 2 teaspoons peppermint leaves, fresh
- ½ teaspoon thyme, fresh
- ¼ teaspoon rosemary, dried
- ¼ teaspoon yarrow flowers, dried

Issy Castillo's Fav (besides Mami's cooking)

Take-Out from Taco Loco!

Acknowledgements

I wish to thank Susanna Nash and Cynthia Price Reedy for having un-flaggingly read this manuscript multiple times without complaining and who always offer superb critiques. You guys are the best! Thanks also to Tim Goodacre, who gave me valuable information about what attracts people to Boulder. And many, many thanks to my editor, Shawn Reilly Simmons, whose astute editorial suggestions have helped improve the story immensely. Finally, I want to thank my husband, John, who has stood by me and encouraged me in my writing endeavors all these years (and never complains about having to order in pizza for dinner because I'm working). I love you, Sweetie.

About the Author

Carolina Dow holds a Ph.D. from the University of Wisconsin. Before becoming a Master Intercultural Trainer, she taught at Brown and Pittsburgh Universities. She has written several nonfiction books on topics ranging from aromatherapy to tea, healthy drinks, esoteric religions, Brazilian folk religions, and how to create a personal sanctuary. She has lived in Mexico, Brazil, Spain, Portugal, and The United Kingdom, currently residing in Boulder, Colorado. In her spare time, she enjoys gardening, remodeling her home, and caring for three unruly kitties.

SOCIAL MEDIA HANDLES:
  https://www.facebook.com/CarolineDowauthor

AUTHOR WEBSITE:
  https://www.carolinadowbooks.com/

Also by Carolina Dow

BA Latin American Studies (32 hours L. A. History), MA Spanish, Ph.D. Luso-Brazilian Studies.

Published books:

Secrets of a Witch's Coven (Schiffer)

Web of Light (Schiffer)

Green Magic (Schiffer)

Witch's Brew (Schiffer)

Complete Book of the Psychic Arts, INATS winner

Saravá Afro-Brazilian Magic (Llewellyn)

Magic from Brazil (Llewellyn)

Pomba-Gira (Technicians of the Sacred)

i Fuego Angelical, a BEA Latino first place winner (Llewellyn)

Tales from the Inside (Lulu)

Tea Leaf Reading for Beginners, State of Colorado Best Nonfiction award winner (Llewellyn)

The Healing Power of Tea (Llewellyn),

What's Your Potion? Liquid Refreshments to Nourish Body, Mind, and Spirit (Schiffer)

A Sanctuary of Your Own: Find a Place for Relaxation and Renewal (Llewellyn).